Ellen Mary Clerke

Fable and Song in Italy

Ellen Mary Clerke

Fable and Song in Italy

ISBN/EAN: 9783744778077

Printed in Europe, USA, Canada, Australia, Japan

Cover: Foto ©Andreas Hilbeck / pixelio.de

More available books at **www.hansebooks.com**

FABLE AND SONG

IN ITALY

BY

E. M. CLERKE

LONDON
GRANT RICHARDS
1899

To

Dr. Richard Garnett, C.B.

*In grateful recognition of
encouragement and advice without
which this volume would
never have been
written*

CONTENTS

PREFACE

THE aim of this little volume is twofold. First, to trace out some of the influences acting on the more popular forms of Italian song; and secondly, to offer to English readers, in the shape of translated extracts, specimens of Italian poets whose works difficulties of language have hitherto rendered inaccessible to the general public.

In carrying out the first part of my programme, I have specially dwelt in the early chapters on the survival of classical myths in popular tradition, and on their transformation and modification at the hands of minstrels and poets. As Boiardo is the great exemplar, among the more polished bards, of this species of assimilation, I have illustrated it by following out some of the episodes in which he has thus blended antique and mediæval mythology, so as to present them in consecutive and intelligible form. It is only in this fashion that the chivalric epic can be rendered readable to contemporaries, since its prolixity and discursiveness make it wearisome to pursue continuously as a whole. Its original composition for piecemeal recitation places it in a totally different category from modern literature, addressed primarily to the mind through the eye.

In the chapters on Giusti and Manzoni I have tried
to emphasise their position as the two great influences
on the growth of modern Italian, the one through his
verse, the other through his prose, the unapproached
and unapproachable masterpieces of their respective
spheres of art.

My second object has been in the selection of passages
for translation, to open up as far as possible new ground,
choosing works that have not as yet been naturalised
in English literature.   Since there is no version of
the "Orlando Innamorato" in our language, I have
drawn largely on it for passages illustrative of my
subject, especially as its beauties are, even in Italian,
disguised by the obsoleteness of the language, and it
has therefore the less to lose in the change of dress.
In my selections from Ariosto, again, I have borrowed
more extensively from his sparkling verse-letters than
from his better known "Orlando Furioso," since the
latter is available in a very adequate English translation.

My versions are in every case line for line transcripts,
that is to say, there is no transposition of the meaning,
which is placed clause by clause as in the original.   I
have made no attempt to reproduce or imitate archaisms
of diction, which would in a modern writer be affectation, but have tried to reflect the simplicity and directness of the language of my text.   A translation must
always be more or less of a compromise between literal-
ness and grace, but I have done my best to make the
new medium as transparent a vehicle as possible for the
transmission of the original author's ideas and intentions.

I have to thank the publishers and editors of the *Dublin*, *National*, and *Contemporary Reviews*, and of *The Gentleman's Magazine*, for permission to republish some chapters which had appeared at different dates in those periodicals.

In conclusion, I have only to say that my little work makes no pretension either to exhaustiveness or scholarship, but if it inspire in my readers any of the interest the subject has had for me, it will have succeeded in its aim.

E. M. CLERKE.

LONDON, *May* 1899.

Fable and Song in Italy

CHAPTER I

The Legacy of the Past

MEDIÆVAL Europe woke up from the long intellectual trance of the Dark Ages like a sleeper suddenly startled from his dreams, still confused as to the boundaries between vision and reality. The newly roused consciousness of humanity was, for a time, disposed to blend the real with the unreal, and to overlook the distinction between the tangible world of sense and the impalpable domain of fancy. All the more was this the case, since to the collective as to the individual soul of man, thrilling to the first supreme sense of self-recognition, ideas were primarily interesting as items of its inner experience, and only in a secondary sense as reflections of external facts. Thus the same visionary attitude of mind which produced mysticism in religion took the form of uncritical receptiveness in the field of secular thought. Fable seemed no less credible than fact, and the most apocryphal legends were accepted on the same footing as the best authenticated statements of history. The faith that so readily digested marvels craved for a perpetual supply of such stimulating food, and fiction flourished in the sympathetic atmosphere of credulity.

A

But, while the myth-haunted imagination of the South clung to the old beliefs, and metamorphosed without renouncing them, the Northern races evolved a new wonder-world for themselves, peopled by real or fictitious heroes of their national story. In Transalpine Europe there were thus formed two great nuclei of romance, round which all the shadowy brain-creations of poets grouped themselves for generations—the Courts of the British Arthur and the Frankish Charlemagne. A series of familiar figures revolving round these centres of action were found, like the stereotyped masks of the Italian Comedy of Art, a convenient basis for an indefinitely varied superstructure of narrative and intrigue.

These stock characters and pieces soon became the common property of Europe, over which there existed then a freer interchange of popular ideas than at the present day, when the literature of culture is, indeed, cosmopolitan, but that of the vulgar strictly localised and circumscribed. The itinerant ballad-singers and tale-mongers who traversed the continent from a very early age were the first seed-carriers of thought; but the Crusades later gave the strongest impulse to that solidarity of popular sentiment of which they were the visible embodiment, and without whose previous existence they would have been impossible.

So thoroughly did the heroes of Northern song become naturalised below the Alps, that they have there to this day a more vivid existence in the imagination of the multitude than any actual historical figures, and among the many stormy episodes that enliven the streets of Naples a pitched battle between two rival " Rinaldi," or chanters of the prowess of that doughty knight, is by no means an uncommon one. But in Italy the luxuriant efflorescence of Northern fancy was grafted on a sub-stratum of classical tradition; defaced, indeed, distorted and disguised, but never wholly obliterated from the long memory of the people. It was this obscure but unbroken link with the past which gave its vigorous vitality to the Renaissance in Italy. There the recovered lore of antiquity stirred associations long dormant in the popular heart, and re-sown on congenial soil, like the mummy wheat of Egypt, fructified to a fresh harvest after its secular burial of oblivion.

The Italian epic epitomises the Renaissance in its fusion of two opposite currents of tradition. Their assimilation was effected by the *bizarre* imagination of Matteo Boiardo, whose single brain, says Signor Rajna,* fulfilled the functions of popular fancy and tradition in its performance of the miracle of recasting antique material in mediæval form. "Nature had endowed him [says this writer] with a precious faculty, stimulated and increased by the age in which he lived, of combining, of harmonising, of bringing forth a new world from a chaos of elements. . . . Every new creation generated an in-definite number of others; every cause drew after it a whole chain of effects. Thus a new world was evolved, which is, after the Dantesque, the most wonderful born of the Italian imagination."

Thus all that he borrowed from legends, from history, from tradition, he coined into new shape and endowed with new life by the power of his vivifying imagination. In the "Orlando Innamorato" he has in this fashion enriched the familiar groundwork of the *chansons de geste* with an embroidery of classical episode,

* "Le Fonti dell' Orlando Furioso." Pio Rajna. Firenze, Sansoni, 1876.

imagery, and illustration, transformed, modified, recreated by the shaping thought, and worked in with marvellous profusion and felicity. Thus his work, though incomplete, effected an artistic revolution, and left a glorious fragment ready to the hand of his successor. If the fame of the latter has eclipsed his own, it is due not to inherent superiority of genius, but to the sudden maturity of intellectual life in the interval between them. During the century covered by the lives of the singers of the two "Orlandos" (1434–1533) man aged fast, and the minute-hand of thought travelled through a large arc on the dial of progress.

In reading Boiardo we feel that the world was still young when he sang. The deathless freshness of an Immortal is on his lips, the limpid faith of childhood in his verse, vivid with the illimitable possibilities of a yet unexplored universe. Who, indeed, could say that marvels should cease in an age which was to make known the one-half of the round earth to the dwellers on the other half? Might not the very laws of nature themselves still have seemed pliant and plastic while the visible horizon of humanity was capable of such indefinite expansion ?

In the succeeding generation this foreglow of auroral promise, vague with unshaped dreams, thrilled with coming revelation, has already given place to the clear noonday of accomplishment. Man has come of age and entered on his inheritance, but in soberer mood; the flush has faded from the face of earth, and the universe in ceasing to be a playground has begun to be a problem.

Ariosto reflects the change ; he is gay, but it is with the calculated mirth of a worldling and cynic, not with the unutterable joyousness of a child or savage. A materialist at heart, the gracious powers of nature have ceased to be living presences to him, and he uses the hobgoblin machinery of his predecessor with no more faith in its reality than a stage manager has in the *diablerie* of his Christmas pantomime. Human passion, most often in its least exalted form, has taken its place as the motive force of his drama, which by its appeal in this respect to the modern spirit, has thrown into the shade the wilder graces of that of his predecessor. The poetical licence of the one degenerates into broad farce in the other, and the leading motive of the elder bard, the representation of the invincible hero as the captive of love, is caricatured by his successor in the extravagances of his madness.

For it must be borne in mind that the exaltation of love as the supreme inspiration of chivalry is the root idea of Boiardo's drama, and that in this, as in his transfusion of the classical material into the mediæval mould, he followed his instinct for assimilation of the most diverse materials. Down to this day the stream of legendary romance had flowed in two distinct channels, the *chansons de geste*, or lays of the Carolingian heroes, forming the repertory of the itinerant minstrel-craft of the marketplace, while the tales of adventure concerning the Knights of the Round Table found more cultivated auditors in baron's hall or lady's bower. Signor Rajna * discusses at some length the theory that the Carolingian cycle was linked on to a still older stock of popular romance dating from the Merovingian period, with the princes of that dynasty as the subjects of its song, and an attempt is made to identify the great Clovis himself with a mythical hero called in French Foovent, and in Italian Fioravante.

* " Le Origini dell' Epopea Francese." Pio Rajna. Firenze. Sansoni, 1884.

Traces, too, have been found of a ruder metrical ditty than the *chansons de geste* in the *cantilene*, a ballad sung in chorus by those who had participated in the events it celebrated, the time being marked by the clapping of hands. These rudimentary forms of song had, however, probably died out in Boiardo's day, and he was dependent for his inspiration on the better known sources with which we are still sufficiently well acquainted.

Although the main theme of the two sets of fable, Breton and Frankish, the struggle of a Christian hero against pagan foes and his final overthrow by treachery, is identical, their treatment of it is essentially different. War, which in the Carolingian epic filled almost the entire canvas, is, in the Breton romances, relegated to the background, and love takes its place as the primary motive of the action. While thus presaging the modern romantic spirit, they reflect, too, a much wider area of contemporary thought, since they embody, on the one hand, the visionary aspirations of mediæval mysticism represented in the Quest of the Holy Grail, and, on the other, the traditions of still older creeds in the witcheries of Morgan and Merlin. These complex sources of inspiration are wanting in the downright fighting epic of Turpin, with its windy clamour of hard buffets unsoftened by any intervening atmosphere of tender influence or phantasmal thought. Thus broadly massed into two distinct groups of fable, divergent in aim, in spirit, and in the audiences addressed, remained the mythical creations of early Europe until the advent of the poet whose mission it was to give them a common and abiding place in literature.

Too broadly sympathetic in his genius to isolate himself from the influence of the masses, Boiardo took the

popular ballad epic of the *chansons de geste* as the
framework of his design, while he grafted on it the
amatory spirit of the more aristocratic chivalric romance, in his novel creation of the enamoured paladin.
Orlando, hitherto celebrated as the type of martial
prowess alone, and scarcely less famed as the con-
temner of the tender passion, is here made to bow to
its yoke, and the supreme triumph of love is attained
in the transformation of the hero of Roncesvalles into
the abject slave of Angelica. The same dual principle
is carried through all the minor episodes, enlivening
them with fresh significance, and breathing life into the
movements of the well-worn set of fighting automata,
which thenceforward stand transfigured in the glow of
passion kindled by the Italian Renaissance. That the
change was deliberately and consciously made by the
poet is proved by the subjoined stanzas, the opening
ones of the 18th Canto of Part II.

> Britain the Great was glorious in its day,
>   And both for love and arms held in renown,
> Whence still its fame resoundeth far away,
>   And honour still King Arthur's name doth crown.
> For valiant knights their arms did there essay,
>   In many a fight, and wandered up and down
> With ladies fair, in venturous quest of glory,
> Whose prowess to this day yet lives in story.
>
> King Charles in France high court did later hold
>   But not to match the first could it aspire,
> Though doughtier far, and more robust and bold
>   Its knights, Rinaldo and Anglante's sire;
> For since to Love it closed its portals cold,
>   Kindled by holy wars alone to ire,
> Not in such honour or esteem 'twas rated
> As was the first whereof I have narrated.

For 'tis from Love that glory first doth spring,
  From Love doth man all worth and honour gain;
Vict'ry and valour, Love 'tis that doth bring,
  'Tis Love that knightly courage doth sustain.
Hence would I fain pursue my theme and sing
  Of great Orlando as enamoured swain,
Returning where by Sacripante greeted,
I left him in the Canto last completed.

But Boiardo's assimilative genius did not restrict itself to the material inherited from his predecessors in art, and the lavish episodical embroidery interwoven into the prismatic woof of his verse is often gathered from more remote sources. Traces of the Druidical forest-faiths of the North are there, as well as reminiscences of demonology shared by all primitive humanity, together with gracious offshoots of classical mythology, handed down in semi-legendary form through the refracting medium of the popular imagination. The result is a bewildering phantasmagoria, wrought of blending and dissolving shapes, defiant of analysis as some rich woof which shows shifting play of line and colour on all its intercrossing threads, as we turn it to the light to examine its design. It is only by detaching one of these recurrent subject-patterns from the involved mass of general detail, that we can trace the manifold fragments of tradition from which it is pieced together. Endless variations on the familiar themes of the twelve Peers of France and the twelve Knights of the Round Table already existed, and in addition to the so-called chronicles of Turpin and Geoffrey of Monmouth, a number of romances such as "Les Quatre-filz-Aymon," "Ogier le Dannoys," and "Regnault de Montauban" were current in France, Provence, and Spain. In Italy similar tales passed from mouth to mouth, and for two centuries previous to

Boiardo, "I Reali di Francia," "Buovo d'Antona" [Bevis of Hampton], and "La Regina Ancroia" had been translated into the vernacular. The second of these romances had been made the subject of a poem in octave stanzas by an unknown poet, probably in the early part of the fifteenth century, who, it is plausibly conjectured, may have sung it about the streets as a wandering minstrel. A more pretentious work in the same metre was "La Spagna," a poem divided into forty cantos and borrowed bodily from Turpin. The events of Boiardo's time made the subject of a war between Christian and Infidel Powers especially appropriate, and the composition of the "Orlando Innamorato," probably begun in 1472 and broken off by the poet's death in 1494, coincided with the Turkish invasion of Europe, bringing it within view of a possible Ottoman conquest. The shock given to Christendom by the fall of Constantinople in 1453, when the poet was in his twentieth year, was still recent when he planned his great work, and the encroachments of the Porte on the Mediterranean continued during its progress. The taking of Otranto in 1480, and the atrocities committed by the Turks, who massacred 10,000 of the inhabitants, spread panic throughout Italy, and caused the Pope to contemplate flight to France. The united forces of the league of the Italian States against the invaders were commanded by Alphonso, son of Ferdinand of Naples, brother-in-law of Boiardo's sovereign, the Duke of Ferrara, and the eventual triumph of the Christians was thus one of personal as well as national interest in the circle of the poet. The Moors were, moreover, still in possession of Southern Spain until very near the end of his life, and the struggle which ended in their expulsion must have lent an air of actuality to his celebration of the earlier wars against them by the forces of Christendom. Through them, too, Europe was in more direct contact with Eastern manners than it has been at any time since, and Mohammedan princes and emirs were more familiar figures to Boiardo's contemporaries than to our own. The preaching of a Crusade during his life-time was another link with the subject of his poem, giving it an epic character in its association with great issues of public policy then in the balance.

Himself a man of action, concerned in all the events of his time, the singer of Orlando had that acquaintance with the motive forces of history which enabled him to realise his theme. We can trace in his handling of it the familiarity with nature gained in out-door life and pursuits, giving his landscape an open-air effect wanting in Ariosto's, which seems in comparison like the painted boards and conventional drop-scene of stage properties. Love of all knightly appurtenances, of splendid armour, of finely tempered weapons, and above all of horses, is apparent in his pages, and his portraits of steeds and chargers are touched with more loving care than those of their riders.

His life is known in little more than outline. Born in 1434 at Scandiano, the family fief, within seven miles of Reggio in Lombardy, he inherited an ancient name and many feudal possessions, entitling him to call himself, not only Count of Scandiano, but Lord of Arceto, Casal-grande, Gesso, and Torricella. His poetic genius was perhaps an inheritance in the maternal line, as the brother and nephew of his mother, Lucia Strozzi, descended from a branch of the great Florentine house, were distin-guished in their day as writers of Latin verse. He was held in great esteem by the princes of the House of Este, and when Duke Borso went to Rome to receive his investiture from the Pope in 1471, was chosen to form one of his train. The death of this patron within a few days of his return was a cause of great grief to the poet, but cost him no diminution of court favour, since he was one of those appointed to escort the bride of the new Duke Hercules I. from Naples to Ferrara, where her marriage took place in 1473. Five years later the governorship of Reggio was bestowed on Boiardo, and this post, save for an interval in which he filled the same office at Modena, he held until his death on December 20, 1494. He was celebrated for the mildness of his rule, and is said to have even held the opinion, very extreme in those days, that capital punishment should not be inflicted for any crime. He was, however, a soldier as well as an administrator, having taken part in the war between Ferrara and Venice in 1482-84.

His marriage to Taddea, daughter of the Count of Novellara, of the noble house of Gonzaga, took place in 1472, when he had reached the mature age of thirty-eight. A previous romantic attachment is inferred from a collection of love poems addressed to a lady, supposed on the evidence of two acrostics to have been a certain Antonia Caprara, born in Reggio in 1451, and consequently seventeen years younger than the poet. Allusions to the rose in some of the stanzas suggest that she may have shared his affections with another lady of that name, or both, perhaps, may have been objects only of the imaginary passion simulated as part of the poetical equipment at that epoch.

There is little doubt, from internal evidence, that the " Orlando Innamorato " was composed for the delecta-

tion of the Court of Ferrara, each canto furnishing the
recital for a single day's sitting. Begun, it is conjectured,
in 1472, it was interrupted on the completion of the
Second Book by the outbreak of the war with Venice in
1482, to be resumed on the conclusion of peace two
years later. Public disaster again came to suspend its
progress, and this time finally, for on the invasion of
Italy by Charles VIII. in 1494 the poem was broken off
abruptly in the middle of the ninth canto of the Third
Book, and the author's death before the end of that
fatal year closed his lips for ever. How much longer it
would have been, or how its protagonist's fortunes would
have ended, no one knows, and the poet himself was
doubtless equally ignorant, as from the episodical
character of the narrative, and its composition for oral
recitation, it was evidently woven from day to day in a
discursive stream meandering rather than progressing.
Its endless reiteration of battles and combats, of which
the incidents must perforce be monotonous, is attri-
butable in the same way to its origin, as the audience
took them in separate instalments, and probably craved
for such stirring scenes. No doubt they spent their
spare time from canto to canto in discussing the characters and actions of their heroes, living in the strange
fantastic world to which the artist's wizardry transported
them.

His function was thus the same as that filled in
humbler fashion by the wandering minstrel-craft, jon-
gleurs, giullari, and cantastorie, who, chanting their
doggrel in the streets and market-places, were the sole
repositories of the popular literature of Europe. Not
seldom a baronial hall was the scene of their improvised
entertainment, when the chatelaine with her maidens,

and the knight with his steward or secretary and chaplain, formed the aristocratic part of his audience.   The serving folk and men-at-arms, with perhaps a mingling of peasants or artisans from the neighbouring villages, filled the lower places in the hall, and cast offerings proportioned to their means into the story-teller's cap as he handed it round after his recitation.   If he were a master of his craft he did not fail to give point to the latter by improvised allusions to current events or the circumstances of those present, adapting to their tastes or proclivities the opening and closing strophes with which he introduced himself and took his leave.   From such lips were heard the first rude strains of the measure which, polished and perfected by an earlier bard than Boiardo, was to furnish the instrument for his many-voiced music.

CHAPTER II

The Theseid and the Octave Stanza

AT two separate points of its orbit of development the Italian Renaissance crosses the path of the English revival of letters. The latter first comes under its influence at its very dawn in its

Morning star of song,

who openly modelled himself on his Italian contemporary, and feels it for the second time in the sources of inspiration furnished by it in the "spacious times" of the Elizabethan dramatists. Later ages may wonder at the former conjunction of names, for Boccaccio's verse, despite the crown of bays it earned him at the Capitol, seems to us moderns scarcely worthy of having directed and guided the inspiration of Chaucer.

The place as a poet of the author of the "Decameron" must, indeed, be determined less by the intrinsic value of his work than by his function as a precursor, essaying a new development of his art, and prescribing its course in the future. Immeasurably below the other component members of the great Triad of the earlier Renaissance, he was, in a truer sense than either, the pioneer of subsequent Italian song. The unapproachable loftiness of Dante's theme forbade imitation, the narrow limitation of Petrarch's condemned it to inane reiteration. But Boccaccio, in giving the metrical romance an established place in literature, supplied the poetry of the future with its main outlet of expression, and opened up to it a new and inexhaustible field of subjects in harmony with modern taste.

The form, moreover, of the later Italian heroic ballad was that first adopted by him as the best calculated for versified narrative. The octave stanza, though not of his absolute invention, since it already existed in popular song, owes to him its introduction to that higher sphere of cultivated letters where it later came to occupy so large a place. The Theseid thus forms a landmark in Italian letters as the earliest attempt to set a heroic subject to that plebeian phrase of melody destined to form the structural basis of all the verse music of the Renaissance. The poem, written in 1341, has the elaborate awkwardness of a first struggle for utterance in an unfamiliar form of diction, while the ideas are still clogged by mechanical difficulties of expression. These difficulties are aggravated, too, by the effort to reproduce classical models, while using, in the Italian vernacular, an idiom as yet untried in such subjects.

For Boccaccio, a diligent and ardent student of the newly-recovered literature of antiquity, was a much more servile copyist of its forms than were his successors. Those hoarded stores, in their time thoroughly assimilated by the Italian mind, had furnished it with materials for fresh growths, and were no longer reproduced in crude incongruity. The Middle Ages are, in this sense, more strictly classical than the later hybrid epoch of the Renaissance, when the complete fusion of antique fable with popular tradition had taken place.

The Italian epic then closely followed the ballad-singers and vagrant story-tellers of the streets, not only in its choice of subjects, but also in the episodical character of the narrative, diverging into an inextricable mesh of collateral channels. Boccaccio, on the contrary, like his classical prototypes, preserves the unity of his design, following throughout a single thread of fable unencumbered by any secondary issues. The difference in tendency between the antique and mediæval mind, shown in this divergence, is highly characteristic of the two epochs, and is still more strongly exemplified in their architecture. The structural simplicity of the Greek temple, with its severe subordination of ornament to design, on the one hand, and the complex vistas of intersecting arches and ramifying pillars in the Gothic cathedral on the other, represent two opposite ideals striven after in all branches of art alike, and typifying respectively the law of rest and the law of growth.

The fable on which the Theseid is founded is described by Boccaccio in his dedicatory letter to Fiammetta as " a very ancient story, found by me and unknown to the generality." Of this original, if it ever existed, no trace has been found, nor does he give any other clue to it. On intrinsic evidence, however, it may be pronounced one of the popular chivalric romances, in which epochs, characters, and manners are jumbled together with the recklessness of an age innocent of archæology. It is this tale of the two Theban knights—Palamon and Arcite, both prisoners in the hands of Theseus, and rivals for the love of the fair Emilia—which Chaucer has familiarised to English readers under the title of the "Knightes Tale." In substance almost a reproduction of Boccaccio's romance, his version differs from it so widely in diction, style of

expression, and metrical form, as to constitute an independent and original poem.

The first book of the Theseid, narrating the expedition
of Theseus against the Amazons, his marriage to Hippolyta their queen, and his return to Athens, accompanied
by Emilia, the young sister of his bride, is of the nature
of a prologue, and as such is omitted by Chaucer altogether.

The siege of Thebes follows, at which Palamon and
Arcite, friends and kinsmen, are made captive, to undergo a long imprisonment in a cell overlooking the garden
of the palace at Athens.   Here they first catch a glimpse
of the heroine, whose appearance is heralded by one of
those descriptions of spring-tide so common among later
Italian poets :

> From the glad aspect of the stars on high,
>   The earth a sweet and gracious influence drew,
> And robed her form so beauteous to the eye
>   In vesture of fresh green and blossoms new ;
> Each sapling tree reclothed its branches dry
>   With verdant leaves, while Spring's sweet stress did sue
> The trees to bloom and fruit in rich redundance,
> And crown the earth with beauty and abundance.
>
> The little birds, in carols blithe and gay
>   Began to chant their amorous joys renewed,
> Sporting on leafy bower and flowery spray,
>   While every living thing its servitude
> To the same power did equally display,
>   And lusty youths inclined to amorous mood
> Felt in their hearts love grow in strength and ardour
> And his enchanted yoke press ever harder.
>   " Teseide," book iii. stanzas 6, &c.

This passage affords an illustration of the verbosity of
Boccaccio, in contrast with the quaint succinctness of his

English disciple, who compresses the essential portion of
the two stanzas into the three following lines :

> The season priketh every gentil herte,
> And maketh him out of his sleepe sterte,
> And seith, " Arys and do thin observance."

In his description of the maiden he follows his predecessor more closely, but with similar condensation of his
ideas.   Boccaccio is at his best when writing of Emilia,
as his sympathy with feminine character enables him to
give her a more distinct individuality than he confers on
the male personages of his tale.   Even through the
stilted conventicnalities of the pseudo-classical style a
penetrating touch of caustic humour here and there
reveals his insight into the cold and narrow nature he is
analysing.

Emilia is a type of woman common enough in real
life, but seldom figuring as a heroine of romance ; with
affections strictly subordinated to self-interest, and a
heart thoroughly under the control of discretion, but
adapting herself, with all her superficial graces of mind
and person, to inspire a love she is incapable of returning.
She is, withal, redeemed from total insipidity by a
childish *naïveté* even in the exercise of her small arts of
fascination, and by a maidenly innocence and freshness
that may be taken to excuse her lack of sensibility.   The
poet's first picture of her is not devoid of grace and
sweetness, despite his redundance of language and
epithet :

> Then fair Emilia, scarce to girlhood grown,
>   Guided and led by youthful fancy's play
> But not by love, yet to her heart unknown,
>   At the same hour each morning took her way

Unto a garden trode by her alone,
  Which close beside her chamber window lay,
And barefooted in morning gown went trilling
Her songs of love, the air with gladness filling.

And this her use and habit did pursue
  The maiden sweet and simple, day by day;
Now plucking with white hand the rose that blew
  In new-born beauty on its thorny spray,
Then twining with it other flowers that grew,
  She wreathed her golden head with garlands gay,
Till on a morn fell out, as chance directed,
A novel chance, by the maid's charms effected.

One beauteous morn, when she had ris'n from sleep,
  And with her tresses blond her head had crowned,
Down to the garden fair her tryst to keep
  She singing went and gaily sported round,
Of blossoms on the sward piled in a heap,
  She swift and merrily her garlands wound,
And still her lays of love she went on singing,
With child-like mirth and angel voice sweet ringing.

At sound of that clear voice that softly flowed,
  Arcite rose, who in his prison lay,
Beside the garden that was love's abode,
  But nought to Palamon his friend did say.
He oped a window that the garden showed
  In haste, to better hear that roundelay,
And thrust his head athwart the iron grating,
To see who such sweet music was creating.
            "Teseide," book iii. stanzas 8, &c.

The reader will doubtless remember Chaucer's description of Emilia, but we insert it to facilitate comparison.

This passeth yeer by yeer, and day by day,
Till it fell oones in a morne of May
That Emelie, that fairer was to seene
Than is the lilie on hir stalk grene,

And fressher than the May with floures newe—
For with the rose-colour strof hire hewe,
I n'ot which was the fayrer of hem two—
Er it were day, as was hire wone to do,
Sche was arisen, and al redy dight,
For May wole hau no sloggardye anight.

Hire yelwe hair heer was browded in a tresse,
Byhynde hire bak, a yerde long I guesse,
And in the garden as the sonne uprist,
Sche walked up and down, and as hire liste
Sche gadereth floures party whyte and reede,
To make a sotil garland for hire heede,
And as an angel hevenly sche song.

Of the two prisoners who became enamoured of this
fair vision, one, as the poet tells Fiammetta in his
dedication, is intended to represent himself, adding that
she will have no difficulty in knowing which.   The story
of his own love is told, he says, as far as the exigencies
of the story and necessary reserve permit, with sufficient
plainness to bring it to her mind.   It was thus a *roman
à clef* that he was writing, but we have not the key which
Fiammetta possessed.   Palamon, whose suit finally
achieves success, is presumably the one indicated, but
his courtship is of so very shadowy a character, not
including the interchange of a word with its object, that
a great deal must have been left to the imagination if it
were intended to portray a less visionary attachment.
Not Palamon, but Arcite, is first cognisant of Emilia's
presence, and he calls his friend to gaze on her as
follows :

And turning inward, in low voice he said
    Unto his friend, " Oh, Palamon, look here,
'Tis Venus self from heaven here downward sped,
    Hear'st thou her song ?   Ah, if thou hold'st me dear

Come hither quick, and see ere she be fled.
   'Twill give thee pleasure to regard so near
The queen of beauty in her charms eternal,
To us descended from the realms supernal."

Uprose then Palamon who heard his call,
   So softly, of his step he scarce was 'ware,
And went with him unto the window small,
   Where both stood still to see the goddess fair,
Whom when he saw, in voice of lively fall
   He said : " 'Tis Cytherea's self is there,
On thing so fair my gaze hath never lighted,
Or looked on aught that vision so delighted."

                 Ibid. stanzas 13, &c.

Chaucer, in narrating this scene, departs from his original in making the captives engage in a hot dispute as to the priority of their respective claims to secure the affections of the lady, and Boccaccio has been censured by modern critics for his failure to indicate any sense of jealousy between them so long as both were in confinement. This may, however, be true to nature, as their passion under those circumstances remained an ideal sentiment without prospect of fruition. He passes on to an analysis, full of keen perception, of the feelings of Emilia when an involuntary exclamation from Palamon betrays the presence of the two spectators.

At that " Ah me ! " the maiden fair to see
   O'er her left shoulder turned with sudden grace,
And to the window straight her eyes raised she,
   Whereon the lovely pallor of her face
Flushed o'er with rosy shame. Who those might be
   She knew not ; but uprising from her place,
With all the blossoms fair she had collected,
Her parting steps elsewhither she directed.

But yet not all unmindful did she go
   Of that " Ah me ! " and though too young in age
Of love's entire perfection ought to know,
   Yet something of its feelings she could gauge,
And deemed herself admired, and felt a glow
   Of pride, to think her charms could hearts engage,
And prized them more, and strove for their adorning,
When to the garden she repaired each morning.
                     Ibid. stanzas 18 and 19.

And while the fair continued still to stray,
   At times in company, at times alone,
For pastime in the garden bright and gay,
   With furtive looks her eyes were ever thrown
Up to the window, whence first heard that day,
   Came Palamon's " Ah me ! " in piteous tone,
Not urged by love, but rather love desiring,
To see if others gazed on her admiring.

And if she knew that others watched to see,
   A mien of frank unconsciousness would feign,
And warble to herself as though in glee,
   With sweetest voice of keen and subtle strain,
And on the grass 'midst bush, and shrub, and tree
   With mincing step and guileless air amain,
Would mimic woman's gait in the endeavour
To charm the eyes of gazers dreamed of ever.
                     Ibid. stanzas 28 and 29.

The subsequent course of the story follows, in both versions, the fortunes of Arcite, released from his captivity at the intercession of Peritheus. But freedom, accompanied by a decree of banishment from Athens, is, in the present state of his feelings, a boon of little value ; and, after protracted wanderings in exile, he risks all to return to the vicinity of the object of his affections. In a menial capacity, and under a feigned name, he reappears at the court of Theseus, where Emilia's eyes alone are keen enough to penetrate his disguise.   The admirable discretion of the young lady, however, prevents her from betraying her recognition either to him or others, but we may imagine her to have been all the more keenly conscious of the silent homage, the opportunity of offering which was all her admirer gained by his proximity.   But in Palamon, who accidentally hears of his rival's appearance on the scene, the mere fact of his presence suffices to excite transports of jealous madness.

Succeeding by stratagem in escaping from prison, he comes upon his kinsman in a wood, to which he had resorted for his amorous meditations, and compels him, though reluctantly, to engage in single combat on the spot.   The knights, absorbed in their duel, are unconscious of the approach of a royal hunting party, until Emilia herself interposes between them, and her appearance is followed by that of Theseus, Hippolyta, and all their train.   An explanation ensues ; the knights confess their identity and their rivalry in love of the fair Amazon. Theseus, a chivalrous monarch, not only condones their breach of prison and parole, but promises Emilia's hand as the prize of a tournament, in which they are to do battle at the end of a year, each attended by a hundred knights of his choosing.

The preparations and preliminaries for the combat offer a congenial field for the descriptive faculty of both poets, and Boccaccio devotes whole pages to the enumeration of the champions, presented by Chaucer with more vigorous brevity.   The most celebrated heroes of antiquity are ranged on both sides, regardless of chronology, and classical personages are freely introduced amid mediæval pageantry.   The English bard's picture of

Lygurge, King of Thrace, may be cited as one of those
in which he adheres closely to his original:

> Ful heye upon a char of gold stood he,
> With four white boles in the trays,
> Instede of cote armure over his harnays,
> With nayles yelwe and bright as eny gold,
> He had a beres skyn col-blak for-old,
> His long heer was kembd behynde his bak,
> As eny ravens fether it schon for-blak.

The same description, as usual at greater length, does
duty for Agamemnon in the original:

> High on a car with four stout bulls for team,
>   Great Agamemnon of Inachia rode,
> A numerous train around, 'mid whom supreme
>   In armour of a baron bold he showed;
> And well the lofty honours did beseem
>   By Greeks in front of leaguered Troy bestowed,
> Keen-eyed, stout-limbed, with beard like wing of raven,
> His piercing look and mien bespoke no craven.
>
> Nor burnished arms, nor mantle fluttering wide,
>   Locks combed or scented, gold or gems he wore,
> But flung around his neck a bear's rough hide,
>   Clasped by the shining claws, so dread of yore,
> In shaggy fold hung down at either side,
>   The bruised and rusted armour covering o'er,
> And to the gazers was the truth notorious,
> That o'er all comers he must be victorious.
>
> Behind him following, but in garb and mien
>   Unlike, the youthful Menelaus came,
> Clad in rich stuffs all precious to be seen,
>   Graceful and fair, unarmed his comely frame;
> And with his locks of gold that glittered sheen
>   The zephyrs toyed, while like a golden flame,
> His amber beard upon his breast descended,
> And all who gazed admired its beauty splendid.

He rode a mighty charger iron-grey,
　　And held a rein clogged thick with massy gold,
Around his neck the fluttering mantle gay,
　　Made music to the breeze that swelled its fold.
Had Venus' heart been vacant, all did say,
　　To gain her love he well might have made bold,
Thus lookers-on his manly grace applauded,
And to the skies his strength and beauty lauded.

Ibid. book vi. stanzas 21, &c.

Each of the interested parties repairs, on the eve of the tournament, to the shrine of a patron divinity, to implore a successful issue.   Arcite has recourse to Mars, to whom he appeals for victory in the fight; Palamon invokes Venus, declaring himself indifferent to success in arms so his love prosper ; and Emilia betakes her to the temple of Diana, to entreat counsel and aid from the maiden goddess.   Each receives a favourable response despite their conflicting wishes, but it is the votary of Venus who in the end obtains the most substantial boon from his patroness.   By a curious and overstrained figure of rhetoric, the prayers of Arcite and Palamon are personified, that they may find their way to the abodes of the divinities invoked.   It is thus that the description of the palace or temple of Mars is introduced, of which, as it is the original of a celebrated passage in Chaucer, we subjoin a portion for comparison.

In the wide Thracian fields, 'neath northern skies,
　　Where never-ceasing storms convulse the air,
And the dark host of clouds for ever flies
　　Before the winds that chase them here and there,
Through reeking wintry climes, where summer dies,
　　And by the curdling cold flung everywhere
Are watery globules and chill snows congealing
To hard and creaking ice o'er nature stealing.

Deep in a barren wood uncouth and drear,
  Where sturdy oaks grew close and thick and high,
All gnarled and rugged, harsh and old and sere,
  Which with eternal shade the light deny
To earth's sad face, by growths of many a year
  Hid from a thousand storms that raved on high,
Strange sounds came thence, and noises wild and eery,
Nor beast nor shepherd sought its shelter dreary.

Of the great god armipotent was seen
  The palace, built of steel that glistened bright,
Which from its surface of resplendence sheen
  Sent flashing back the sun's reflected light,
Abhorrent of that dismal place, I ween.
  Strait was the iron door and scant in height,
The gates were all of adamant immortal,
And metal-plated was each massy portal.

The ideas here are undoubtedly striking, and only the
diffuse nervelessness of style prevents the passage from
rising to the high level of poetic eloquence to which it is
brought nearer in Chaucer's condensed rendering. Arcite's
prayer, on reaching the abode of the war-god, finds it
peopled by metaphorical abstractions like herself.

There Fury she beheld enthroned in glee,
  With horrid visage all ensanguined o'er,
Death fully armed, and Stupor did she see,
  And every altar reeked with floods of gore,
Which, shed on fields of battle, running free,
  From human veins in crimson floods did pour,
Their fires were lit with brands from smoking cities,
And wrecks of war which nothing spares or pities.

With storied tales the temple walls were lined,
  Above, around, by cunning hand made plain,
And first was all the booty there outlined
  By night and day from captive cities ta'en,

Victims of brutal force in bonds confined,
  And captives in sad garb, a piteous train,
Whole peoples bound in chains, strong places battered,
And iron gates and forts all rent and shattered.

And ships of war were seen equipped for fight,
  And hollow cars, and faces marred with blows,
And doleful plaints were heard of grief and fright,
  And Force was there triumphant in repose.
All wounds and hurts were sanctioned there by right,
  And earth oozed red with blood of slaughtered foes.
On all sides round, in every aspect direful,
Dread Mars was pictured, tyrannous and ireful.

                    Ibid. book vii. stanzas 30 *et seq.*

Chaucer's rendering of this passage is a masterpiece of vigorous compression, in which the essence of the original is conveyed with added swiftness and energy of expression. The octave stanza, despite its musical charm, does not lend itself to concentration, and Boccaccio's fine conceptions are often disguised by the accumulation of detail with which they are overloaded. As, moreover, he is impartial in his allotment of space to the other divinities invoked, the triple multiplication of the idea in the description of their respective abodes becomes wearisome from iteration. Emilia's invocation to Diana is, however, interesting from its candid simplicity in uttering her girlish doubts and uncertainties.

And if the gods already have disposed
  In their eternal and august decree,
That all shall happen as hath been proposed,
  Then bring unto my arms him who shall be
Most welcome to my heart and unopposed,
  And who with firmest will desireth me.
To speak his name my lips I cannot tutor,
So lovable to me seems either suitor.

And let the other, wounded with the shame
  Of losing me, be hurt by this alone,
And if this word to utter I may claim,
  To me, oh goddess! in these flames make known
Whose incense to thy godhead flies—what name
  Shall his be who my future faith shall own.
So this pyre of Arcite then be reckoned
The emblem—and of Palamon the second.

At least my troubled soul shall feel less pain,
  Less sadly for the vanquished party sigh,
And with a lighter heart the sight sustain
  When from the lists I shall behold him fly.
My will, now so divided, then must fain
  Take sides with one of those in arms who vie,
And see the other fly with heart made steady
By knowledge of the future fixed already.

Ibid. stanzas 86 et seq.

The omen that follows is ambiguous like most revelations of the future, the flame first quenched being subsequently rekindled, and Emilia, interpreting the prophecy according to her desires, fails to discern its true significance. The tournament takes its course, affording the poet's imagination a large field for recounting incidents of battle, enthralling to contemporary as they are wearisome to modern readers. Arcite triumphs over his rival, but Venus, mindful of Palamon's invocation, sends a Fury to frighten the horse of the victor, who is unseated, and receives a fatal injury from the fall. He lingers long enough to celebrate his nuptials with Emilia, but subsequently languishes and dies, leaving her as a legacy to Palamon. In his description of the death of Arcite the poet touches a chord of human feeling rarely sounded in that age, and showing him as the precursor of modern pathos.

If she perchance, touched by my early fate,
   In tender grief let fall one pitying tear,
Oh, haste to soothe, and bid her woe abate,
   For that sweet face so lovely and so dear,
Hath filled my heart with love for her so great
   That me her smile more than herself doth cheer,
I, more than she, am saddened by her sadness,
And change with her loved face from grief to gladness.

Thus, if the parted soul beyond the tomb,
   Aught of what passes in this world can know,
Amid the dismal throng in realms of gloom,
   Less sad and more courageous mine will go.
This said, he ceased ; nor speech did more resume,
   While with a voice of tender grief and woe,
And words whose broken tones with anguish quivered,
His soul as follows, Palamon delivered.

Ibid. book x. stanzas 46 and 47.

The poem concludes with the funeral rites of Arcite and the nuptials of Palamon, to whom the favour of Venus thus secures the fruition of his hopes. With many defects, it forms a landmark in literature, not merely from its introduction into it of a new metrical form, but also as containing the first true picture of girlhood in European poetry. In her innocent coquetry, her childish artificiality, and her unfailing correctness of deportment, Emilia stands alone as an attempt to realise feminine character at a period when its types were purely conventional, and is still perhaps the most lifelike *ingénue* in ancient or modern art.

The Theseid is memorable, too, as the earliest versified love-tale of the Middle Ages, in which sense it forms a connecting link between mediæval and modern letters, no less than as the first attempt to give permanent form to a class of fable extensively circulated among the un-

lettered vulgar by oral tradition. The popular imagination, fed by the recitations of the vagrant rhapsodists
of the market-place, ran riot in similar subjects, and
the names of Lancelot and Guinivere, of Tristan and
Iseult, of Fiordiligi and Brandimarte, with endless variations on their loves and sorrows, were handed down from
lip to lip, and from generation to generation. It was on
this legendary store that Boccaccio, Sacchetti, and Ban-
dello, nay, Shakespeare himself, drew for the raw material
of their narratives; it was here that Boiardo, Pulci, and
Ariosto found the inexhaustible supply of marvel and
adventure that enliven their brilliant verse.

Chaucer, too, appropriated to his own uses some of
this common stock of early romance, borrowing it at
second hand from the pages of Boccaccio with a frank
licence which was not in those days dubbed plagiarism.
How closely he adhered to his text, not only in the
general outline of the work, but even in its imagery and
illustrations, may be judged from the few passages here
quoted for comparison. Yet his version is rather a paraphrase than a translation, and, according to Mr. Furnivall's
analysis, out of 2250 lines only 270 are direct transcrip-
tions, while 374 bear a general likeness, and 132 a more
distant one to the corresponding ones in the original.
The superior brevity of his rendering, in which some
10,000 lines are represented by little more than a fifth of
their number, is sheer artistic gain, attained by judicious
compression and superior concentration of language.

The influence of foreign writers over Chaucer's mind
is explained by the absence in his own country of any
literature worthy to be so called, until created by him on
the basis of general European culture. The break in the
continuity of language effected by the Norman Conquest

had cut the country off from its earlier history and traditions, and the Anglo-Saxon tongue, surviving only as the barbarous dialect of the rude vulgar, lost all power of developing to any more advanced use. Hence the new English language, slowly evolved from the fusion of the two elements of population, and perfected in the fourteenth century almost to its present form, found itself without a past of its own on which to found the superstructure of its future growth. It had reached a stage of maturity in which the French *fabliau* and the Teutonic myth were alike alien to it, and required a new starting-point and a fresh fulcrum of thought from which to work out the latent capabilities of its compound nature. This Chaucer, a man of wide sympathy and many-sided intelligence, gave it, by linking it to the awakening intellectual life of continental Europe.

The rapid extension of international trade relations helped to the same end, and their influence on literature is strikingly illustrated by the English poet's mission to Italy. Sent thither to establish a closer commercial connection between England and Genoa, he spent the year 1372–73 in the northern Italian cities, and was thus brought into familiar contact with the poetry and letters of that country. His visit to "the worthy clerk, Fraunces Petrarch," is matter of tradition, and if there be no record of his having been brought into personal relations with Boccaccio, he at least came well within the sphere of his artistic influence.

Nor is his debt to be exhausted with the loan of a subject from the Theseid. The "Decameron," too, was laid under contribution, supplying him with the tale of the patient Griselda, and probably suggesting by its central plan of a group of narratives linked to a central situation the similar framework of the Canterbury Tales. In his Troylus and Criseide he has given again an even closer adaptation of Boccaccio's " Filostrato " than that of his Theban lovers in the " Knightes Tale." The edition of this work by Rossetti, in which the English text is collated with a literal prose rendering of the Italian original, supplies all the material for a comparative study of the two. Of the Theseid, on the contrary, no English version exists, although it was considered worthy of appearing in a Greek translation as early as 1529.

Boccaccio had the rare fortune, shared with the two modern novelists Manzoni and Scott, of eclipsing by his fame as a prose-writer that which he had previously acquired as a poet. Crowned as such in the Capitol in 1342, six years previous to that plague of Florence which supplied him with the tragic setting of his Decameron, he shone among his contemporaries as the second luminary of Italian song, with a lustre surpassed only by that of Petrarch. The founder of modern Romantic poetry, who set the key to the master-singers of the Renaissance, and exercised through Chaucer so potent an influence on the germination of English letters, we may well ask why as a poet he is now almost forgotten and his verse practically unread save by the historian of literature.

The answer is to be found in his want of dramatic expression, and in the dilution of thought which swamps the subject under a flood of words. Every sentence is a circumlocution, every epithet an irrelevance, every phrase an ambiguity. Nowhere lucid, the style is often obscure, and in some passages corruption of text seems to have supervened on original defect of construction. Hence it is scarcely wonderful that semi-oblivion should have overtaken Boccaccio's poetical works, and that while in his own country they are never read and little remembered, English students are satisfied to know them in the more vigorous verse of their own chanti-cleer of song, the clear-voiced herald of their dawning prime of letters.

CHAPTER III

The Preludes of the Ballad Epic

THE gradual evolution of the Italian chivalric epic from
the songs of the people can be best traced in one of its
most characteristic features, the address to the audience
at the opening and close of each canto.   These invariable
apostrophes, called Saluto and Commiato, or greeting
and adieu, had, with the *giullari* and *cantastorie* of the
street corners, a religious character, recommending the
auditors to the care of Heaven or the Saints in a spirit
of piety often startlingly at variance with the theme of
the intervening entertainment.   The tenth canto of one
of the earliest chivalric poems, "Spagna," closes in the
prevailing fashion, with the subjoined invocation—

> In my next canto fitly to describe
> This fierce and furious fight I will endeavour,
> Christ and His Blessed Mother keep ye ever.

In a similar spirit the fiftieth canto of an early version of
Rinaldo's adventures concludes as follows :

> When next I sing I'll with the end reward ye,
> The king of heavenly virtues ever guard ye.

Matteo Boiardo, in giving the street ballad its courtly
and classical form, shaped, too, its simple prefatory

utterances into that consummate perfection which only waited at the hands of Ariosto the stamp of his powerful individuality to gain currency for all time. Through the cantos of the "Orlando Innamorato" we can trace this progressive transformation of the homely greetings of the barn or the market-place into a series of melodious preludes, to whose infinitely modulated cadences the chords of the poet's lyre are swept with all the freedom of improvisation. Adopting the form as well as the matter of their humbler prototypes, the masterpieces of Renaissance song still retained the character of recitations, each canto being designed either in appearance or reality for a single day's enter-tainment. Their aim being thus different from that of a purely literary work, the production of a succession of striking episodes giving independent interest to each chapter, rather than the sustained development of a continuous action, we find in them the faults and beauties entailed by such a plan of construction : on the one hand absence of unity and sequence in the different parts ; on the other, inexhaustible fertility of invention, lavish profusion of incident, and florid bril-liancy of descriptive detail. Abounding in rhetorical perfections and constructive defects, they scarcely bear to be read as a whole, and would perhaps be best appre-ciated by modern readers in the form of extracts con-nected by a slight thread of explanatory narrative. In contrast with the severe unity of design exhibited by the "Divina Commedia," they produce somewhat the same effect as a gorgeous specimen of flamboyant architecture compared with the majestic outlines of an Early Gothic cathedral. And as the former, while defective in contour, is rich in suggestion for the artist's pencil when studied

in detail, so the romantic poems of Italy gain rather than
lose by analysis of their parts, and we do them no injustice in detaching from the general mass of the
structure some of its ornamental capitals for separate
examination.

In his earlier chapters, Boiardo, still mindful of his
plebeian models, occasionally recurs to the religious
ejaculatory form, as in the following lines closing the
nineteenth canto of his First Book :

> But since this canto over long hath been,
> Another day the rest I will recount,
> If you return to hear the pleasant story,
> So keep ye all the mighty king of glory.

Throughout the earlier part of his poem the prologue
stanzas are invariably recapitulations of the previous
situation, and of this explanatory formula the two
following are specimens :

> Erewhile ye saw the havoc and dismay,
>   Wrought by King Agricane fierce of soul,
> Like torrent through the coast that cleaves its way,
>   Or petard breaching ranks where it doth roll,
> So with his sword he makes no idle play,
>   But strikes each standard and high banner pole,
> Hews down the foe, and his own men doth scatter,
> Nor cares which falls, the former or the latter.
>   " Orl. Inn." book i. canto ii.

> Fair sirs, in the last canto I left off,
>   Where at the Saracens Astolfo jeers,
> And, " Villain," saith, " thy vaunting fashion doff,
>   Unless thou vaunt in hell amid thy peers,
> Of barons proud laid low to be thy scoff :
>   To what I plan for thee now ope thine ears,
> Since with thy giant frame such rank doth tally,
> First boatswain I will make thee in a galley."
>   " Orl. Inn." book i. canto iv.

It is not until the fifteenth canto that he first breaks through the trammels of prescription by introducing one of those passages of abstract reflection definitely adopted by him as an invariable prefatory form from the twenty-sixth canto onwards, and handed down by him as a legacy to his successor.   We subjoin this first example of the newer form of introduction, which thus super-seded the older fashion :

> All things beneath the moon—wealth's vast increase—
>   Kingdoms, and realms, and rule, the whole world o'er,
> Are subject to Dame Fortune's light caprice,
>   Who, when least thought of, opes and shuts the door,
> And seeming white turns black, nor e'er doth cease
>   From change, but doth in war display her more
> Unstable, fickle, shifty, and ungracious,
> And beyond all things flighty and fallacious.
>   *Ibid.* book i. canto xv.

It is in these preliminary passages that the poet, liberated from the restrictions of convention, had free scope for the development of his personal genius, suppressed in the narrative portions of his work by the exigencies of his theme.   Thus his vivid fancy, expatiating in its enlargement, seizes on every mood of nature or his own mind, as a means of reintroducing himself to his audience.   Here is a stanza in the form of a spring greeting, a class of opening in which he evidently took especial delight :

> The season that doth heaven with light illume,
>   And gives the trees a vesture green to wear,
> That fills the air and earth with love and bloom,
>   And tuneful birds, and flowrets blushing fair,
> My song of love incites me to resume.
>   And bids me to all here once more declare

The prowess and the deeds in lofty fashion
Wrought by Orlando in his am'rous passion.

Ibid. book ii. canto xx.

In the same spirit is the May carol with which he opens
the nineteenth canto of his Second Book :

I found myself one merry morn in May,
   In a fair meadow decked with blossoms rare,
'Twas on a hill, the sea beside it lay,
   All tremulous with splendour shining there,
'Mid roses on a thorn-bush green, her lay
   Of love a damsel sang, and thrilled the air,
So sweetly moved her lips to dulcet phrases,
The thought of it my heart still stirs and raises.

A classical simile furnishes another introduction to his
auditors, with which he presents himself as follows :

A story-teller, Arion was his name,
   In the Sicilian sea, or near those bounds,
Had voice and words so sweet that round him came
   Dolphins and tunny-fish to hear the sounds.
That music fishes in the sea should tame
   Is, in good sooth, a thing that much astounds,
But for my lyre 'tis greater grace and glory,
If it draw ye, fair Sirs, to hear my story.

Ibid. book ii. canto xxvii.

Sometimes he stimulates the curiosity of his hearers by
a foreshadowing of the exciting subject of his narrative
in the following fashion :

Morgana and Alcina and their charms
   Have long delayed my Muse in her career,
Nor have I shown one brilliant feat of arms,
   Nor the sky full of shivered lance and spear,
Now must the world all shake to war's alarms,
   And blood above the saddle bows rise clear,

For, towards this canto's close, or I'm in error,
You'll come upon wounds, flames, fire, sword, and terror.
Ibid. book ii. canto xiv.

Again, when, in the following strain, invoking inspiration from his subject, he contrives to herald its importance :

Now must my voice to my song's level soar,
    And lordlier measure I must seek to find,
With bow more rapid sweep my lyre-strings o'er,
    Since of a youth to tell I have a mind,
So rude and fierce, in ruin drenched with gore
    To lay the world he well had been inclined,
Hight Rodamonte was this braggart heady,
Of whom I more than once have spoke already.
Ibid. book ii. canto vi.

It was this hero's name, immortalised in our language in its derivative, rhodomontade, the invention of which caused the author so much trouble that when he hit upon it he galloped home straightway and desired all the bells to be rung in token of rejoicing. The following exordium ushering in the second canto of the Third Book has all the triumphant glory of the dawn in its imagery and versification :

The sun, crowned gloriously with golden rays,
    His face uprist from ocean's rim afar,
And roseate dyed the sky, and from the gaze
    Already hid the waning morning star,
Within the palace, from all sides, the lays
    Were heard of pilgrim swallow, bar by bar,
And birds that in the garden dwelt, saluted
The rising day, with verse their joy that fluted.

The date of the commencement of the concluding portion of the poem is fixed by the stanzas with which the author addresses his audience in opening the first

canto of the Third Book, showing him to have resumed
the thread of his narrative at the close of the war with
Venice.

> As sweeter doth to mariner appear,
>   Whom stormy gales have buffeted about,
> The sight of tranquil deep and ripple clear,
>   Of air serene, and sky where stars look out ;
> And as the pilgrim doth rejoice to near
>   The smiling plain when day puts dark to rout,
> Since in the open he doth safely find him,
> With night and rugged mountains left behind him.
>
> Thus, since from us the infernal storm and stress
>   Of ruthless war departed has, I trow,
> And joy and mirth return the world to bless,
>   And fairer than before this Court doth show.
>   will with greater pleasure, I confess,
>   Resume the jocund tale planned long ago,
> Then come in courtesy to hear my story,
> Fair ladies, lords, and knighthood high in glory.

He thus addressed himself to the Court of Ferrara,
alluding to events familiar to all present, and in which
he and his hearers had borne their part, but which
require the interpretation of history to make them intelligible to the modern reader.

In another preface he takes the audience into his
confidence, expounding the plan of his work with consummate grace and beguiling simplicity in the subjoined
stanzas :

> With many a flower, blue, yellow, red, and white,
>   Of every kind that in the woodland grows,
> With fairest herbs I've made a nosegay bright,
>   Pinks, gillyflowers, pale lily, blushing rose,
> Come forward all whom fragrance doth delight,
>   And pick and choose as fancy may dispose,
> For some delight in lilies, some in roses,
> And each and all show varying taste in posies.

So I in divers mode have planted o'er
  With fights and love-affairs mine orchard plot,
Fierce hearts with joy on tales of battle pore,
  The soft and gentle on the lover's lot.
Now to Ruggiero, left in battle sore
  With Rodamonte on the meadow spot,
'Mid blows so stormy, and assaults so cruel,
That ne'er was seen the like of this fierce duel.

Idem, book iii. canto v.

The foregoing specimens will serve to show how completely the traditional forms, at first adhered to in the
composition of the "Orlando Innamorato," were discarded ere its completion, and how great was the variety
of prefatory addresses by which they were gradually
superseded.   Now it is somewhat remarkable that
Ariosto, having so wide a field of choice open to him,
should have contracted instead of enlarging its limits,
practically confining himself to one style of exordium—
that couched in the sermonising vein of didactic or
philosophical reflection.   The key to this anomaly must
be sought in the bent of his mind, which instinctively
selected human nature as its first, if not its sole, subject
of study.

Some modern critics see in the author of the "Furioso"
the embodiment of the pictorial genius of the Renaissance, but to me it seems as though they had mistaken
his temper and tendency, misled by the wonderful command of language which not only clothed but decorated
his ideas.   For he was in reality totally wanting in the
painter's first gift, that discriminating power which seizes
on the salient and suggestive features of the subject and
assigns due artistic proportion to its relative parts.   His
descriptions are of the catalogue order, mere unclassified
inventories of qualities or objects, and there is not

throughout the " Orlando Furioso " a single passage that calls up such a clear vision of any external scene as Boiardo evokes with a sketch in verse like that of the May morning just quoted.

Ariosto's strength lay in a different direction — in dramatic power of describing and dramatic insight in analysing human actions and motives; in a keen, if not profound comprehension of character; in realising, in short, the world within, instead of the world without. With nature he has little or no sympathy, and there is scarcely a trace in his works of his having been touched by her varying aspects. We know that he passed three years as Governor of the Garfagnana, in the heart of some of the finest scenery in Italy or the world. Morning by morning he must have seen the conflagration of the dawn tossed in flame from peak to peak of the blanched and shattered pinnacles of Carrara, day by day watched the Modenese Apennines stand out sculptured in sunshine, with the violet shadows on their flanks deepening and shoaling as the light went and came above them; year by year seen the moving pageantry of the seasons roll to and fro over the wide valley of the Serchio, winding like a highway among the hills to where it was lost in their blue gulfs of distance. Yet of all this we find no hint in his verse, in which, despite its elegant garrulity, the references to scenery are of the scantiest. At most a garden or two, planted with ornamental flowers carefully enumerated, a well-kept shrubbery with fruit-trees and shady arbours, occasionally a fountain, and more rarely a low hill, are mentioned with approval. Some of the adventures he records take place during maritime travel, and Notus or Boreas is duly invoked to call up a storm, which is, however, introduced as a purely conventional piece of stage mechanism, and in the strictest subordination to the human action it promotes. Boiardo, on the contrary, when he describes the sea quivering in the morning splendour, suggests the whole ocean in a single line, as does the skilled artist with the pencil-sweep limiting its horizon.

Keeping in mind this difference in mental constitution from his predecessor, it ceases to be surprising that Ariosto should have rejected for his exordiums all the models of pictorial and descriptive imagery left by him, to follow him only in those which gave free play to his own analytical and reflective turn of thought. His initial stanzas being thus devoted to moral generalities, we can reconstruct from them with tolerable accuracy the poet's scheme of life, regarded from the genially cynical point of view befitting a man well satisfied, in the main, with himself and his surroundings. For it must be remembered that all the philosophy handed down to us is necessarily, from the mere fact of its survival, the philosophy of success, and that the real bitterness of life remains mute in the inarticulate oblivion of obscurity. Your true cynic is the man who has failed, but whose opinions are consequently of no account, while triumph, trumpet-tongued, has the ear of the world and of futurity. Diogenes in his tub, blazoning obtrusive self-abnegation in the pride that apes humility, is but a sham pessimist compared to Lazarus amid his potsherds, and the latter, though propounding no paradoxes and enunciating no theories, is the more genuine if less noisy philosopher.

Ariosto's cynicism we feel is but the imaginative cynicism of prosperity, just sharp enough, like the *agro dolce* sauce of Italian cooks, to give piquancy of savour to dainty viands, not to strew ashes on the homely or insufficient fare of the less well served at the banquet of life. The foibles and inconsistencies of humanity he touches with a light hand, as much in caress as in chastisement; but its struggles and sufferings, its doubts and self-questionings, he leaves unexplored in his brilliant verse. Theology has no place in his system, and there is no longer a trace of those religious invocations so long adhered to by his predecessors. His code of morality, indeed, is rather of a pagan than a Christian type, and inculcating, as it does, only a certain measure of truth and kindliness without any ascetic self-restraint, would have sat lightly on an ancient Greek. The following stanzas (first and second of canto xxi.) emphasising the obligation of good faith, represent about the highest moral level to which he soars:

> No hempen rope doth bind a load so fast,
>   Or nail hold wood with such a forceful strain,
> As faith, when o'er a lofty soul is cast
>   The bond of its indissoluble chain.
> Nor was true faith by artists in the past
>   Depicted save in vesture without stain,
> Draped in a fair white veil like a religious,
> Since slightest soil or speck would make her hideous.
>
> Good faith should be maintained then without spot
>   Whether to thousands pledged, or one alone,
> Though in lone forest or sequestered grot
>   Remote from towns 'twere plighted all unknown,
> As though before tribunals, and the knot
>   Of witnesses, in deed or parchment shown,
> So, without oath or vow or any token,
> The simplest promise should be kept unbroken.

In the two stanzas next quoted, opening respectively the sixth and twenty-third cantos, sound moral lessons

are inculcated, perhaps all the more effectively that the
motive invoked is none of the highest :

> Ill fares the evil-doer who doth trust
>   That secrecy will hidden crime aye shroud,
> For if all else were mute, the entombing dust
>   Of earth—nay air itself—would cry aloud.
> And heaven ordains the sin itself shall thrust
>   The sinner—spent his term—to stand avowed ;
> His own accuser, though by none suspected,
> In unforeseen betrayal self-detected.
>
> Let each one help the other, rarely fate
>   Omits the recompense good actions claim,
> Or if she do, at least they bear no freight
>   Of death or loss, or ignominious shame.
> Who injures others payeth soon or late
>   The unforgotten score against his name.
> The proverb says, Men go forth nimble-footed
> To meet each other, but the hills stand rooted.

Ariosto, however, is not seen to advantage in this commonplace garb of sententious morality, which ill beseems
his gay and worldly temperament.   He is at his best in
the vein of playful sarcasm which characterises most of
his philosophical utterances and is his favourite method
of rebuke for falsehood or folly.   His caustic irony,
indeed, spared nothing, not even himself, for we can
scarcely believe that the following stanzas on poetical
chroniclers were penned without conscious satirical
reference to his own servility to princely patrons.   They
form an exception to his ordinary rhetorical outbursts in
being placed in the middle instead of at the opening of
a canto, and are part of St. John's discourse to Astolfo
during his journey to the limbo of lost property in the
moon, in search of the vanished reason of Orlando :

Less pious was Eneas—nor so bold
   Achilles as Fame tells—less Hector's fire—
And thousands there have been in days of old
   Who might to higher place than these aspire :
But palaces and villas, lands and gold,
   Conferred by their descendants were the hire
Paid for transcendent and immortal glory,
Bestowed on them by writers of their story.

Scarce was Augustus so benign and good,
   As Virgil's sounding trumpet doth proclaim,
His taste in poetry, 'tis understood,
   Doth cancel the proscription's debt of shame.
Of Nero's crimes far less perchance we should
   Have heard—and glorious yet might be his name,
Though earth and heaven he equally offended,
If scribes and authors he had but befriended.

In Homer's page Atrides now we see
   With triumph crowned—the Trojans dull and cold,
And, faithful to her spouse, Penelope
   Bear from her suitors insults manifold.
But whoso wishes truth from falsehood free
   Reversed and changed should have the story told :
Troy should victorious be, and Hellas routed,
And as a flirt Penelope be scouted.

And then, again, by history see betrayed
   The fame of Dido, who, though pure of heart,
Is now reputed as a worthless jade,
   Since Virgil played her an unfriendly part.
Nor marvel if some warmth I have displayed,
   Or if my views at some length I impart,
Writers I love, as suits my former station,
Since I on earth pursued the same vocation.
             "Orl. Fur." canto xxxiv. stanzas 24 *et seq.*

Like all flatterers, Ariosto occasionally gave a surreptitious vengeance to truth in an outburst of candour,

in the style of the subjoined sly hit at his fair auditors on their most sensitive point :

> Oh, happy cavaliers of elder days,
>   Who in lone valley or sequestered dell,
> In cavern dark, or savage forest ways,
>   In dens of serpents, bears, or lions fell,
> Found what in palaces scarce meets the gaze,
>   In our time, e'en of eyes that seek it well,
> Women, I mean, who in their youth's fresh morning,
> With beauty's title merit the adorning.
>
> *Ibid.* canto xvi. stanza 1.

And in another passage, under the form of a defence of the fair sex against their calumniators, he contrives to strengthen rather than weaken the case against them by a reference to his own very unfavourable experiences. His standard of constancy does not, however, seem to have been sufficiently high to justify recriminations against others, as we argue from what follows :

> 'Mid these complaints, and many more beside,
>   Along his road the King of Sarza spurred,
> As now in murmurs low he faintly sighed,
>   Now spake in tones that distant echo stirred ;
> While thus the female sex he vilified,
>   We must allow his reasoning was absurd,
> Since for a bad one here and there detected,
> At least a hundred good might be selected.

> Though 'mid the many I have loved, I vow,
>   I have not found a single constant dame ;
> That all are false I never will allow,
>   But on harsh destiny throw all the blame.
> Many there are, and have been before now,
>   'Gainst whom to lodge complaint no man can claim,
> But 'tis my fate if 'mid five score nonsuches
> There be one jade, to fall into her clutches.

Nor will I cease to seek till, ere I die—
    Nay, ere my locks more threads of silver show—
One day I yet may boast that even I
    Some fair have found whose faith no change doth know,
If this occur (and yet my hopes are high
    That it may be) I ne'er will weary grow
Of crowning her, as best I can, with glory,
With pen and tongue, in prose and verse, and story.
                    Ibid. canto xxvii. stanzas 122 *et seq.*

Ariosto's tone in speaking of women, of whom his real estimate was evidently very low, alternates between raillery and panegyric. We subjoin a specimen of the latter, selecting two stanzas from the long opening passage of the thirty-sixth canto, leading up to a tribute of flattery to Vittoria Colonna :

Not Tomyris or Harpalyce dread,
    Nor those who came to Turnus'—Hector's aid—
Not she who Tyrians and Sidonians led
    Across the sea to Libya's shore embayed,
Zenobia not, nor she before whom fled
    Assyria's, India's, Persia's hosts dismayed,
Not these alone, with others famed in story,
Deserve to shine for ever crowned with glory.

For women strong and faithful, pure and wise,
    Not Greece and Rome alone have had to boast,
But every land on which the sun doth rise,
    From the Hesperides to India's coast,
Whose worth and fame are smothered in such guise,
    That of a thousand one is known at most,
Since of their deeds there then were none to tell us,
Save only writers masculine and jealous.
                    Ibid. canto xxxvi. stanzas 5 and 6.

The ethics of love occupy the largest space in the poet's lucubrations, as the vicissitudes of the tender passion itself supplied, no doubt, the subject of his most frequent meditations, and the source of his most poignant emotions. Adhering to the principle of allowing him as far as possible to speak for himself, we extract one of the few passages in which he takes an ennobling view of that sentiment.

> In love full many a one feels pangs most sore,
>   Of which the greater part I have essayed,
> Unto my hurt so varied o'er and o'er
>   That I can speak as one who's of the trade,
> Hence if I say, as I have said before
>   In speech and writing, and have ne'er gainsaid,
> That pain is light, or sharp and keen this latter,
> Accept as truth my verdict in the matter.
>
> I say, and said, and will say till I die,
>   Who knows himself entrapped in worthy snare,
> Although he find his lady cold and shy,
>   Averse and distant to his burning prayer ;
> Though hope be none, though love all wage deny,
>   Though toil and time be vainly wasted there,
> If high his heart be set, in deepest anguish
> He need not weep, although he droop and languish.
>
> But weep should he who hath enslaved his will
>   To a fair tress of hair and bright eyes twain,
> 'Neath which doth hide a heart defiled with ill,
>   Where nought is pure and only dregs remain ;
> The wretch would fly, but with him carries still
>   Like stricken deer, the arrow's rankling pain,
> Shame of himself and of his love he feeleth,
> Nor dares disclose a wound no balsam healeth.
>
> *Ibid.* canto xvi. stanzas 1 *et seq.*

Ariosto always treats this subject from an autobiographical point of view, alleging his experience or bemoaning his weakness with ingenuous *naïveté* and frankness. The following three stanzas were evidently penned in one of those moments of disillusion which were doubtless frequent with him :

Who sets his foot in love's entangling snare
    Withdraw it ere his wings are limed as well.
That love is madness all the wise declare
    With concord that our doubts should sure dispel.
Though all may not Orlando's fury share,
    Some other sign their lunacy doth tell ;
And of insanity what proof more striking
Than sacrifice of self for others' liking ?

By varied symptoms shown, the cause is one,
    Alike the frenzied folly whence they spring ;
Like a great wood, untracked and vast, where none
    Finds the straight road 'mid paths all wandering,
To left, to right, and here and there they run—
    In short, my reasoning to an end to bring,
He who in love grows old deserves no better
For all his pains, than manacle and fetter.

Well might ye answer me—Another's fault,
    Friend, thou dost show, unmindful of thine own,
Full well (I answer), now my mind makes halt
    In lucid interval, my case is known,
And much I strive and hope (the last assault
    Repelled) to rest and leave this dance alone,
But all at once to do't my strength exceedeth
Since on my very bones the poison feedeth.

Ibid. canto xxiv. stanzas 9, &c.

From the following stanzas on jealousy we should have
inferred the susceptible poet's liability to this passion,
even if his biographers had not expressly stated it :

What happier or more joyous state had been
    Than that of tender heart in amorous mood ?
What life more beatific and serene
    Than to be bound by love's sweet servitude ?
Were man not goaded by that sting so keen
    Of black suspicion—by that fear pursued—
And martyred by that dark and deadly passion
Of jealousy, whose rage takes every fashion.

While every other bitter interblent
  Amid the honey of this sweetest sweet
Is but additional perfection lent
  To love, its joy to heighten and complete,
More dainty tastes the liquid element
  From thirst prolonged, and after fasting meat ;
Nor can the joys of peace be duly rated,
Save first the ills of war are known and hated.

Though eyes behold not what the heart would see,
  And ever craves—e'en this may be made light,
The longer the slow hours of absence be
  The greater joy when time doth reunite.
To service without wage we may agree
  If hope survive, however faint and slight.
For service true is in the end rewarded,
Though long it seem to pass quite unregarded.

The angers, the repulses, and in short
  All pains and torments love has to endure,
Do by their recollection but exhort
  To fuller sense of joy that we secure.
But this infernal plague, if it distort
  And poison the sick mind with ills past cure,
Makes even mirth and gladness when they follow,
Seem to the lover flavourless and hollow.

                    Ibid. canto xxx. stanzas 9, &c.

In the next prologue quoted a genuine note of manly
tenderness for women escapes the mocking bard, suggesting the idea of an utterance called forth by some actual
incident at the moment.

All other animals beneath the sun
  Or live in peace, to quietness inclined,
Or if they come to blows, the male doth shun
  To war upon the female of his kind.
Safe with her mate through woods the bear doth run,
  The lion next the lioness you'll find,
Wolf is to she-wolf mild as gentle zephyr,
Nor doth the bull with fear inspire the heifer.

What plague accurst then lends Megaera power
   Dissension within human hearts to sow?
That man and wife must wrangle by the hour,
   And scold and rave in language vile and low.
Fresh blows on scratched and livid faces shower,
   And bathe the marriage bed with tears of woe,
Nor tears alone do plenteously bestrew it,
But blood, oft shed in anger doth bedew it.

Methinks that man doth grievous outrage dare
   On nature—and 'gainst Heaven's high law rebel,
Who a fair woman's face to strike can bear,
   Or hurt one hair of hers in anger fell.
But whoso poisons her, or doth not spare
   With cord or knife her spirit to expel,
A man I'll ne'er believe such wretch as this is,
But fiend in human form from hell's abysses.

Ibid. canto v. stanzas 1, &c.

Though Ariosto's views of life may not seem to the modern reader very novel or profound, we can well believe that his contemporaries, dazzled by the florid and brilliant language in which they were expressed, may not have perceived that his sparkling epigrams in octaves embodied only commonplace and obvious truths. They may be best summed up in the celebrated definition of a proverb as "the wisdom of many and the wit of one." For he converted the common stock of ideas round him into an intellectual currency, stamped with the impress of his genius and coined in the authority of his name.

This novelty of form may be accepted as a substitute for originality of substance, but it does not atone for the absence of moral elevation in the utterances of the laughing philosopher of Ferrara. The best that can be said for him in this respect is that his morality, if not lofty, was sincere; that he assumed nothing he did not feel; and that if his ideal was placed low, he at any rate lived up to it.   There is abundant evidence in his biography that he practised the facile virtues he preached, and that if the standard he proposed to himself was not a very exalted one, he at least attained its level.

That the scoffing attitude towards feminine charms assumed by the singer of Orlando's madness was but a pose may be inferred from the love poems addressed to Alessandra Bennucci, the fair widow whom he certainly loved and probably married. The following sonnet is one of the many inspired by the golden locks which were one of her real or fancied charms :

> How can I worthily the praise unfold,
>   Due to thy charms angelic and divine,
>   Since e'en at thought of those fair locks of thine,
> The tongue doth fail and speech grows dull and cold?
>
> Though lofty style and phrase of dulcet mould,
>   Taught by all Greek and Latin schools, were mine,
>   Not half or part the meed could they assign
> Of praise to those bright rippling knots of gold.
>
> To see them shine so even and so long,
>   In wealth of silken skeins, to many a lute
> Might furnish matter for eternal song.
>   Ah! had I bit, like Ascra's bard, the fruit
> Of laurel, so my praise would I prolong,
>   That I should die a swan, where I die mute.

Here we have more of Ariosto's real feeling than he displays in the persiflage of the brilliant prologue stanzas which were part of the framework inherited from his predecessor, already out of date in the change in the conditions of art effected in the brief interval between the two. The extension of the use of printing had wrought a revolution which, in obviating the necessity for oral declamation, had deprived poetry of its original *raison d'être*. The exquisitely finished exordium and close of each canto in the "Orlando Innamorato" divided it into separate instalments for recitation by the singer, who resorts to the device practised by all story-tellers from Scheherazade onwards, of holding on the interest of his auditors by suspending his narrative at the most thrilling crisis. The "Orlando Furioso," on the other hand, though cast in the same mould as its predecessor, was printed and published in strictly modern fashion before being submitted to its author's patron, the Cardinal of Este. The poetical forms adopted from the earlier poem have therefore lost their real meaning, and only survive as stereotyped and fossilised conventions. The canto has become a chapter, the glorified ballad-singer is merged in the courtly poet laureate, and the romantic poem has become literature in ceasing to be song.

CHAPTER IV

Charlemagne's Tournament

In the brilliant opening of the "Orlando Innamorato" we have the pure creation of Boiardo's imagination, as the incidents are entirely of his own invention. True, he introduces the stock figures of popular romance, assuming a certain familiarity with their previous history on the part of his audience, but he invests them with an absolutely new invididuality, and clothes them for the first time with the semblance of flesh and blood. The puppet heroes of mediæval fable take on the lineaments of living actors on his crowded stage, and if his heroines are of more conventional type, they are, at least, strongly differentiated. While flagrantly violating all historical, geographical, and archæological truth, he adheres closely to the unalterable facts of human nature, and never loses sight of the essential distinctions of character between his personages amid all the fantastic wizardry of his narration. Their introduction on the scene in the first act of his drama is perhaps the most vividly descriptive passage in early song. The curtain rises on it in the following fashion :

> Fair Sirs and gallant knights assembled here,
>   To list to stories rich in new delight,
> In silence, prithee, give attentive ear
>   To the fair tale my song shall now recite,

Then shall ye hear of actions without peer,
  Of lofty toils and deeds of wondrous might,
By bold Orlando wrought 'neath Love's constraining,
What time King Charles as Emperor was reigning.

Nor deem it, Sire, so strange a thing if I,
  Of great Orlando as enamoured tell,
For nought there is so proud beneath the sky
  But is subdued by Love's o'ermastering spell,
Not strength of arm, or soul of courage high,
  Not shield or mail nor sword so sharp and fell,
Nor other power, what might soe'er it wieldeth,
But unto Love succumbeth straight, and yieldeth.

This novel tale to few indeed is known,
  By Turpin's self concealed—who deemed perchance,
Its tenor, to the valiant Count if shown,
  Might umbrage give, and eke be viewed askance,
Since he was loser, matched 'gainst Love alone,
  Who conquered all things else, as tells romance,
To wit Orlando—knight of fame and glory—
No more of preface—come we to my story.
            "Orl. Inn." book i. canto i. stanzas 1 *et seq*.

He here claims originality for his tale with the fiction
that Turpin had deliberately suppressed it out of deference
to Orlando, and he then digresses to the doings of another
personage, Gradasso, for which he cites the Archbishop's
chronicle as authority, as was his wont for many incidents
not to be found in it, returning then to the tournament as
follows :

But here I leave him to his projects vain,
  Since of his coming ye shall duly hear ;
To turn once more to France and Charlemayne,
  Who musters baron stout and chevalier
And calls all Christian princes to his train,
  Each duke and lord, and paladin and peer,

To the great tournament which he proposes
To hold in May-tide, at the Pasch of Roses.*

In court are gathered peer and paladin,
    The feast to honour with observance due,
And from all sides and furthest bounds flock in
    To Paris, crowds of people not a few;
And thither Saracens their way too win,
    For royal court was cried the world unto;
And all received safe-conduct, say narrators,
Save only they were renegades or traitors.

And folk of Spain swarmed thick in every place,
    Come in the train of barons great and high;
Of King Gradonio with the serpent-face,
    And Ferraguto of the dragon-eye;
King Balugante, kin to Charles's race,
    And Isolier, to Serpentin aye nigh,
And many more of noble rank and title,
Who shall be mentioned in the joust's recital.

With instruments did Paris all resound,
    And bells and drums and clarions stirred the air;
And war-horses with trappings were led round,
    Of antique fashion now disused and rare;
And gauds of gold and jewels did abound,
    And tongues past counting were heard spoken there,
For all, to do the emperor's good pleasure,
Adorned their persons without stint or measure.

And now, as the eventful day drew near,
    When the great joust they should begin to fight,
King Charles, in royal robes with festive cheer,
    Unto his banquet-table bade invite
Each noble baron, lord, and cavalier,
    Who came his feast to honour with their might;
The numbers at that banquet ranged with cover,
Were thousands twenty-two, with thirty over.

* Whitsuntide, in Italian Pasqua Rosa, a favourite season for
tournaments in the old romances, Arthurian and Carolingian.

King Charlemayne, with jocund face and mien,
  Amid his paladins on golden chair,
High-seated at the table round, was seen,
  In front of him the Saracens grouped there,
Who neither bench nor table used, I ween,
  But lay like couchant hounds on carpets fair :
Their custom and their wont herein retaining,
And usages and modes of France disdaining.

To left and right the tables fair to see,
  Were duly ordered, as my volume sings,
Crowned heads sat at the first, of high degree,
  The English, Lombard, and the Breton Kings ;
Otho, and Solomon, and Desiderio, three
  With whose renown all Christendom yet rings :
And next them came in order of gradation,
The Christian princes, ranged by worth and station.

To dukes and marquises the second place,
  To counts and belted knights the third doth fall,
The House of Mayence doth high honour grace,
  And Gano of Pontier above them all,
Rinaldo's glances blazed, for that vile race
  Of traitors, with proud mien and words of gall,
Derided him amongst themselves with laughter,
Because his garb theirs was not fashioned after.

                      Ibid. stanzas 8 *et seq.*

Since the modern reader is less well informed than
Boiardo's contemporaries as to the history and position
of these personages, he should bear in mind that Gano
or Ganelon is always mentioned with detestation as the
traitor who, out of jealousy of Orlando, betrayed Charlemagne's rearguard at Roncesvalles to Marsilio, one of the
Saracen kings of Spain. His personal appearance was
forbidding, as he was six-and-a-half feet high, with fiery
hair and glaring eyes. Silent and moody, he disbelieved
in friendship or any form of moral good, and was a pre-

cursor of modern pessimism. His castle stood on the Blocksberg, the loftiest summit of the Harz Mountains, afterwards accurst as the haunt of witches and demons. Rinaldo's poverty was evidenced in his old-fashioned doublet, the subject of the traitor's mockery. This paladin, the cousin and rival of Orlando, was the eldest of the sons of Aymon, whose castle of Montalbano or Montauban stood on the banks of the Tarn, near its junction with the Garonne. His virtues were those of a soldier rather than a citizen, as he was no less rapacious than valiant, and paid his armed followers out of the plunder of travellers. When outlawed by Charlemagne for killing one of his knights by throwing a chess-board at his head, he and his three brothers lived as freebooters in a wood, like English Robin Hood and his merry men. When he and Orlando come to blows the latter does not fail to throw these adventures in his face, with that plainness of speech in which the paladins indulged when excited.

The banquet is progressing gaily, the courses, ushered in with trumpet flourish, are borne round in dishes of massy gold, and wine is served in cups of fine enamel from the Emperor's table to those he delights to honour, when the festivity is suddenly interrupted by an un-expected apparition.

> Then all is mirth and festive revelry,
>   And low-voiced converse fair the ear delights,
> King Charles, who on such height himself doth see,
>   Girt round by kings and dukes and doughty knights,
> All Paynimrie holds worth no greater fee
>   Than ocean sands the whirling tempest smites;
> When lo! a sight both novel and amazing
> Holds him and all around in wonder gazing.

For at the great hall's end, in stern array,
  Four giants entered, fierce and overgrown,
And in their midst a damsel made her way,
  Behind whom walked a single knight alone;
The morning star she seemed at break of day,
  A golden lily, or a rose new-blown,
In short, to sum the truth and reach a sequel,
No charms were ever seen that hers could equal.

Though in that hall was Galerana seen,
  Though Alda, great Orlando's spouse, was there,
Clarissa, Armellina mild of mien,
  And many another one whose praise I spare,
And fair was each, and virtue's mirror sheen,
  Or rather fair had seemed, till showed more fair,
That flower of loveliness whose radiant glory
Eclipsed all other beauties famed in story.

Ibid. stanzas 20 *et seq.*

The bevy of fair ladies described here may require
some introduction to the reader, although they disappear
henceforward from the page, humdrum wives standing a
poor chance of remembrance in competition with the
bewitchments of Angelica. Galerana was the wife of
Charlemagne, sister of one of the Moorish kings. Alda
or Aude "La Belle," as she was styled, daughter of the
Count of Genoa and sister of Oliver, was married to
Orlando, and Clarissa or Clarice, sister of Yon or Huon,
King of Bordeaux, to Rinaldo. Angelica tells her tale
and makes her petition to Charlemagne, introducing her
attendant knight as Hubert of the Lion, unjustly
despoiled of his dominions, and herself as his sister. He
desires to be allowed to challenge all the knights to
single combat, on condition that if once unhorsed they
are to consider themselves his prisoners, but if the like
mishap befalls him, she is to be the prize of the victor.

These terms being granted by Charlemagne, who is represented as prolonging his interview with her for the pleasure of gazing on her, despite his venerable years, she withdraws to the rendezvous, a solitary pine beside Merlin's Rock. The next actor in the drama is Malagisi the sorcerer, a famous character in romance. He and his brother Vivian, twin sons of Duke Bevis of Aygremont, and cousins of Rinaldo, were both stolen in infancy. The slave woman who carried off Maugis or Malagisi was devoured by a lion and a leopard, who then killed each other in disputing for the child. The latter was found under a hawthorn, whence he is called d'Aubespine, by Orianda the Fay, who brought him up and taught him magic and necromancy. By these arts he took from the Saracen, Anthenor, the sword Fusberta, and from a demon, whom he cheated by personating another fiend, the enchanted horse, Bajardo, who understood human speech. Both these fairy gifts he bestowed upon his kinsman, Rinaldo. No sooner has Angelica left the hall than this potent enchanter discovers by the evocation of his familiars that she is a false and foul witch, the daughter of Galafrone, King of Cathay, while the pretended Hubert is his son, Argalìa, equipped with an enchanted steed and armour, especially a gilded lance whose touch unhorses the stoutest knight. Even more celebrated than this magic weapon is the ring of Angelica which worn on the finger counteracts all spells, but transferred to the mouth renders the bearer invisible. By this talisman the incantations of Malagisi, who tries to take her captive while sleeping, are frustrated, and he is made prisoner by Argalìa, while she takes possession of his book, and is mistress of all his magic in addition to her own.

Meantime the number of knights claiming to do battle for Angelica is so great that they have to draw lots for precedence, and the first chance falls to Astolfo of England, whose beauty, insouciance, and tendency to harmless braggadocio combine to make him one of the most vivid and genial figures on Boiardo's canvas. Here is the picture of him riding forth to the combat at Merlin's Rock.

> The day to eve already had declined,
>   Ere all the lots were fully drawn at last,
> And Duke Astolfo, high and proud of mind,
>   Demands his armour, nor is aught downcast,
> Though coming night the day makes dim and blind,
>   He saith, as one in valorous mood set fast,
> That he will bring this fray to swift decision,
> Unhorsing Hubert in the first collision.
>
> This Englishman, fair Sirs, I'd have ye know,
>   Astolfo, was of beauty past compare,
> Rich, but his courtesy made fairer show
>   Than e'en his wealth ; of goodly dress and air ;
> Less skilled perhaps in arms, for oft o'erthrow
>   In fray or joust unhorsed, fell to his share,
> But to ill chance ascribed he each fresh stumble,
> Remounted dauntless, dauntlessly to tumble.
>
> But to our tale ; in armour he was seen
>   Well worth a kingdom's ransom fairly paid,
> For round his shield were set great pearls of sheen,
>   And gold the shirt of mail where'er displayed,
> But priceless must the helmet be, I ween,
>   For there a mighty jewel was inlaid,
> Which, unless Turpin's volume be misleading,
> A ruby was, a walnut's size exceeding.
>
> His charger trappings wrought with leopards bore,
>   Embroidered thick, and all with gold o'erlaid,
> Alone he started forth, nor any store
>   On danger set, as on his path he strayed.

The day was spent, and unto night it wore,
   When unto Merlin's Rock his way he made.
And there the gorgeous knight the horn uptaking,
Blew a loud blast, far distant echoes waking.

Uprose stout Argalìa at his note,
   From where his bulk beside the fountain lay,
And armed him *cap-à-pie* from heel to throat,
   In harness all complete without delay,
And on Astolfo rushed in white surcoat
   Which o'er himself and charger flowed away,
His shield braced on, his lance set firm and steady,
Which had so many knights unhorsed already.

A courteous greeting changed the pair between,
   The terms of combat were defined anew,
The damsel next was shown upon the scene,
   And then to proper distance both withdrew,
Ere charging each 'gainst each across the green,
   Their shields advanced, knees gripped, with balance true,
But lo! scarce touched, Astolfo at six paces,
Dropt, while his heels did with his crest change places.

Stretched lay the Duke upon the sand full low,
   And cried indignant, Fortune false and fell,
Thou in despite of reason art my foe,
   My saddle's was the fault, thou know'st right well,
My seat I sure had kept an' 'twere not so,
   And won yon beauteous dame by valour's spell;
Thou hast contrived the chance to earth that bore me,
To give yon Pagan knight a triumph o'er me.

Astolfo ta'en those giants huge between ·
   Is led within the tent by their stout arms,
But when he of his harness stript is seen,
   The beauty of his face the maid so charms
Shown in its dainty grace and comely sheen,
   That pity for his case her bosom warms,

And he by her was with such honour treated,
As to a prisoner might be duly meted.

Unbound and all unguarded did he stray,
    In pleasant dalliance the fount beside,
While fair Angelica by moonlight's ray,
    Gazed on his beauty when she could unspied,
And when 'twas dark, his limbs she bade him lay
    Upon the couch the curtains' screen inside,
She and her brother with the giant warders,
Kept watch outside lest he transgress their orders.

Ibid. stanzas 59 *et seq.*

The first light of day brings on the scene the next
champion, Ferraguto, a Saracen giant, spell-charmed, like
Achilles, against hurt, save in one vulnerable spot. Unhorsed, nevertheless, by Argalia's magic lance, he refuses
to be bound by the terms of the duel, renews the fight,
puts his opponent to flight, and slaying the four giants,
pursues Angelica, who spurs her palfrey towards the
forest of the Ardennes in haste to escape from her rude
wooer. Astolfo, left alone upon the field, picks up
Argalia's lance, which has been forgotten in the confusion
of the Saracen's onset, and returns to Paris with the news
of what has occurred. Rinaldo and Orlando, both consumed with jealous passion, set out secretly on the track
of the enchantress, who has thus lured the two mightiest
paladins from their duty. Orlando only yields to his
impulse after a protracted struggle with his better nature,
in portraying which Boiardo shows himself not without
psychological insight. Meantime the tournament goes
on in their absence, the terms being that one knight is to
hold the lists against all comers until defeated, when the
victor takes his place. Serpentino was chosen to open
the battle, whose initial stage is described as follows :

The day broke fair, and dawned with blithesome cheer,
    Nor ever sun arose more fair and bright,
First on the field King Charles was to appear,
    Unarmed save for his greaves, in public sight
High on a mail-clad steed did he career,
    With staff in hand and sword upon his right,
And round his feet in service meet and decent,
Flocked counts and knights, and barons high and puissant.

Lo Serpentino to the field doth pace,
    Armed *cap-à-pie*, a wondrous mien he wore,
A mighty war-horse did he curb with grace,
    Which pawed the ground with ardour fretting sore,
This side and that curvetting o'er the place,
    With eyes like coals, and bit all frothèd o'er,
Neighs the fierce brute such strait place ill-befitting,
And snorts with nostrils through which flames seem spitting.

And in like mood his daring cavalier,
    With visage set and stern doth him bestride,
Arrayed in splendid arms doth he appear,
    Firm in his seat with mien and air of pride ;
Men, women, children, point at him and peer,
    Such nerve and valour are in him descried,
As give to all full reason for discerning,
That none save he the prize hath hope of earning.

As cognizance and bearing of this knight,
    On azure shield a golden star doth shine,
And on his lofty crest all richly dight,
    And surcoat fair, was wrought a like design ;
His shirt of mail and helmet strong and light,
    Were counted to be worth a royal mine ;
And all his costly armour shone resplendent,
With gem and stone, and precious pearl and pendant.

So in the lists this champion takes his place,
    And after he had duly paced them round,
He like a tower stood in the central space,
    While from all sides the trumpet blast 'gan sound ;

E

The jousters from the corners inward pace,
  Outvying in rich attire whereon abound
Such gems and gold and pearls for every wearer,
That Paradise their presence had made fairer.

A paladin comes first to claim the fight,
  Whose armour is with silver moons besprent,
The lord of Bordeaux, Angelino hight,
  Well skilled in war, and joust and tournament;
Then Serpentin made sudden movement light,
  So swift he seemed a whirlwind as he went,
While from the other side like tempest heady,
Comes Angelino, lance in rest made ready.

Then full in front, where helm and shield unite,
  Doth Angelin strike Serpentin a blow,
But backward yielded not the doughty knight,
  Who 'neath the stroke bent to his saddle-bow;
With fall so sudden doth the other light,
  That both his heels he to high heaven doth show,
The cry goes up from all the field uproarious,
He of the star is up to this victorious.

Ibid. canto ii. stanzas 32 *et seq.*

The series of combats that follows are described with
amazing life and spirit, so that the interest is never
allowed to flag for a moment, until a critical stage of
the mimic battle is reached in which after the defeat of
the principal Christians, Grandonio, a pagan giant of
irresistible strength and ferocity holds the lists. The
princes of the house of Mayence, true to their nature,
slip away lest they should be called upon to answer to
his challenge, after they have seen the mighty Oliver
flung from the saddle and carried from the lists insensible
with his helmet cleft in twain, but help comes from an
unexpected quarter, for the high-spirited Astolfo, who
had been partially disabled by the fall of his horse early in

the day, determines at least to strike a blow for Christendom, although unaware of the potent auxiliary he possessed in the lance of Argalìa. A characteristic description of his demeanour as he takes his place as a spectator among the ladies is given in stanza 55 of the Second Canto.

> Astolfo hath returned the crowd among,
>   Borne by a palfrey white of easy pace,
> Unarmed, save that his sword beside him hung,
>   And midst the ladies he with smiling face
> Disports him with gay speech and ready tongue,
>   As one who overflows with witty grace,
> But while he lounges thus, Grifon unseated,
> Is by Grandonio flung to earth defeated.

The like fate having befallen all his subsequent antagonists, he is left master of the field, and with intolerable arrogance loudly taunts the Christians with their cowardice.

> But if ere this that Pagan proudly spoke,
>   His insolence doth now all bounds defy,
> He cries to all in words that ire provoke,
>   Ye Paladins, who wine-cups love to ply,
> The tavern seek ye, vile and dastard folk,
>   In other games than drinking skilled am I,
> Bravely this Table Round the world defieth,
> So long as to its challenge none replieth.

> When now King Charles these insults heard dismayed,
>   And saw his Court the scoff of Paynim foe,
> With troubled look and mien that fear betrayed,
>   He cast around his eyes that seemed to glow ;
> Where now are those who homage should have paid,
>   And who forsake me in this day of woe ?
> Where Gano of Pontier, Rinaldo great, or
> Orlando's self, vile recreant and traitor ?

Vile offspring of vile dam, false renegade,
    An ye return, may I this instant die,
If these my hands hang thee not without aid !
    These words and many more King Charles doth cry.
Astolfo from behind heard his tirade,
    And slipped away, unseen of every eye,
Then home returning, all so quick arrayed him,
That armed within the lists he soon displayed him.

Not that the valiant baron deemed in sooth,
    A vict'ry o'er the Paynim stout to gain ;
But only sought in loyalty and ruth,
    To do his duty unto Charlemayne.
Firm on his horse, he seemed in very truth,
    A peerless knight, surpassing all the train;
But those who knew him said, By gracious Heaven
Some other help than this to us be given.

With graceful mien, his head inclining low,
    Before King Charles, he said, My Lord and Sire,
This haughty foeman to unhorse I go,
    Since such, I understand, is thy desire,
The King, with troubled face, where scorn doth show,
    Said, Go, and help ye Heaven in strait so dire !
Then to those round he cried in indignation,
We wanted but this last humiliation.

Astolfo vowed that Pagan to enslave.
    A captive at the oar upon the sea,
Whence the fierce giant doth so rage and rave,
    That never equalled could his anger be.
Now will I tell in my next canto's stave,
    If by the sovereign Lord 'tis granted me,
Chances more strange, and deeds and marvels greater,
Than e'er were sung or written by narrator.

                        Ibid. canto ii. 63 *et seq.*

The amazement of the beholders at the result of the
encounter, in which the magic lance proves its efficiency,

causes a scene of great commotion, and the astute Gano, guessing that Astolfo's victory must have been due to a "fluke," returns with his followers, thinking to wrest his easily earned laurels from him. Foiled in this expectation, they resort to their usual expedient of treachery, and after one has been detected and disgraced for an attempt to hold his own against Astolfo by having himself bound to the saddle in contravention of all the laws of the game, the champion is finally unhorsed by a blow from behind in an encounter in which three set upon him together. Thereupon ensues a row royal, as Astolfo, assailed by the whole house of Mayence, first lays Grifone low with a broken head.

> His helm of steel alone kept life within,
>   Now in the lists behold the melley rage,
> For Gano, with Macarius, Ugolin,
>   Armed 'gainst Astolfo furious battle wage ;
> While Turpin and Duke Namo both strike in,
>   With Richard, and in aid of him engage,
> From all sides rush the folk in tumult swelling,
> The scandal brings King Charles to aid its quelling.
>
> Who soundly doth belabour each and all,
>   And more than thirty heads hath broke, I wis ;
> What traitor, or what rebel, hear him bawl,
>   Hath dared disturb my feast with scene like this?
> He turns his charger through the seething brawl,
>   Nor e'er a chance to ply his staff doth miss ;
> His path the mighty Emperor soon cleareth,
> As each in fear or homage disappeareth.
>
> _Ibid._ canto iii. stanzas 23 _et seq._

Astolfo is naturally infuriated when the house of Mayence tries to prove him the author of the disturbance, and Grifone kneels at Charles's feet to invoke justice upon him.

Inform ye, Sire, from all here, high and low,
    I do beseech ye, how the case hath been,
And if ye find that I to strike the blow
    Against the Englishman, the first was seen,
All pains will I in patience undergo,
    Though I be quartered here upon the green ;
But if contrariwise proved his wrongdoing,
Let him who wrought the ill accept its ruing.

With error wrath so clouds Astolfo's mind,
    That Charles's presence he esteemeth nought,
But cries, False traitor ! ill to thee comes kind,
    Vile offshoot of vile seed, with malice fraught,
Thy heart within thy breast my hand shall find,
    And tear it forth, ere we from hence are brought.
Grifone saith, I fear thee not a tittle,
And in more fitting place will show how little.

But here by reason's sway I hold me bound,
    Lest I dishonour my good liege and lord,
But still the Duke doth cry, Malignant hound,
    Thief, ribald, curst of Heaven, by man abhorred ;
King Charles with clouded brow then darkly frowned,
    And cried, Fore Heaven ! Astolfo, by my word,
An ye mend not your manners and your speeches,
A lesson ye shall learn that sorrow teaches.

                Ibid. stanzas 26 *et seq.*

But Astolfo's rage has become uncontrollable, and the whole series of incidents is brought to a close by his consignment to prison for brawling in the royal presence. They form in one respect the most instructive example of Boiardo's style and genius, as entirely created by his own invention without aid from chronicle or fable, and they show that supreme power of narration which makes him one of the first of story-tellers. The animated scenes which he unrolls before us, from the stir and hum in the streets of Paris, and the great banquet interrupted by the appearance of Angelica, to the combats at Merlin's Rock, and the varied passages of arms in the tournament itself, have all the life and movement of the animated pictures in a kinematograph, and the action, while its separate threads remain distinct, never flags for a moment. Consummate art of construction is displayed, too, in the way in which it is made to prelude the main subject of the poem, in the departure of Orlando, lured from his duty by a fatal passion, and in the anticipation of the treachery of the house of Mayence, to which we may suppose him in the poem, as well in the chronicle on which it was founded, to have fallen a victim at Roncesvalles. The first act of the great poem is thus like the overture of an opera, which heralds its music by preliminary and prophetic strains.

Tasso, who borrowed many suggestions from Boiardo, has followed on the lines of Angelica's arrival to lure the knights from their allegiance, in the appearance of Armida in the camp of Godfrey of Bouillon on a similar mission. She, too, entices the Christian champions from the crusading host under pretext of seeking redress for her supposed wrongs, and like her prototype relies not merely upon her personal charms but on her necromantic arts to aid her in the accomplishment of her purpose. The Damascus enchantress plays, however, a double part and embodies a dual thread of traditions, as her ensnarement of Rinaldo associates her with that other group of sorceresses of whom Circe was the classical original.

CHAPTER V

The Hercules Saga in Mediæval Song

THE earlier Renaissance in Italy might more truly be called a *Reveillé*, since it was rather an awakening than a new birth. Literature slept in the infancy of tongues and dialects resulting from barbaric invasion, but the hoarded wealth of fable and fiction handed down from antiquity had a vivid and abiding life in the popular imagination. Dante, with the instinctive craving of genius for the widest possible audience, first divined the possibilities of the new hybrid speech, which he found, by a philological miracle, ready shaped to his lofty use. There is no Italian literature behind him, yet the "vulgar" idiom becomes in his hands an instrument of the widest range, capable of uttering the most sublime flights of thought, the most abstruse ideas of philosophy, the most exalted forms of religious symbolism. The divorce between folk-speech and letters effected by the divergence of the Romance languages from the parent Latin having been thus set aside, the store of oral and traditional material for tale or verse accumulated in the long memory of ages was ready to be poured through the newly opened channel of expression.

But the host of phantoms that peopled the brain of Europe had not dwelt there without undergoing some process of transformation or development. Fable bred fable, and legend branched into legend, dropping some of their original features and assimilating new ones as they grew. And as mythology naturally lost its religious associations in a Christian atmosphere, divinities became humanised, and demi-gods were deprived of their celestial kinship, in their later avatars. Shorn of many of their attributes, they survived rather as personifications of some persistent abstraction, than as personages with a definite life history.

The favourite ideal of this fantastic world, like that of the elder past from which it sprang, is that of the embodiment of irresistible strength exercised on behalf of right, representing in both cases the craving for justice of a rude age, when violence could only be matched with violence, and the brute strength of the oppressor vanquished by that of the deliverer. The classical hero and the mediæval knight-errant are thus but variations on a single type, around which gathered the most motley accretions of fable and fancy. Hercules, the "strong man" of Greek and Asiatic tradition, was the prototype of many other rude saviours of society, and his name sums up the most characteristic features of all.

In mediæval legend, again, the nebulous fame of many a doughty knight has gathered itself into the aureole of a single figure, and folk-rhyme and epical romance are agreed in immortalising Orlando as the supreme incarnation of the heroic nature. Thus, while the surviving fragment of the French epos and the two great chivalric poems of Italy are alike dedicated to his name, it receives still more widespread glorification in the humbler apotheosis of popular speech. "A Roland for an Oliver" is an English equivalent for scoring off an adversary, as "Faire le Roland" is, in French, synonymous with swagger; while presumptuous boasting is chidden in the Italian adage, "Chi parla d'Orlando, che non vide mai il suo brando" (To prattle of Orlando some make bold, Who ne'er his mighty broadsword did behold).

The Orlandian legend, with which the Rhine country is especially rife, owing to the vicinity of Aix-la-Chapelle, Charlemagne's capital, survives there in the name of Rolandseck, while in Italy the Paladin's name clings to many a spot, from the Sasso d'Orlando at Susa to the Passi d'Orlando on the Appian Way, from the Torre d'Orlando at Gaeta to the Vicolo della Spada d'Orlando in Rome, and to the Padiglione d'Orlando, as the old church of St. Angelo in Bologna is styled. The village of Corciano in Umbria proudly bears as its municipal insignia the "Quartiere," or shield of Orlando, quartered red and white, deriving the privilege from a legendary duel between the hero and one Cornaletto, a Pagan magnate of the place, who in accepting baptism at the hands of his conqueror obtained permission to wear his cognizance.*

In a little shrine at Roncesvalles the relics of the hero were long venerated, and an Italian traveller, Domenico Laffi of Bologna, saw there, as late as the seventeenth century, not only his stirrup, mace, and boots, the latter said to have been occasionally worn by the priest when saying High Mass on great solemnities, but also the famous horn Olivant, still showing the split with which it was cleft by the mighty dying blast

<blockquote>O'er Fontarabian echoes borne</blockquote>

to the distant host of Charlemagne.

---

* "Una Leggenda Araldica." Alessandro d'Ancona. Imola. 1880.

Although it is the elder Orlando of Boiardo and Ariosto, as well as of the song of Taillefer, who is most familiarly known in European letters, the youthful hero, styled in caressing diminutive Orlandino, has a history of his own, still more fondly remembered by the peasantry of Southern Europe. This part of the Orlandian legend is embodied in a book which may perhaps boast the most enduring popularity of any ever written, since after more than five centuries of existence it still forms the Italian rustic's chief repertory of fiction. " I Reali di Francia " dates in its present form from about 1350, but still earlier authorities for the traditions of Orlando's youth are found in the French language, in the "Chanson d'Aspremont" and "Les Enfances Roland,"* composed in the end of the twelfth and beginning of the thirteenth centuries respectively. As, however, the principal scene of both is laid in Italy, they may have originated in that country, from a desire to naturalise there the great champion of Christendom. Both stories are combined into a continuous narrative in "Le Prime Imprese del Conte Orlando," a comparatively modern poem in the favourite octave stanza by the Venetian poet, Lodovico Dolce, who lived from 1508 to 1568-69.

Orlando, according to these traditions, though not, like Hercules, Jove-born, is at least of the highest earthly lineage, since he springs, on his mother's side, from the royal house of Pepin. Charlemagne's fair sister, Bertha, having formed a clandestine attachment to a comparatively obscure young knight, Milo of Anglante, a cadet of the illustrious house of Chiaramonte, her birthday

* Professor Saintsbury ascribes this *Chanson* to the twelfth century. " The Flourishing of Romance and the Rise of Allegory." Edinburgh : Blackwood. 1897.

festivities furnish the occasion of his surreptitious introduction into her presence among her girl friends,
disguised in female attire. The Emperor's rage is so
great at the discovery of the trick that he condemns the
hapless lovers to the stake, and the sentence is only
commuted on the intercession of the sage, Namo of
Bavaria, into one of perpetual banishment. The pair,
now wedded, set forth on a long and toilsome journey
which brings them finally to Sutri, and here, in a cave
still known as the Grotta d'Orlando, the future Paladin
is born. Proving, like his classical prototype, a most
irrepressible infant, he rolls across the floor ere he
can be swaddled, whence a fanciful derivation of his
name from Rotolante, and requires four nurses to
supply his prodigious appetite.   The serpents strangled
by the cradled son of Alcmene are paralleled by a
she-bear and cubs disposed of by the baby hands of
Orlandino, while his biographer dwells as follows on
the resemblance of his lineaments to those of the elder
hero :

> The likeness of the child might truly know
>   Whoso the infant Hercules had seen,
> Alike in limbs and stature did he show,
>   And kept that mould in after life I ween.
> 'Tis true his look was fierce, for there the glow
>   Of spirit bold, informed both glance and mien,
> Yet was he aye in act humane and tender,
> And white of heart as swan of milky splendour.
>   " Le Prime Imprese del Conte Orlando," canto ii. 61.

A little later on the poet describes his hero as accoutred
in a fashion that recalls the traditional garb and arms of
Hercules :

But ten short years he counted—yet in might
  The Hebrew Samson truly seemed to be,
A goat-skin was the garment of the wight,
  And for a sword a sturdy staff grasped he.
Bertha, who bore her sorrow's crushing blight
  And absent from her side did Milo see,
Laments that threat, or prayer, or wrath, or wailing,
In aught to curb the boy are unavailing.

Idem, canto iii. 54.

The parti-coloured quartering of Orlando's shield is traced by one tradition to this period of his career, when, having organised his little companions as juvenile guerillas, he wore a garment patched together from contributions of cloth levied on them. Such a patch-work blouse, called a "schiavona," was, in point of fact, the prescribed livery of a beggar or slave, and adopted as such by pilgrims.

Meantime the sturdy little vagrant's imperial uncle had arrived in Italy, and in returning from Rome chanced to make Sutri one of his halting-places. Here he banqueted daily in mediæval fashion, in a great hall open to the public, and among the crowd who flocked to gape at the royal meal, a winsome beggar-lad soon became conspicuous by his bold bearing. The culminating point of his audacity, when, taking literally a jesting remark made by one of the gentlemen in waiting, he snatched the first dish from the imperial table, is described as follows by his poet-biographer:

But lo! there comes with royal pomp, to meat,
  The Emperor, with all his knightly train,
And at the festive board now takes his seat,
  Where lords and marquises to wait are fain,
Poised Orlandino stands on ready feet,
  Like hawk on wing, with eager gaze astrain,

To watch the cupbearers in turn appearing,
Of whom the first is seen the table nearing.

Then Orlandino waiteth not I ween,
   For him who should the part of butler play,
But without bow or reverence is seen
   The vase with nimble hand to snatch away,
Regarding not those lords of haughty mien,
   Nor caring right or justice to obey,
Off darts the boy in flight the bird's outspeeding,
Or Parthian arrow's airy rush exceeding.

                    Idem, canto iv. 28, 29.

The youthful marauder, encouraged by impunity, on
the following day lays sacrilegious hands on no less a
prize than the Emperor's own drinking-cup, thereby
attracting the attention of the monarch, who has him
tracked to his cavern home. The recognition of his
mother, and her reconciliation to her imperial brother
form the natural sequel of the episode. The theft of the
cup and the bestowal of the royal favour in requital of
an act of daring violence recall an incident of the
Herculean legend, of which they seem a distorted
version. For the Theban hero, firing an arrow at the
sun in resentment for the inconvenience suffered from its
rays, receives not only the pardon of Phœbus for his
impiety, but a reward for his intrepidity in the shape of a
golden cup.

The close of "Les Enfances Roland" having thus left
the child triumphantly reinstated in his natural position,
the "Chanson d'Aspremont" takes up the thread of his
adventures, when, as a boy of thirteen, he is confided to
the care of Archbishop Turpin, and detained in the
Castle of Laon, in order to prevent him from following
the Emperor on a fresh expedition into Italy. The
passage of the army, however, excites his martial ardour

to such a pitch that he finds means of escape, and presents himself in the camp with four companions mounted on horses unceremoniously requisitioned from some Breton bumpkins.

In this campaign he performs two of his most famous exploits, often the subject of allusion in the records of his later career, the successive defeats of the Saracen warrior-kings, Almonte and Troiano. The horse Brigliadoro, the sword Durindana, and the horn Olivant are all trophies of his victory over the first of these antagonists, from whom was also adopted, according to this version, the celebrated cognizance of the quartered shield.

Thus accoutred with all his heroic paraphernalia, Orlando had no other gift to solicit from fortune than that of a wife, and with this the siege of Vienne enables the chroniclers to provide him. Here, while Charlemagne is engaged in reducing to submission his rebellious vassal, Girart, the fair Alda, daughter of this chieftain's brother, Renier of Genoa, is forcibly carried off by Orlando, while inadvertently straying beyond the walls. Rescued with difficulty from his tempestuous wooing by her brother, Oliver, she eventually becomes the bride of her ravisher, after her fate has been decided by the issue of the famous five days' duel fought by the two paladins on an island in the Rhine.

The story of Orlando's later career grows in complexity in the hands of the two great Italian singers who have chanted it, interweaving those exploits in which he follows in the footsteps of his classical prototype with what may be termed the stock business of mediæval knight-errantry. The strange alchemy of Boiardo's genius fused without apparent incongruity the two

opposite classes of adventures, metamorphosing at will
the material inherited from the elder past. The unconscious freedom with which he recast his subject is
manifested in his treatment of the hydra fable, of which
the essential idea is retained in the power of self-multi-
plication possessed by the monster, while it is here
incarnated in a giant instead of in the classical dragon.
This formidable antagonist forms the last of a series
defeated by Orlando at the several gates of Falerina's
enchanted garden, and the description of the battle is a
specimen of the poet's wonderful power of vivifying the
ancient myths. The difficulty of the task is declared to
be apparently insurmountable,

> Because a giant of vast strength and size
>   Doth, sword in hand, the entry guard amain,
> And if in combat slain perchance he dies,
>   Two more spring from his blood upon the plain ;
> The same as he, for each of these likewise
>   Doth other four produce if he be slain,
> With infinite increase of his posterity
> In ever growing numbers and temerity.

> But ere unto that portal he attain,
>   All built of massy silver glittering sheen,
> Much more for him to do doth yet remain,
>   And skill and knowledge will he need I ween,
> Yet doubting fears the Count do not detain,
>   Too full of courage lofty and serene,
> But to his heart he saith, that nothing feareth,
> " He conquers all things who but persevereth."

> Thus with himself communing did he stray,
>   Down by the slope upon its northern side,
> Where, as he reached the plain, before him lay
>   A flowery vale with level surface wide,
> There tables white were spread in fair array,
>   In readiness a gushing fount beside,

And golden goblets on all sides were gleaming,
With savoury viands in abundance teeming.
"Orlando Innamorato," Part II. canto iv. 63, &c.

A book with which the paladin has been provided by
a friendly damsel warns him of a hidden snare, a chain
held by a Faun ambushed in the thicket, and designed
to entangle the unwary adventurer who should fall into the
trap so temptingly baited. Forewarned of the danger,
he slays the Faun, and proceeds to encounter the hydra-
natured monster at the gate.

When towards the giant doth Orlando fare,
    Nor feels a moment's dread of such a fight,
His life had known so many, that no care
    Of this one's issue can his soul affright,
On comes the monster huge, and from mid air
    A furious sword-stroke deals with all his might.
The Count, on one side stepping did evade it,
And with his fairy brand full soon repaid it.

Above the hip he smote his bulky foe,
    And chain and plate of mail were all in vain,
For through cuirass and hauberk crashed the blow,
    And cleft him to the other thigh in twain,
With joy now did the son of Milo glow,
    And deemed the combat o'er, the foeman slain,
And in the upshot took great pride and pleasure,
As his dead foe on earth his length did measure.

For dead he was, and in such streams around
    His blood gushed forth that earth was flooded o'er,
But as beyond the bridge it touched the ground,
    A fire enkindled round the pool of gore.
As soared the flame with living radiance crowned,
    A mighty giant grew within its core,
Armed was he and seemed breathing fire and passion,
And then was born a second in like fashion.

F

They seemed in very sooth true sons of fire,
   As swift and fierce as though all flame within,
With mien aglow, and looks ablaze with ire,
   And e'en the Count delayeth to begin,
Nor plan of action doth his mind inspire,
   Since lose he will not, yet 'twere loss to win,
For though he overthrew them both, his trouble
When they were born again would but redouble.

                     Idem, Part II. canto iv. 72, &c.

The chain with which the vanquished Faun had sought
to ensnare him is his resource in this dilemma, and with
it he eventually succeeds in binding fast both his
monstrous antagonists. To another series of his heroic
labours belongs one in which two famous classical feats
are combined, since he sows with the dragon's teeth of
the Cadmian fable a field ploughed by a pair of furious
bulls like those yoked by Jason. The supernatural
machinery is set in motion by a blast from an enchanted
horn, according to time-honoured prescription.

He raised the horn, and blew from lusty throat
   As one who with its use was well acquaint ;
A peal of thunder seemed the mighty note,
   Prolonged in distance ere its sound grew faint,
As on the ear its closing echoes smote,
   A rock split open 'neath the spell's constraint—
A hundred fathom towered that cliff of wonder,
Which now with great convulsion gaped asunder.

And when the rock was cloven through and through,
   Two bulls thence issued forth with dreadful sound,
In terror each his fellow did outdo,
   Such fire and fury in their looks were found :
Their horns were iron, hair that backward grew
   Did with strange hues each monstrous head surround,
Since here with black, and there with green 'twas tinted,
Now red, now gold, it shone and gleamed and glinted.

Orlando paid the book no more regard,
  But turned to where the rock had split in twain,
Nor aught too soon was he upon his guard,
  For with a crash the bulls rushed out amain.
Dismounted from Bajardo on the sward,
  He firmly stept to meet them o'er the plain;
The first came on, and stooped its head stupendous,
And struck the Count in flank with force tremendous.

Eight fathom was he flung, ere down he slipt
  To earth again, with heavy shock and fall;
On came the second, and with horn steel-tipt
  Broke through chain-armour, plate, and hauberk all.
Skyward once more he flew, then earthward dipt,
  Till bones and flesh did sorely ache and gall,
No wound, 'tis true, had either foe implanted,
Since the bold knight was 'gainst all harm enchanted.

Ask not if turmoil did his soul confound,
  No human tongue its state to tell might dare;
As with his feet firm planted on the ground,
  He showed his sovereign strength sublime and rare,
And strokes terrific dealing all around,
  Made Durindana whistle through the air,
While on the horns and hide of each tormentor,
The doughty knight rained blows right, left and centre.
                    Idem, Part I. canto xxiv. 26, &c.

The bulls show signs of giving in sooner than the
champion, who on this occasion outdoes the feats of the
most famous Espada of the Corrida of Seville or Madrid.
The climax comes when,

At last Orlando seized, to end the battle,
One of the mighty horns of those fierce cattle.

His left hand grasped the horn, and thus held fast,
  The beast, which bellowing loud, raged to and fro,
With bounds prodigious tried its forces vast,
  But not for this Orlando would let go,

Bajardo's bridle he had loosed and pass'd
    Beneath his belt, and yet did wear it so,
This, of stout chain-work wrought, the Count now seizes,
And with it leads the bull where'er he pleases.

And while the one he thus had tricked and tamed,
    Still gripping fast the horn by which he held,
The other bull, to wrath more dire inflamed,
    Wheeled round, and struck with ardour nothing quelled.
The Count then dragged the first to where, far-famed,
    A marble pillar rose from days of eld,
To mark the tomb where King Bavardo rested,
As the inscription round its shaft attested.

Then with the bridle which the first had ta'en,
    The second he made captive to his power ;
When to the column he had led the twain,
    On both such furious blows he 'gan to shower
That all the rage of one and each did wane,
    Nor halts that warrior bold, earth's pride and flower,
But so betwixt the bulls his sword disposes,
Its point in front, its hilt behind reposes.

Then of a trunk a cudgel stout he made,
    And like a rustic set himself to plough,
Before him urging those fierce bulls dismayed,
    Compelled to tread the furrow straight, I trow,
With threats and blows his tree-trunk on he laid,
    Such merry farming ne'er was seen till now,
As Durindana shears the ground it passes,
And cuts through sticks and stones, and roots and grasses.
        Idem, Part I. canto xxiv. 35, &c.

The next blast of the horn brings forth a monstrous
dragon, glittering in iridescent mail, and breathing flames
which consume in a trice the Count's shield and armour.
Even thus defenceless, he triumphs eventually and proceeds to complete the task imposed on him. The
passage descriptive of its fulfilment is especially charac-

teristic of the poet, since it exemplifies the strong realism
with which he works out his theme, never shrinking from
pursuing it to its ultimate details, however extravagant.

> Thus striking at haphazard, to and fro,
>   In that blind struggle, dark and dim and drear,
> Right on the neck at last he smote the foe,
>   And from the trunk the gory head did shear.
> Which, taken by the Count, a horrid show
>   Made, as he grasped and gazed upon it near,
> Streaked green and brown, vermeil and red and yellow,
> The teeth he drew, each grislier than its fellow.

> The valiant Count then doffed his helm, and laid
>   The dragon's teeth its concave space within,
> Next to the new-ploughed field his way he made,
>   As the book's rhymes had taught—the field wherein
> Was King Davardo's sepulchre displayed,
>   There all the poisoned seed he planted in.
> Turpin, whose word is nowhere to be doubted,
> Says knightly plumes from the bare earth then sprouted.

> Gay plumes, I say, that knightly crests adorn,
>   Rose by degrees from out the soil all round,
> Then helms and mail-clad breasts grew up like corn,
>   Till bust and arms were clear above the ground.
> First footmen, and then horse, came forth new-born,
>   All shouting Arms! To Arms! with martial sound.
> With drums and flags and cries they come in surges
> While on Orlando's breast each lance converges.

> The Count, while gazing on this wondrous sight,
>   Saith in his heart, This foul and evil seed
> With Durindana I must reap in fight.
>   If ill I fare, 'tis thanks to mine own deed,
> Why doth the human race still take delight
>   In blaming others for their folly's meed ?
> But he, in sooth, hath double cause for weeping,
> Who evil sows, to harvest in worse reaping.

The Count, this said, delayed not to be gone,
  Since little time to arm himself remained;
The doughty knight his armour buckled on,
  But neither lance nor shield had he retained,
Sprung from the ground Bajardo's back upon,
  He spurs him on, by lofty pride sustained,
Against the folk whose myriads round extended,
Doomed, though scarce born, to die ere day was ended.

Now to what purpose one by one to tell
  The blows that rained—the wounds and bruises sore?
Since Durindana, charmed by fairy spell,
  Nor arms nor shield can stand as fence before.
Suffice it, Count Orlando, fierce and fell,
  Despatched them all before the day was o'er,
When slain, upon the field their burial followed,
For corpses, arms, and steeds the earth straight swallowed.

Then, when the Count had gazed around each way,
  And saw dispersed and slain those numbers vast,
Who in this life had made so brief a stay,
  And in one spot from birth to burial pass'd,
He set unto his lips without delay,
  The horn, to blow a third and final blast,
Achieve the quest, and be its trophy's captor,
As I shall tell you in another chapter.
                    Idem, Part I. canto xxiv. 52, &c.

The reward earned by the knight as the sequel of the
long series of preliminary labours successfully accomplished proves a disappointment to his martial ardour.
With faculties strung to the highest pitch in expectation
of the culminating struggle, he raises the horn once more
to his lips, with the following result: .

So loud a blast he blew, that tired outright
  Was the stout champion by the horn so weird,
Nought came to view, while day declined to night,
  And much some mocking trick or jest he feared;

When lo ! a little spaniel, snowy-white,
   Loud barking on the bloomy mead appeared.
The Count gazed on the hound, and said, By Heaven !
To me some worthier quest than this be given !
              Idem, Part I. canto xxv. 2, &c.

He flings the book of instructions on the ground, and is
departing in disgust, when the damsel who had been his
prompter throughout implores him not to throw away
the transcendent gift now proffered by fortune. The
white spaniel is, she explains, the emissary of the Fata
Morgana, the dispenser of wealth, the guardian of
treasure, and by the assistance of the little beast the
favour of its mistress may be secured through the capture
of another spell-wrought quadruped, whose place in her
witcheries is set forth as follows :

Morgana, she of whom I speak to you,
   Who doth, as queen, o'er all things joyful reign,
Hath sent her stag to roam the wide world through,
   Which, white of hair, hath golden antlers twain ;
By magic art so wrought this end unto,
   That never in one place doth it long remain,
But ever speeds, to flight than pause far apter,
And seeks through earth, but never finds a captor.

Nor could it e'er by any force be ta'en,
   Save by assistance of the spaniel white,
Which first doth find it, then pursues amain,
   And chases in full cry with all its might ;
Led by its voice, you then must track the twain,
   For like an arrow's is their airy flight;
Six days untired the dog with clamour chases,
Then on the seventh, makes halt, nor further races.

For on that day a fountain's brink they gain,
   Wherein the stag doth plunge in sore affright,
And without hurt or trouble there is ta'en,
   To give its hunter fortune and delight,

For six times daily doth it shed full fain
    The antlers of its brow—each left and right
Of thirty branches, and their mass furcated,
May at a hundred pounds be roughly rated.

And thus such treasure shall you have in store,
    When the enchanted stag you captive lead,
That you shall be content for evermore,
    If wealth and riches make men blest indeed ;
And to the love of that bright Fay moreo'er,
    Of whom I tell, you may perchance succeed,
I mean Morgana, beauteous, radiant-seeming,
And fairer than the sun at noontide beaming.

Ibid. Part I. canto xxv. 9 *et seq.*

This phantom animal resembles the brazen-hoofed, golden-antlered, Arcadian stag chased by Hercules, and fulfils a like function in drawing down on the champion the wrath of its protecting divinity. But while the Greek hero is visited with Diana's vengeance for the slaughter of her nimble-footed favourite, it is for the contrary offence of despising the chase of such a prey that Orlando becomes the object of Morgana's persecution. The slighted Fay evokes a fresh series of enchantments in order to make him her captive, ending, after many surprising adventures, in his triumph and her subjugation.

The number and variety of the Orlandian giant-combats recall those of the stout Theban. Thus in one he vanquishes his adversary as Hercules does Antæus, by lifting him bodily from the ground and squeezing him till he is senseless. ("Orlando Innamorato," Part I. canto xx. 23, &c.) In another he overcomes by shattering his opponent's head with a blow of a club used as a substitute for Durindana, then temporarily lost. (*Idem*, Part II. canto iv. 15, &c.) In voracity, too, he rivals his classical model, and the quarter of horse con-

sumed by him on his arrival at Albracca corresponds to
the quarter of an ox which forms a meal for Hercules.
One of the Herculean adventures is, on the other hand,
assigned by Boiardo to Rinaldo, who is robbed of a
damsel by a Centaur in crossing a stream, just as Deianira
is carried off by Nessus.

But in the interval of over half a century that had
elapsed before Ariosto took up the dropped thread of
his predecessor's story, the Greek myths had lost their
lately renewed vitality, and no longer put forth fresh
blossoms of gracious fantasy. The Olympian machinery
and nomenclature survived as properties inherited from
the past, but faith had faded into mannerism, and their
use was retained only as a form of literary affectation.
The new element of caricature enters into the later
Renaissance renderings of such fables, and there is
already a foreshadowing of Cervantes in Ariosto. Thus
the Herculean deliverance of Hesione from a sea-
monster is rather parodied than recast in the similar
intervention of Orlando on behalf of a fair captive, whose
plight is described as follows :

> Approaching to the naked rock as near
>   As a strong hand might cast a stone with ease,
> A plaint he seems—yet scarcely seems—to hear,
>   So faint his ear it reaches on the breeze.
> He leftward turns, and 'neath the crag-wall sheer
>   Down by the water's edge a woman sees,
> Bare, as when newly-born, of fold enswathing,
> Bound to a trunk ; her feet the ripples bathing.
>
> Because as yet too distant—and because
>   Her face is stooped—he knows not who is she.
> Both oars he pulls in haste, and nearer draws,
>   All eagerness hereof informed to be ;

When lo ! the bellowing shore resounds, nor pause
  Doth echo make from cave and wood and lea,
The waves boil up, and lo ! the monster neareth,
Beneath whose bulk the ocean disappeareth.

As from dark valley steaming doth ascend
  A tempest-swollen cloud all big with rain,
And darker than blind midnight doth impend
  O'er all the world, and daylight quench amain,
Thus swims the beast, and seaward doth extend,
  And seems to fill afar the watery plain,
The ocean thrills ; Orlando nothing falters,
Looks proudly on, nor heart nor aspect alters.
                    " Orlando Furioso," canto xi. 32, &c.

The burlesque tendency suggested by the arrival of the
deliverer in a boat pulling a pair of sculls is carried still
further in the ensuing combat, whose issue is decided by
his cramming the anchor down the monster's throat.
These modernising touches show how completely the
feeling of the older world had vanished from later
Italian art, while its decadence is explained by its retention of the dead forms from which the animating
spirit had departed.   Ariosto with his farcical treatment
has given the *coup de grace* to antique fable, and in this
closing travesty of the Herculean myth we have a foreshadowing of the pantomime and musical farce of our
own day.

   But the inexhaustible vitality of Greek fantasy has
secured for it yet another Renaissance in the revived
Hellenism of which, in English letters, Shelley and
Keats were the earliest, and William Morris the latest
exponents.   French poetry has found a wealth of inspiration at the same source, and as a contrast of modern with
mediæval classicalism we quote one of the six sonnets
which M. de Hérédia, the most brilliant living master of

the neo-classical school, has dedicated to the illustration of the Herculean legend. "Centaurs and Lapithae" is the title of this specimen of the latest embodiment of the undying creation of Hellenic fancy.

> Unto the feast the nuptial throng doth crowd,
> Centaurs and warriors drunk with merriment,
> And flesh of heroes shows in torchlight blent
> With fulvous hair of Children of the Cloud.
>
> A laugh, a din, a shriek—the Bride, scarce vowed,
> Struggles in hairy arms, her purple rent,
> And hoof-strokes clatter on bronze armament,
> While sinks the table 'mid the tumult loud.
>
> But he who dwarfs the greatest rises now,
> A lion's muzzle wrinkling on his brow,
> Bristling with tawny hair—'tis Hercules.
>
> And through the mighty hall, from end to end,
> Cowed by the eye which flames of wrath doth send,
> The monstrous herd with snorts reluctant flees.

CHAPTER VI

Circe the Island Goddess

THE early popularity of the fable of Circe is shown by its appearance in the Odyssey in two forms, both doubtless traditional variations of the same original. That Calypso is but a duplicate of her sister-enchantress is evident from the identity of epithet and language, both obviously prescriptive, applied to them, as well as from the general similarity of outline in their story. Both island goddesses, they become enamoured of the wandering mortal cast on their shores, and detain him in gilded captivity, but eventually consent to speed the parting guest on his way. They share the same descriptive epithet, "of the braided tresses," * are similarly engaged when first introduced in "singing with a sweet voice," as they fare to and fro before a loom, and are clad in the same fashion, "in a great shining robe, light of woof and gracious," with a golden girdle cast about the waist and a veil on the head. Mercury is in each case the agent of deliverance, and " the goodly Odysseus " makes both his fair hostesses swear a like oath "not to plan any hidden guile to his hurt." Calypso is, however, a much more shadowy personage than Circe, whose previous career,

* The translations are from Messrs. Lang and Butcher's " Odyssey."

her murder of her husband, the Prince of Colchis, and consequent exile by her family to a lonely island, seems to give her a footing in the actual world on a substantial basis of human turpitude.

Popular piety in the Middle Ages by no means called in question the existence of the heathen divinities, but, while dethroning them from the supernal heights of Olympus, assigned them place and power in its own demoniac mythology. Circe, however, underwent a more gracious transformation, and was relegated to that elfin world in whose fantastic creations Northern fancy ran riot. Here we find her under many names and in varying disguises—as the baleful but beautiful fairy queen who selects a favoured mortal to share the sensuous joys of her existence. In early British fable she appears as the sister of Arthur, she who transported

Mystic Uther's deeply wounded son

to her enchanted Isle of Avalon when he passed from earth. The mortal love of this fair dame was the knight Ogier, called the Dane, though his country was not northern Denmark, but the "Dennemark" or Ardennes frontier between France and Belgium, the district which conferred pseudonym and patronymic on William de la Marck, "the wild boar of Ardennes." Legend tells how Ogier was one day carried by his horse, Papillon, along a track of light to Avalon. There, beside a sparkling fountain, he sees a beautiful maiden who offers him a golden crown wreathed with flowers. He no sooner puts it on than all memory of his former life is obliterated from his mind, and he becomes the contented slave of the fairy. But one day his crown slips off into the fountain, his memory returns, and all the dormant feelings of his former self

reawaken within him.   He revisits earth to find that two
hundred years have passed away in what seemed a few
rapturous hours in Avalon.   Charlemagne and all his old
associates have departed, and earth has no longer a place
for him, so he finally returns to fairy-land, where he still
dwells in a long trance of bliss.*

The fountain in this legend is no chance accessory, for
Morgain in all her phases is invariably connected with
water ; and we must remember that Circe herself was not
only of oceanic lineage, but that her four attendant
maidens " were born of the wells and the woods and the
holy rivers which flow forward into the salt sea."

Now the water-loving nature of the fay is not only a
link with Circe, but serves also to connect her with a still
wider set of associations.   For in Breton speech her
name, slightly disguised as Marie Morgan, is the desig-
nation of the mermaid or woman-fish, the form under
which Derceto or Atergatis, the Phœnician Venus, was
worshipped.†

In some cities of Asia Minor the fish, originally sacred
to this divinity, are still held in superstitious reverence,
though the pond in which they are enclosed has been
generally re-christened after Abraham or some saint ;
and even in Ireland a relic of the same Phœnician
worship survives in the "holy fish" believed by the
peasantry to inhabit the "holy wells" that abound
through the country.   The water-fairy, Melusina, is

---

* "Curious Myths of the Middle Ages."   By S. Baring-Gould.
† An early Greek coin represents Aphrodite standing on two
dolphins with tails coiling right and left, while she passes her
fingers through her long tresses with the traditional action of the
mermaid.   The mirror, too, bestowed on the latter was part of
the paraphernalia of the Paphian Goddess.

of the same origin, but the class of stories in which she figures diverge into channels foreign to the Circe myth. The thread of legendary romance is thus ever twined of many strands, baffling the attempt to trace it home to a single starting-point.

The Fay Morgain or Fata Morgana is, as we shall see later on, the most conspicuous representative of the classical enchantress. The many-facetted invention of Boiardo, however, gave a multiform aspect to every theme he dealt with, and he created a group of guileful goddesses, differing more or less from the original type. But in the enchanted palace of the first of the series he puts before us, as though to strike the keynote of similar situations, the tale of Circe in its classical form, availing himself of a favourite device of mediæval poetry by describing it as the subject of decorative representation. Such an arcade or loggia as he portrays, with its frescoes of successive scenes, must often have been before his eyes in the cloisters and churches of Modena and Ferrara.

Orlando, the most redoubtable champion in Christendom, having incautiously drunk from a bowl proffered him by a lovely damsel on a bridge, has been thereby deprived of memory, and enthralled to the fairy, Dragontina, who keeps a preserve of knights similarly bewitched to fight her battles and do her bidding. The paladin's entry into the enchanted garden takes place as follows :

> On Brigliadoro enters by the gate
> The mighty Count of Brava dazed in mind,
> He sees a palace wrought with art so great
> As all imagining to leave behind.
> A cloister fair and wide doth rest its weight
> On amber shafts and base of gold refined ;

With marbles white and green the floor is gleaming,
And gold and azure on the roof are beaming.

The Count then turned to view the fair arcade,
   With walls three-fronting, painted every one—
The master's hand such cunning had displayed
   That Nature here might see herself outdone.
'Mid other rare and curious things portrayed,
   Through varied scenes a story seemed to run:
Damsels and knights than buds in May were rifer,
And each one's name was writ in golden cipher.

There stood a damsel on the salt-sea beach,
   Her face so tinted with life's vivid hue,
That whoso gazed half seemed to hear her speech,
   As with soft words men to the shore she drew,
And then to beasts transformed them all and each,
   Bereft of human shape, a bestial crew :
As boars or wolves or lions some imbruted,
And some to griffins winged or bears transmuted.

And here a ship to reach the land is seen,
   Thence stepping to the shore a cavalier,
Who, with his honeyed words and gallant mien,
   Inflamed to love that damsel without peer.
The key that locked the magic draught, I ween,
   In act to give him she doth next appear,
The potion yielding, by whose virtue aided
So many knights to beasts she had degraded.

Next was she shown by love so blindly led
   For that bold Baron come across the main,
That, lured by her own arts, herself instead,
   To drink of the enchanted cup was fain.
Turned to a milk-white hind as then she fled,
   In hunter's snare behold her trapped and ta'en.
Circella hath the painter writ above her,
And giv'n the name Ulysses to her lover.
        " Orl. Inn." book i. canto vi. stanzas 47 *et seq.*

The story of the transformation of the enchantress into a hind, unless of Boiardo's own invention, shows that the myth of Circe had become sufficiently popularised in mediæval Italy to receive additions and modifications. The situation of this, and similar regions of enchantment, beyond a river, which must be crossed to reach them, invests them with the island character traditionally required for their isolation from the everyday world, true marine islands not being easily accessible to the paladins, who travelled generally by land. After some tremendous encounters, in which the enthralled knights are compelled to do battle with their friends and kinsfolk, the Garden of Dragontina is finally destroyed by Angelica's ring, the *deus ex machinâ* of the poem.

Orlando meets a still more formidable sorceress in the kingdom of Orgagna, where Falerina, princess of that country, holds a number of knights in durance by the potency of her spells; but, like Circe, retains one by the witchery of love alone. The Paladin, warned of the dangers to be encountered here, is, of course, doubly determined on the enterprise, and is presented by his friendly informant with a book containing directions for counteracting the various forms of enchantment about to be encountered. The description of Falerina's garden is interesting as an ideal mediæval landscape, faithfully reflecting the surroundings of an ordinary Italian villa, and suggestive rather of fresh and flowery pleasantness than of any of the more sublime aspects of nature :

> On the right hand a fountain spouted wide,
>   Its living wave in bounteous plenty shed ;
> A marble figure standing in the tide,
>   Forth from its breast the gushing water sped,

G

And on its brow was writ, This stream will guide
   To the fair palace whoso will be led.
To lave his brow and hands the Count doth hasten
In the refreshing coolness of its basin.

Flanked was by a tall tree on either hand
   That fountain all embowered in verdure green,
A stream it poured that gladdened all the land
   With purest water of crystalline sheen.
It ran 'twixt blossoms on a flowery strand,
   And was the same the writing meant, I ween,
Which on the forehead of the image printed,
The peerless Count had read, as has been hinted.

To reach the palace then he took his way,
   There to resolve on further enterprise ;
And as his path beside the margin lay,
   He gazed on the fair scene in mute surprise.
It was the very blossom-time of May,
   That broke in flush of bloom before his eyes ;
Such perfumed breaths from all the place were stealing,
As filled the heart with every blithesome feeling.

Soft dales and pleasant heights the eye did greet,
   And beauteous woods of larch and pine were there,
And birds on verdant boughs in cadence sweet,
   Sang their wild wood-notes on the fragrant air ;
Rabbits and kids and stags with flying feet,
   All creatures harmless and of aspect fair,
Swift hares and does, amid the trees were chasing,
The pleasant garden with their antics gracing.

Orlando took the streamlet for his guide,
   And after he had gone some way, full soon,
Beneath a hill, the rising ground beside,
   He saw a palace all of marble hewn ;
Yet saw not all ; since partly it did hide
   Behind the trees around it thickly strewn ;
But when its stately mass he came close under,
He fairly lost himself for very wonder.

Since not of marble was that pile, the which
    Had caught his eye athwart the green arcade,
But on the palace-walls of lofty pitch,
    Enamels glowed, and scales of gold inlaid.
A gate it had of treasure all so rich,
    The like to human eyes was ne'er displayed,
In height it measured ten, in width five paces,
With emeralds lined, and rubies on both faces.

        Ibid. book ii. canto iv. stanzas 20 *et seq.*

Wall decoration has certainly made a great stride here since the days when the companions of Ulysses in the forest glades came upon "the halls of Circe builded of polished stone, in a place with a clear prospect." The dwelling of Homer's goddess would evidently have seemed a very unadorned and unpretending structure to the luxuriant imagination of the Italian poet.

The entry into Falerina's garden proves a task of superhuman difficulty, one door only being visible at a time, which vanishes as soon as its guardian-monster is disposed of, a process repeated at each in succession. Orlando, however, is instructed by his guide-book how to proceed in these emergencies, and when about to engage in single combat with one of the formidable janitors, a bull, the touch of whose horn consumes like flame, takes the preliminary precautions recommended. He fills his ears and helmet with roses so as to exclude sound, and thus protected, like the companions of Ulysses, proceeds with the adventure :

Thus both his ears he had so firmly sealed,
    With roses thickly crushed and closely wound,
That to his sense no outer stir appealed,
    Though strained to listen for the faintest sound.
So to the stream beneath whose wave concealed,
    Full many a one had watery burial found,

A tiny lake it formed, in calm reposing,
With tranquil wave pellucid depths disclosing.

The Count had scarcely reached the brink, when lo !
    A gurgling eddy 'gan to fret and boil,
Up rose a Siren singing from below,
    Hid from the sight her beauty's hideous foil ;
All woman what above the wave doth show,
    All fish beneath, with writhing scaly coil,
Plunged to the waist, her lower limbs she covers,
What's foul doth hide, and what is fair discovers.

Then 'gan she sing in dulcet tones so sweet
    The birds flocked round to listen to her strain ;
But scarce had come on airy pinions fleet,
    Ere, lulled with sweetness, they to sleep were fain.
Nought heard the Count, but by the book's receipt,
    A semblance of attention did maintain,
And listening feigned—then, as the volume bade him,
Down on the sward beside the marge he laid him.

                              Ibid. stanzas 35 *et seq.*

While he feigns to sleep, the Siren approaches the shore
to slay him thus helpless, but has the tables turned on
her by the knight, whose stratagem enables him to take
her by surprise.   Having slain her, he proceeds to dye
his armour in her blood with the following result :

No spot he leaves but is in gore imbrued,
    His harness else, like wax upon the pyre
Had melted piecemeal 'neath the onset rude
    Of the terrific bull, whose nature dire
When stirred to rage nought earthly had withstood,
    Who hath one horn of steel and one of fire,
Consuming all with touch of flame and iron,
Save what had drunk the life-blood of a Siren.

                              Ibid. stanza 43.

We have here the fusion of the singing Siren with the
monstrous form of Scylla, which produced the mediæval

mermaid. This hybrid, while endowed with the vocal
spells of the bird-woman of classical art, a creature not
of the sea, but of the shore, is adorned with the fish-tail,
wherewith the jealousy of Circe disfigured the maiden
Scylla. The association of the whirlpool with the
woman-fish is dimly conveyed by the Italian poets in
the eddy which always precedes her appearance, as in
the passage just quoted and a similar one in "Tasso,"
while the original scaly-tailed woman or goddess was the
aquatic Venus of the East.

The Siren recipe having proved effectual in securing
him victory over the bull, Orlando encounters with equal
success an armour-plated ass and a hydra giant. The
three preliminary contests, in each of which one of
the senses, as in the one narrated, is the subject of
allurement, probably symbolise temptation in various
forms.

The destruction of Falerina's garden is eventually
effected by cutting down a tree, the golden fruit on
whose high and slender stem the Paladin had been
instructed how to pluck. The fairy herself, found con-
templating her image in a sword which she is endowing
with spells for his destruction, is made prisoner and
compelled to act as guide to another man-trap filled with
ensnared knights, in the realm of Morgana.

This elfin queen, the typical fairy of Italian song, is
associated with a curious natural phenomenon. In calm
weather, the inhabitants of Reggio, on the Straits of
Messina, see a phantom city, with towers and walls and
moving population gleaming beneath the gentian-blue
waves, and call this submarine mirage the palace of the
Fata Morgana. Whether her fictitious existence originated solely in the refraction spectre, or her name was

only fancifully bestowed upon it, the association truly indicates her position as a sea-witch, and Boiardo accordingly not only establishes her in a subaqueous realm, but assigns her, among other supernatural insignia, two mysterious fishes who feed on gold and silver. Teutonic fable, however, with which as a North Italian he came in contact, steps in to modify her character, making her the guardian of a treasure suggestive of the Rhine Gold, the submerged hoard of the Nibelung, whence the poet, embroidering his theme as he goes along, proceeds to give her an allegorical signification as the goddess of Fortune in general.

Orlando is forcibly introduced to her kingdom by a giant who seizes him in a combat on a bridge, and leaps bodily into the stream, carrying him in his arms. The wonders of the under world are then disclosed to him as follows :

On through the grotto goes he without fear,
    And travels there some three miles' length or so,
Without a ray the darkling path to cheer,
    When marvel strange encounters he, for lo !
A stone that shone with radiance bright and clear
    Its ray like fire, in vivid burning glow,
Illumed his way, all things around defining,
As though the noonday sun in heaven were shining.

And by it was a stream before him shown,
    Some twenty fathom wide, or maybe less,
And from beyond it shed its light the stone,
    In a field piled with gems in such excess
As 'twould a volume take me to make known,
    For in clear sky not stars so thickly press,
Nor spring such plenty hath of flowers and roses,
As there of pearls and gems the light discloses.

That river whereof I have sung before
 Was by a bridge so scant and narrow spanned,
Scarce a half palm's breadth did it measure o'er,
 An image iron-wrought on either hand
Stood, like a man-at-arms, to guard the shore;
 Beyond the bridge did the wide plain expand,
Where lay the treasure by Morgana hoarded,
Now hear the marvel strange that place afforded.

For scarce the son of Milo had set foot
 Upon the narrow bridge, across to fare,
When lo! the graven image standing mute
 Lifts from the other side a club in air,
That blow, indeed, had fall'n with little fruit
 If the Count's magic sword had met it there;
But parrying stroke were vain, for, hear the wonder,
The bridge it smites, and straight the bridge goes under.

While yet the Count doth on this portent brood,
 And greatly marvel as he thinks it o'er,
Lo! now behold another bridge protrude
 By slow degrees, where that had been before.
Orlando steps thereon in daring mood,
 But need is none to tell the tale once more,
The figure bars the way across the river,
Doth strike the bridge, and straight the bridge doth shiver.
   Idem, book ii. canto viii. stanzas 18 *et seq.*

This spell is frustrated by the simple expedient of jump-
ing across the stream, which Orlando, though in full
armour, clears at a bound, to find himself confronted
with fresh prodigies on the other side.   Of these the poet
weaves a further web of mystery as he goes along, blending Oriental fable with the fantastic creations of his own
brain into a new phantasmagoria:

When he had come the meadow bank unto,
 Where her vast treasure had Morgana rolled,
Before him, stiff and upright, came in view
 A king who did a numerous audience hold;

All stood, while he was seated 'mid the crew,
  His limbs were all compact of massy gold,
And o'er them layers closely were adjusted
Of rubies, pearls, and diamonds, thickly crusted.

All seemed that king to reverence and to dread,
  Before him was a table laden fair,
With viands, as though for a banquet spread,
  But all was wrought of hard enamel there.
A shining brand was hung above his head,
  Which threatened death each moment from the air,
And on his left, removed by distance narrow,
Was one who held on bended bow the arrow.

And one stood by his side who seemed his twin,
  So close resembling him in mien and air,
Who held a written scroll his hand within,
  And this was what the legend did declare :
Nor wealth, nor all the goods that man doth win,
  Which he possesses with such fear and care,
No power avails, nor pleasure finds admission,
Where they are gained or held in dark suspicion.

Wherefore that king such gloomy mien did wear,
  And cast suspicious glances all around ;
Before him on the banquet table fair,
  A golden lily the Carbuncle crowned.
Which like a lamp illumed with vivid glare,
  The hall and every nook within its bound,
Although the square its mighty space did cover
A hundred fathom stretched each way and over.

With living rock all roofed and vaulted o'er
  The place was, and round closely walled was it,
Thence exit was obtained by portals four,
  Each richly wrought and carven bit by bit,
No window had it through which light could pour,
  But solely by the Carbuncle 'twas lit,
Which in that cavern shed such radiant splendour,
That scarce the sun the day more bright doth render.

The Count, who this meantime but little heeds,
   Unto an entrance door directs his way,
But all so dark the vault as thence it leads,
   The Paladin knows not which side to stray ;
But doubling back he from within proceeds,
   In turn the other portals to essay ;
And tries them all with endless pains and labour,
More dark is each and dismal than its neighbour.

But while he stood absorbed in musing slow,
   The wondrous stone enchained his heart and eye,
And to his mind seemed living fire aglow ;
   But as in haste to snatch it he drew nigh,
The brazen figure with the bended bow,
   Incontinent a hurtling shaft let fly :
The Carbuncle it struck, and its diffusion
Of radiance quenched 'mid clamour and confusion.

And on the instant lo ! an earthquake shock
   Swayed all the place, and moaning shook the ground,
Bellowed on every side the hollow rock,
   Nor was there ever heard more dreadful sound.
The Count stood firm and moveless as a stock,
   As one in whom no fear was ever found :
When lo ! the Carbuncle, the lily crowning,
Once more sheds light, the dark in radiance drowning.

Once more Orlando did its theft essay,
   But scarce had touched it with his hand, when lo !
The archer next the king without delay
   Let fly a golden arrow from his bow ;
An hour this time endures the earthquake's fray,
   The cavern rending as in earth's o'erthrow ;
The light vermeil, once more, when all is stilly,
Returns to crown with fire the golden lily.

Now doth Anglante's Count reflect how he
   Can seize the beauteous stone of light the source ;
His shield he took, and placed a screen to be
   Between the archer and his arrow's course,

Then the Carbuncle snatched, and instantly
   The arrow struck the shield with ringing force ;
But the vain blow it fully met and parried,
And the Carbuncle thence Orlando carried.

Ibid. stanzas 24 *et seq.*

Finding his way through the grotto by the light of the stone, the Paladin succeeds in rescuing Rinaldo and a number of other knights enclosed in a crystal prison as the captives of Morgana. Her affections are centred in Ziliante, a beauteous youth, who is eventually rescued also, after she has changed him into a dragon to guard her bridge by the terror of his aspect. It is noteworthy that she is the only one of Boiardo's elfin queens who exercises this power of transformation, which is, indeed, as in the case of the classical enchantress, a faculty generally reserved for oceanic divinities in the fable of all countries. Queen Labe, the Circe of the " Arabian Nights," who transforms Prince Beder into an owl, is an island sorceress ; Queen Gulnare, similarly endowed, is a Princess of the Sea ; and it is in her capacity as an ocean or water nymph that Morgana is equally gifted. Boiardo was here the faithful interpreter of a tradition, which he followed, perhaps, rather instinctively than consciously.

In " Mambriano," a chivalric poem, of which the composition intervened between that of the "Innamorato" and "Furioso," its author, Francesco Bello, known as " Il Cieco di Ferrara," introduces an island fairy, Carandina, who resembles Circe in her attentions to shipwrecked sailors. Mambriano and Rinaldo, who successively arrive in this fashion, are rivals for her favour, until the friendly wizard, Malagisi, plays the part of Mercury by rescuing the latter with the aid of a counter-potion.

The personal charms of Carandina are described in the hyperbolical fashion of the day:

> Had she but lived when Troy still ruled the land,
>   And Venus from the shepherd gained the prize,
> Not to the goddess had he stretched his hand,
>   Nor Troy been burned to ashes in such wise;
> For as those fair and tender limbs he scanned,
>   And caught the lovely looks of beauteous eyes,
> Not the mere apple for which gods had striven,
> But Troy and his own self had Paris given.
>
> As every star that gems the vault on high,
>   'Tis said its splendour from the sun doth take,
> All beauty that on earth enchants the eye,
>   Is loved and honoured solely for her sake;
> As Zephyr lulls all storms with gentle sigh,
>   So her sweet speech a calm of soul doth make;
> Cheers noble hearts, and e'en the pusillanimous
> Uplifts to actions lofty and magnanimous.
>   " Mambriano," canto ii. stanzas 31 *et seq.*

The abundance of water in Carandina's garden recalls Calypso's island, where " the wells of four streams set orderly were running with clear water, hard by one another, turned each to a separate course," and the fish-tank formed by the converging rills is not without a suggestion of the ponds of Atergatis:

> Full in the garden's midst a fountain gushed,
>   All bordered round with trees of beauty rare,
> The home of birds, whose voices never hushed,
>   Poured dulcet music on the pleasant air.
> Forth from the hill the sparkling waters rushed,
>   In many a rill to course the garden fair,
> All hastening towards a basin broad and brimming,
> Where various fishes in the depths were swimming.

With every fruit that ripens 'neath the sun
    Or teems on earth, the garden did abound,
And there, moreover, many a beauteous one
    To earth denied was in perfection found ;
There all spoke love—there speech of war was none—
    There Venus' self as reigning queen was crowned,
'Mid music, song, feasts, games, and joys yet rarer,
In all which Mambriano was made sharer.

                    Ibid. canto i. stanzas 64 *et seq.*

The burlesque genius of Ariosto found a congenial subject in the episode of the fay Alcina, left unfinished
by his predecessor, and devoloped by him into a true
Circe fable.   Characteristically introduced with a faint
flavour of Phœnician tradition, while exercising her
power over fishes, this sea-witch is endowed by her latest
bard with those irresistible spells of transformation generally ascribed to her oceanic kinsfolk.   The hero, Ruggiero, borne to her island by the Hippogriff, or flying-
horse, ties up that ærostatical animal to a myrtle-tree,
which remonstrates in a human voice against such treatment, and proves to be the Paladin, Astolfo, thus transformed by Alcina. Ariosto, in his usual colloquial strain,
describes the newly-arrived knight as refreshing himself
after his journey when surprised by this marvel :

His parching lips in the wave cool and sweet
    He laves, and through its tide his hands doth pass,
From out his throbbing veins to draw the heat,
    Enkindled by the weight of his cuirass ;
Small wonder if it irked in course so fleet
    Since not for brief parade he wore its mass,
But had, thus fully armed as for a tourney,
Made at one stretch three thousand miles of journey.

                    " Orl. Fur." canto vi. stanza 25.

The poet's vigour of language is exemplified in the

following homely metaphor borrowed from Dante; while the idea of the human myrtle was originally derived by both poets from Virgil:

> As when a log of wood with empty core
>   All void and sapless on the hearth is flung,
> And the moist air that filled each gaping pore
>   By the flame's ardour from its veins is wrung,
> With inner groans it seethes and splutters o'er,
>   Till its internal rage find vent and tongue,
> So plains and moans and querulously grieveth
> The injured myrtle, till its bark it cleaveth.
>
> *Ibid.* stanza 27.

The courteous knight apologises, full of remorse for the sufferings unwittingly inflicted on a sentient being, and requests to hear the story of so strange a metamorphosis. The imprisoned spirit introduces itself as Astolfo, the English Paladin who, with the air of a lady-killer with which Ariosto has endowed him, cannot refrain from boasting of his conquest of Alcina:

> Of gracious mien, triumphant still in wooing,
> My very charms have been my own undoing.

He then goes on to tell his story, beginning with his release with others from Morgana's prison by the arms of Orlando:

> Returning from those islands far and lone,
>   Washed on the eastward by the Indian sea,
> Where in a dark and dismal grotto thrown
>   Rinaldo and some others were with me;
> Whence with that prowess for which he is known,
>   The Cavalier of Brava set us free.
> I held my way along the sandy reaches,
> Where in its rage the north wind howls and screeches.

Led by our pathway and an adverse fate,
  Upon a lovely shore one morn we came,
Where, looking o'er the sea was situate
  The castle of Alcina, mighty dame.
And her we found, just issued from the gate,
  Alone upon the beach, before the same,
Where without hook or line she drew the fishes
Unto the shore according to her wishes.

There nimble dolphins swam, and at their heels
  Came the gross tunny-fish with mouth agape,
And oily-headed sharks and ancient seals,
  Stirred from their drowsy sleep by many a cape,
Gilt-heads and mullet, salmon, blackfish, eels,
  Swam round in shoals of every size and shape,
Sawfish and whales, all monsters of the ocean,
Thrust from the deep their mighty backs in motion.

Ibid. stanzas 38 *et seq.*

Among the other marine monsters assembled is a whale
which the Paladins take for an island. Alcina, meanwhile, receives them courteously, but looks on Astolfo,
as he declares, with especial favour :

Alcina drew these fish from out the sea,
  By virtue of mere words and muttered spell,
The Fay Morgana's fairy sister she,
  Twin-born, but first or last I cannot tell.
And straightway when Alcina looked on me,
  As her face told, my aspect pleased her well,
With plotting skill and cunning she proceeded
To part me from my comrades, and succeeded.

Ibid. stanza 40.

She effects her purpose by entrapping him on the whale's
back under the following pretext :

And if you would behold a siren fair,
  Who with her song doth pacify the deep,
To yonder island strand we will repair,
  Where at this hour she ever tryst doth keep.

> The mighty whale she showed, which floating there
>   We deemed, as I have said, an islet steep,
> I ever rash and bold (in lamentation
> I say it) ventured on the great cetacean.
>
> <div align="right"><i>Ibid.</i> stanza 40.</div>

The monster instantly puts to sea, carrying him and the fay, who has also embarked on it, to her island realm. Here he shares her power and splendour until the moment comes for him to expiate his folly by his penitential transformation :

> Too late I knew her nature false and vain,
>   Which loves and unloves in a moment's space;
> But two brief months' duration had my reign,
>   Before a brand-new lover took my place.
> The Fairy drove me from her with disdain,
>   An outcast from her favour and her grace.
> And then I learned, since mis'ry truth discovers,
> Like fate had met a thousand former lovers.
>
> Lest they her life of wickedness declare,
>   When wandering hence by her caprices spurned,
> On this rich soil she plants them here and there,
>   To olives some, and some to larches turned,
> To palms and cedars some, while others share
>   The form which I by this green shore have earned;
> Some flow as streams, some rage as beasts ferocious,
> As most doth please this Fairy's pride atrocious.
>
> <div align="right"><i>Ibid.</i> stanzas 50 <i>et seq.</i></div>

Ruggiero, even though thus forewarned, falls headlong under the spell of the fickle dame, to whose allurements the poet gives a secondary allegorical significance, which may, indeed, point his moral, but which rather mars than adorns his tale. The interposition of the good, but prosy fairy, Melissa, rescues him and all the other knights from their degraded condition, finally vanquishing the potent and perfidious Alcina.

The idea, however, embodied in her and her sister-hood, of female fascinations rendered irresistible by alliance with the supernatural had not yet disappeared from Italian song, and it was reserved for a later age to reverse the Homeric tradition by associating witchcraft exclusively with age and deformity. Tasso's Armida conquers more hearts by her beauty than by her incantations, though it is by means of the latter that she first leads Rinaldo, the young Achilles of the Christian Iliad, a captive to her island bower. In his description of her emergence from the water preceded by an eddy in the stream, as well as in the lulling power of her song, Tasso closely follows Boiardo, though, unlike the earlier Siren, she is entirely human in shape. The description of Armida's palace, where the triumphs of love are depicted on the walls, recalls, too, the passage descriptive of Falerina's dwelling in the " Orlando Innamorato " :

> A circle forms the rich and sumptuous hall,
>   And in its heart, the centre of the ring,
> A garden is enclosed abloom with all
>   Of rare or treasured flowers on earth that spring,
> Round in confusion rise arcade and wall,
>   By demons piled in mass bewildering,
> And in their tangled snare of pathways winding,
> The garden lies close hidden from all finding.

> The greater entrance-way the pair pass through
>   (Since by a hundred the vast pile is gained),
> There gates of sculptured silver fair to view,
>   On massy golden hinges creaked and strained,
> But since art here material doth outdo,
>   They stopped to gaze upon the figures feigned,

Which lacked but speech alone for life's perfection,
Nor even that to cheat the eye's detection.

Distaff in hand, Alcides there tells o'er
    Tales to Maeonian handmaids; even he
Who routed Tartarus, the stars upbore,
    Now turns the spindle, while Love laughs to see ;
With deadly arms that erst the hero wore,
    Iole's feeble fingers sport in glee,
The lion's hide flung o'er her person slender,
Seems raiment all too rough for limbs so tender.

A sea is opposite; with surges hoar,
    Its broad cerulean fields are foaming white,
Its central space a double row spreads o'er
    Of ships and arms, and weapons flashing light ;
Gold flames the deep, and all Leucadia's shore
    With martial conflagration blazes bright,
Cæsar leads Rome, Mark Antony the legions
Of Egypt, Araby, and Ganges' regions.

You might have deemed the Cyclades afloat,
    Or crashing mountains in collision there,
So each on other rushed, so fiercely smote
    The tow'ring ships together, pair and pair,
There darts and torches flew, there might ye note
    The deep a ghastly load of slaughter bear,
But lo ! ere Vict'ry knew which side to favour,
The fair Barbarian Queen in flight doth save her.

And Antony, too, flies, forsaking those
    Fond hopes of empire which had filled his breast,
He flies not—nay, no fear the hero knows,
    Her flight he follows, led by her behest ;
In him behold a man in whom as foes
    Love, wrath, and shame contend in fierce unrest,
As now on the fierce battle and its chances,
Now on the flying sail he turns his glances.

                              " Ger. Lib." canto xvi.

                                        H

Tasso has modelled whole passages on corresponding ones in Virgil, and Armida's reproaches, when Rinaldo is released by the arrival of his comrades with a counter spell, are copied almost literally from those which Dido heaps on the departing Eneas.   And as the woman has vanquished the sorceress in her case, so modern romantic sentiment here triumphs over the classical and mediæval spirit which had so long clung to the ancient story, and it is henceforward invested with a new character.

In Spanish literature we find it treated from this later point of view, which Calderon has emphasised in the title of his Circe drama, " El Mayor Encanto Amor " (" Love the Greatest Enchantment ").   In this version it triumphs, indeed, on all hands, for only to its spell is Ulysses vulnerable, while the enchantress, dying in despair at his departure, finds all her witchcraft helpless against its power.

Thus in the modern Circe the purely human element alone survives, and the kernel-thought she embodies, asserting the supreme spell of beauty over men's hearts, stands out at last in bare simplicity stripped of all the husks of fiction that had overlaid it.   For a certain recrudescence of popular taste had, in the Middle Ages, again obscured what classicalism had tended to make clear, restoring some of the ruder legendary forms discarded by Greek culture.   So while Hellenic Aphrodite rises from the Paphian foam in undimmed loveliness, having cast the scaly slough of the Eastern fish-goddess, her deformed progenitor, the grotesque mediæval imagination revives that monstrosity in the mermaid or siren, whose close connection with the water-witch of Italian song is proved by the identity of Morgana's name with the Marie Morgan, or woman-fish of Breton folk-

lore.   The shadowy association which linked this hybrid
of the deep to the class of ideas more gracefully embodied in the island goddesses, Venus,* Calypso, and
Circe, may be dimly traced in the gold-fed fish of Morgana, in Caradina's well-stocked tank, in Alcina's pisca-
tory sport, and in the holy fish, the object of mysterious
veneration to the Irish peasantry.   But if such survivals
do little more than remind us how completely we have
broken with the past to which they belonged, they also
show how deeply rooted in human nature must be a tradition which has so long haunted the brain of mankind.
They point the moral that if Circe the sorceress is finally
deposed, Circe the woman lives and reigns for ever, and
that, as the motto of Calderon's drama puts it, Love is
still the greatest enchantment.

* Among other fables connecting Venus with the fish avatar
is one narrating how she and Cupid, meeting the giant Typhon
by the banks of the Euphrates, were so terrified at his aspect
that they jumped into the stream and took the form of fishes.
The Italian *pesce d'aprile* is perhaps connected with this worship,
April being the month of Aphrodite.

CHAPTER VII

Fountain Magic

BELIEF in the magical virtue of wells and springs was part of the universal nature worship common to primitive man, and survived long enough in Northern France to be denounced by Christian bishops, together with other remnants of the ancient Druidical faith. But the more exclusive association of love-spells with fountain magic may be traced to the rites of the Syrian moon goddess, identified under her various synonyms with water as the source of fertility, and venerated in many localities in connection with sacred ponds. Hence Boiardo interwove, as usual, a double strand of fable, when he linked the love-fountains of the Ardennes to the spells of Merlin, the Cymric wizard. There is, indeed, a parallel in Irish legend to the exercise by the latter of his power in this region for the cure of a fatal passion. The champion, Cuchullain, we are told, having, like so many heroes of romance, been enticed away to visit the fairy Fand on her happy isle, leaving his own true love, Emer, pining in his absence, the wrongs of the latter are avenged by the inconstancy of her rival, who deserts her mortal admirer to return to her own realm in the Isle of Man. He loses his senses and flies to the mountains in delirious rage, but is cured by the Druids by the administration of "the drink of oblivion," which he has no sooner swallowed than all memory of the fairy and her enchantments is obliterated from his mind. A similar potion cures the jealousy of Emer, which was of the nature of insanity, and both are restored to their normal state of mind. In Boiardo's version of the story of Merlin's Fount, it had an analogous origin, having been designed as an antidote to the philtre whence sprang the fatal passion of Tristan and Iseult. Rinaldo, enamoured of Angelica, is here the sport of its power.

> Within the wood the amorous Baron tries
> To peer, and what it hideth to seek out ;
> A grove of shady bushes he descries,
> Girt by a clear and rippling stream about.
> Charmed with the fair and festive spot, he hies
> Toward it straight, with neither fear nor doubt,
> Where in the midst a fountain meets his vision,
> Work not of human hands, but art Elysian.
>
> Of alabaster wrought, all gleaming white
> Its structure, and with gold so thick o'erlaid,
> So richly ornamented and bedight,
> It shone like flame within the flowery glade ;
> Merlin 'twas built it, that the doughty knight,
> Sir Tristan, by its magic might be stayed
> From longer that fair Queen with love pursuing
> Who later, as we know, was his undoing.
>
> Sir Tristan, hapless wight, by dire behest
> Of evil fate, ne'er reached the fountain shore,
> Though often he rode forth upon the quest,
> And far and near that country travelled o'er ;
> Such virtue by its waters was posse'st,
> The knight who drank it, hot with love before,
> Was of the am'rous passion straight divested,
> And her he erst adored thenceforth detested.

High stood the sun, and sultry was the day,
　　When Prince Rinaldo reached the flowery shore;
All dewed with heat, and weary with the way,
　　He, tempted by the water bubbling o'er,
Leaped from Bajardo's back without delay,
　　And quenched both love and thirst, now felt no more;
For that chill draught, once tasted, wrought its mission,
And straightway changed his am'rous heart's condition.

Now in his soul as vile doth he despise
　　Pursuit of thing so shallow, slight, and vain,
And e'en those charms which to his dazzled eyes,
　　Before seemed superhuman, doth disdain,
And from his memory drops in careless wise;
　　For such strange spell that water doth contain,
That now his will, beneath its transformation,
Holds fair Angelica in detestation.
　　　　　" Orl. Inn." book i. canto iii. stanzas 32 *et seq.*

Upon the feelings of the latter the counter-spell of the
Fountain of Love works a contrary effect somewhat
later, and the meeting of the pair with their sentiments
towards each other reversed is described by the poet
with the subtle self-mockery characteristic of the Renaissance, but less often found in Boiardo than in his successors.

Forth from the wood in mood of lofty pride,
　　That warrior rode, who knew no thought of fear,
Thus lost in thought, he reached a river-side,
　　Where flowed a sparkling stream crystalline clear,
Its bloomy marge had nature prankt and pied
　　With every flower that spring-time bids appear;
To shade the lovely shore from sun and weather,
A pine and beech and olive grew together.

The stream of love it was that sparkled here;
　　Not witched by Merlin's magic like the first,
For innate virtue in the waters clear
　　Here wakes in hearts of men love's fiery thirst;

Full many an ancient knight and cavalier,
    By error led, hath sipped its wave accurst ;
Rinaldo drank not, since as was narrated,
His thirst he at the other fount had sated.

Lured by the beauteous spot, the knight was fain
    Here for a while to rest and take his ease,
So loosing from Bajardo's neck the rein,
    He let him graze the mead as he should please ;
In heedless mood he then reclined amain
    Upon the marge to sleep 'neath shady trees.
The Baron slept, nor sense kept watch to tell him,
The chance, as you shall hear, that next befell him.

Angelica, when from the dreadful fight
    So fierce and obstinate, she fled away,
Reached the same stream, where thirst bade her alight
    On the green sward, to drink without delay.
Now list to novel chance, how Love the sprite
    Chastised the haughty dame that said him nay.
For, as the Baron 'mid the flowers reclining
She saw, love filled her heart with sudden pining.

Her snowy palfrey to the pine made fast,
    Unto Rinaldo sleeping she draws nigh,
Looks on the knight, and feels her strength ebb fast,
    And knows not, hapless maid, what course to try.
The mead was thick with blossoms strewn broadcast,
    And lilies fair with moss-rose buds did vie,
Her fair hand strips and strews them ever faster
Right on the face of Montalbano's master.

Whereon Rinaldo waking lifts his eyes,
    And sees the damsel stand above him there,
Who greets him with all honour, friendly-wise ;
    But he, with clouded brow and altered air
Leaps to his saddle and in surly guise,
    Rejects her gentle speech and greeting fair,
Through the dense thicket he before her flieth,
Who at his heels upon her palfrey hieth.

                        Ibid. stanzas 48 *et seq.*

Bajardo's fleetness makes the race a hollow one, and Angelica is hopelessly distanced by her quondam lover. But as there is always a touch of nature even in Boiardo's farcical situations, he infuses a ring of genuine emotion into the lamentations of the fair pursuer, which enables her to appeal, however remotely, to our sympathy.

> Now would he but at least permit mine eyes
>   To rest a little while upon his face,
> And thus to check or temper in some wise
>   The fire of love that me consumes apace,
> All reason, well I know, my love defies,
>   But where love is, there reason hath no place;
> As harsh, and stern, and rude though I accuse thee,
> Be whatsoe'er thou wilt, I thus would choose thee.
>
> And while lamenting thus, she turned toward
>   The shady beech her gaze bedimmed with dew,
> Ye blessed flowers, she cried, and blessed sward,
>   Who the dear touch of that fair visage knew.
> How envious I of partial fate's award,
>   Which happier lot than mine bestows on you,
> Since I would die this moment on condition
> That unto me should come such blest fruition.
>
> *Ibid.* stanzas 48 *et seq.*

But Rinaldo is not allowed to escape with impunity the wrath of the divinity defied, and love's vengeance is brought about by a fanciful episode, perhaps suggested to the author's mind by some antique representation of Cupid or Apollo and the Graces. The scene is thoroughly characteristic of his power of invention in handling the threadbare themes of classical mythology, and is described in what is perhaps one of the most exquisite passages of purely fantastic description ever evolved from the more sportive moods of poetry. In a glade of the forest Rinaldo comes upon Love and his three com-

panions dancing on the green, and all four, immediately
turning upon him with reproaches for his treason to the
laws they hold sacred, pelt him with the flowers they
are carrying. The fair petals sting and wound like fire,
and the anguish they inflict almost reduces the knight to
death's door. The passage is one of those translated in
Dr. Garnett's admirable work on " Italian Literature," so
it would be superfluous to quote it here, and we only
append the stanzas descriptive of the termination of the
scene.

> Nor could he tell if gods or men were those,
>   Nor prayers availed, nor aught such foes could rout,
> And thus they tarried, nor e'er took repose,
>   Till on their shoulders wings began to sprout,
> Of white and gold, vermilion blent with rose,
>   And from each plume a living eye looked out,
> Not peacock-orbed, or other fowl's in seeming,
> But like a lovely maiden's softly gleaming.
>
> Then straight did they uplift themselves in flight,
>   And one by one unto high heaven upsoared.
> Rinaldo on the lawn in doleful plight,
>   Now left alone, with tears his state deplored,
> O'erwhelmed so sore with pain and woe, that quite
>   His senses ebbed away in grief outpoured,
> And in the end such anguish did invade him,
> That as one dead upon the sward he laid him.
>
> *Idem*, book ii. canto xv. stanzas 30 *et seq.*

Thus ends the vision, which seems real while it lasts,
yet has the iridescence of a soap-bubble in its swift
transit across the stage. The neglect of Angelica's
flower greeting is avenged by a floral chastisement, and
the only cure to be found, as the knight is informed by
Pasithea, who returns with the message, is a draught from

the Fountain of Love. He obeys the prescription, and is at once healed of his wounds and restored to his passion, which is, however, still doomed to frustration, as its object, ere he meets her again, has steeled her heart against him once more by a chance draught from Merlin's Fountain. Thus the game of cross purposes is played to the end by the working of these opposite spells.

The idea of two fountains mutually counteracting or correcting each other has its root in Eastern fable. Thus in the Book of Sindibad, a youth on his way to marry a princess is first changed into a woman by a draught from one spring and then restored to his sex by drinking from another endowed with opposite virtue. In another tale a monkey is seen to transform himself into a man, and *vice versâ* by plunging alternately into two adjoining pools. This miraculous quality of water becomes a love-spell in classical legend, according to which oblivion of passion was attained by a plunge in the river Selinus, while the opposite character of Cupid's two sets of arrows, the one sharp and golden, to act as the stimulus of love, the other blunt and leaden as its soporific, was acquired from immersion in different fountains.

In his version of the story of Narcissus, Boiardo treats it as another instance of Love's retributive justice, and grafts fresh outgrowths on his theme with the usual licence of his luxuriant fancy. The sepulchre of Narcissus thus becomes the centre of a whole cycle of love stories and fountain magic.

> Beyond the bridge a plain was seen to fold
>   Around the rock whence welled the fountain's wave;
> A sepulchre of marble did it hold,
>   Not wrought by human art that gorgeous grave,

A script above in letters all of gold,
   Ran thus: That soul in dreams doth idly rave,
Which of its own fair face enamoured sigheth,
Here sepulchred the young Narcissus lieth.

Narcissus was in times antique and dim
   A youth so lovely and of charms so rare,
No picture painter's brush did ever limn
   Could image forth a thing so passing fair;
But scornful he as beauteous, for in him
   As oft in others, grace with pride did pair,
For rarely are these qualities found parted,
Whence many a one hath perished broken-hearted,

And as the Queen of Orient did in sooth
   The fair Narcissus love with fond excess,
And found him void of pity and of ruth,
   Indifferent to her love and tenderness,
She pined in sadness for the lovely youth,
   And wept from dawn to dark in sore distress;
Addressing him such words of supplication,
As might have moved the sun from heav'n's high station.
             Ibid. canto xvii. stanzas 49 *et seq.*

The imprecations of this slighted fair one on her death-bed move the gods to grant the vengeance she claims, and a fountain is again the instrument of retributive chastisement.

And so did it befall, for to the place
   Where gushed the fountain as my lay hath told,
Narcissus came, chance-led by sylvan chase,
   Through having run a stag far through the wold;
He stooped to drink, and saw his own fair face
   There imaged, which he now did first behold,
And, gazing on't, was in such error taken
That his own semblance love in him did waken.

Now who such strange event hath heard amain ?
    Oh Love's stern justice, how thy bolts destroy !
Since o'er a fountain's brink he sighs in vain
    For that which having, he can ne'er enjoy.
That soul so pitiless of others' pain,
    By kneeling dames adored, who to the boy
Gave worship rather to a god belonging,
Now self-enamoured dies of hopeless longing.

And gazing on his image, fairest sight
    The world contained, for beauty without peer,
Doth waste away for utter sheer delight,
    And pine like withered lily, pale and sere ;
Or severed rose—so drooped the winsome wight,
    Till the fair face of white and damask clear,
Dark eyes and merry glance, Love's food and fuel,
Fell Death destroyed, the world's destroyer cruel.

                       Ibid. stanzas 53 *et seq.*

With the classical legend here narrated Boiardo in his
habitual fashion proceeds to weave additions of his own,
connecting it with the fanciful beliefs of a later chapter
of popular romance. For the Fairy Silvanella, coming
on the body of the dead Narcissus, still beautiful in
death, is smitten with his fatal beauty, and also pines
away after having erected for him the beautiful sepulchre
described above. She bequeaths to the fountain a fresh
set of maleficent spells, whose working is told as follows :

For she, desiring partners in that pain
    Which lingering death in amorous pining brought,
Such malice in her woe did still retain,
    That fairy spells she on the fountain wrought,
And whoso passed that way, nor did refrain
    From looking on the wave with magic fraught,
Saw 'neath its surface girlish faces gleaming,
With wreathèd smiles and fair and gracious seeming.

And such a charm is in their glances seen,
  That whoso looks departeth thence no more,
But all dissolved in love, upon the green
  Must die at last upon the flowery shore.
Here passed, in evil hour for him, I ween,
  A gallant king, for daring famed, and lore,
Who with his lady rode, her name by token
Was Calidora, his Larbin was spoken.

Ibid. stanzas 59 *et seq.*

This lady, widowed of her lord by the fatal fountain, has taken up her abode close by, with the humane purpose of warning others of the danger, and has engaged a knight to prevent any from passing that way by force if necessary. Here the story is linked on to the adventures of Orlando, who with his companions chances upon the spot, and is only dissuaded from doing battle with its warder by the recital of its strange history from the lips of the bereaved Calidora.

Here we have a perfect example of the amalgamation of classical and mediæval material by Boiardo, and can trace step by step the process by which the watery mirror-spell of antique myth shapes itself into a shadowy suggestion of the Naiads' Pool of Teutonic fable. The latter idea, in its fully developed form, is carried out in his next specimen of water-magic. It will be observed that the entire series forms a cycle, in which the subject undergoes a species of evolution, assuming gradually a more materialised, and, so to speak, anthropomorphic form. Thus the original fable of a philtre in which water acts as a love-medicine, either for cause or cure, passes into the shadow myth, and this mirror-spell again into the visionary glimpses of phantom faces. We shall now see how this latter invention embodies itself in the actual flesh and blood water-nymph, enjoying a festive and frolicsome subaqueous existence in stream or haunted well.

The germ of this phantasy, to which the Naiad fountain in which Hylas was drowned furnishes a classical analogy, may be traced still further east, and in Persia a well near the city of Kashan is to this day believed to be of un-fathomable depth, and to have enchanted groves and gardens at the bottom. The Persian hero, Hatim Tai, again, jumps into a well in search of a certain vizier's son, who had been enticed down by the beauty of the Naiad Queen. He succeeds in his mission, but only persuades the young man to return to his friends after he has received his fair hostess's promise to visit him above ground.

Of a similar character is the Rhine-country legend of the origin of the celebrated spring of Baden, according to which three young men, riding through the forest, are accosted by three nixies, who rise from a well and invite them to dance upon the sward. They do so, nothing loth, but find themselves by a sudden subsidence of the ground deposited at the bottom of a lake and confronted with an irate water-king, who is with difficulty pacified by his daughters' entreaties. The visitors are whirled by an eddy to the surface after three magical pebbles have been bestowed on them. The first is accidentally dropped into the lake, raising a storm accompanied by a flight of pursuing serpents; the second falls on a rock whence the Baden spring gushes out; and the third is retained by its possessor without any noteworthy result, showing that the end of the tale must have been forgotten, as popular fable never reaches so "lame and impotent a conclusion."

Water-fays, with Morgain at their head, play a leading

part in Breton romance, and the Lady of the Lake, who
bestows Excalibur on Arthur, inhabits a subaqueous
palace, declared by Merlin to be "as fair a place as any
on earth." The mysterious Isle of Avalon, to which the
water-witch, Morgain, transports Ogier, belongs to the
same class of watery elysium, and the wreath of oblivion
with which she crowns his brow has its counterpart in
many aqueous spells. We shall now see how Boiardo
deals with all this legendary matter, letting him tell for
himself how his hero finds his way to the Naiads' Bower.

> But first will I recount what chance befel
>   Brave Count Orlando, led so far astray,
> As ye have heard, by false enchanter's spell,
>   To where Great Charles seemed worsted in the fray ;
> He deemed that all before him fled pellmell,
>   In headlong rout of terror and dismay,
> Until they reached the sandy flats and surges,
> Where Ardennes forest on the ocean verges.
>
> A thicket there of verdant laurel grew,
>   Girt by a gushing fount's pellucid stream,
> Where the accursèd host was lost to view,
>   Dissolving into smoke like empty dream ;
> That the Count wondered at a chance so new,
>   And portent so unheard, ye well may deem,
> Who in that heat with droughty fever burning,
> Passed to the wood, much evil fortune earning.
>
> From Brigliadoro's back, when once inside,
>   He sprang to sip the fount that sparkled near,
> And leaving him fast to a laurel tied,
>   Stooped from the bank above the ripple clear ;
> Within its depths a structure fair he spied,
>   Which held him there intent on it to peer,
> For there a crystal chamber met his glauces,
> With ladies thronged, who vied in songs and dances.

Those lovely ladies through the dance did wind,
    And sung in cadence tuned to love's device,
In the fair crystal palace walled and lined
    With gold and gems, inlaid with stones of price:
The day already to the west declined,
    When bold Orlando bent him in a trice,
To see the end of chance so marvel-freighted,
Nor further thought, debate, or counsel waited.

But as he was, all armed into the tide,
    He plunged, and to the bottom went full soon,
To find him standing in a meadow, pied
    With all the flowers that ever bloomed in June.
The gallant Count then to the palace hied,
    With heart so light and in such merry tune,
That for sheer joy he never more bethought him,
Whence he had come, or what had hither brought him.
        Ibid. book ii. canto xxi. stanzas 43 *et seq.*

The poet breaks off here to close his second book with
a peroration to his audience, leaving his hero in inglorious
captivity, and six whole cantos of the third book inter-
vene before he returns to his rescue, bringing three other
knights to effect it, with Fleur de Lys, the lady of one of
their number.

He in the camp—of Agermant I tell,
    Was hailed with honour by the warlike train,
But now to further speech of him farewell,
    While to my former tale I turn amain,
And of Anglante's Count narrate the spell,
    Who found himself in strangest error ta'en,
Amidst the Naiads in the Fount of Laughter—
Now shall ye hear what chanced to him thereafter.

Within their watery home these Naiads dwell,
    And like to fish disport themselves therein,
And mighty fabrics raise by magic spell,
    For all designs of theirs attainment win;

The knights of earth they ofttimes love full well,
　　For life unmated doth fair dames chagrin,
Such fays abound from whom no art delivers,
Nor hidden only in the depths of rivers.

These in the fount that is of laughter hight,
　　A mansion beautiful beyond compare
Had built of gold and silver shining bright,
　　And in the festive dance disported there.
Already have ye heard Orlando's plight,
　　When from his steed dismounted unaware,
He in the dainty tide found fond illusion,
As I have told at the last book's conclusion.

And how the ladies welcomed, and were fain,
　　With pomp and revelry him there to treat,
Who all unfettered freely did remain,
　　Ensnared by love of the enchantment sweet ;
His face he mirrored in the watery plane,
　　While sense and feeling from his mind did fleet,
The Naiads, gay and mirthful beyond measure,
In gazing on him found their joy and pleasure.
　　　　　　　Ibid. book iii. canto vii. stanzas 6 *et seq.*

An enchanted wood is among the defences with which
they have girt round their bower, and here surprising
adventures await the rescue party, consisting of Ruggiero, Gradasso, and Brandimarte.　Fleur de Lys has
armed herself with counter-spells, and bids them hew
manfully with their swords at the trees that oppose their
progress, but sore temptation assails them when they do
so.　Ruggiero has no sooner cut down a laurel than dis-
comfiture overtakes him in the following fashion :

But when the beauteous tree was stricken low,
　　And in the dust its crown of triumph lay,
From out its trunk a lovely maid did grow,
　　With golden tresses shining like the day,

I

And vivid eyes like living stars aglow,
    Who wept as one to torment sore a prey,
With speech so soft and voice so modulated,
The fiercest heart its rage would have abated.

Canst be so cruel, Baron fair, said she,
    As to take pleasure in my wretched plight?
If in my present state thou leavest me,
    My feet as roots deformed will clasp this site,
My body to a trunk transmuted be,
    My arms as rigid boughs stretch left and right,
This face rude bark will mask, these golden tresses
As leaves and frondage meet the wind's caresses.

                                    Ibid. stanzas 18 *et seq.*

The distressed damsel persuades the courteous knight
to lead her to the river, and the result may be imagined
by any expert in fairy tales:

As on the river bank the pair arrive,
    The lovely nymph there took him by the hand,
And of his former self did so deprive,
    One burning longing did his soul command,
Headlong into the living wave to dive;
    Nor did the lady his desire withstand,
But as they stood, thus arm and arm together,
They sprang into the stream's abysses nether.

Below in the fair palace crystalline,
    They were made welcome with all festive glee;
There Sacripant did with Orlando pine,
    And many a baron and much soldiery;
The Naiads with them danced in glittering line,
    And flutes and tabors piped of revelry,
And thus, in song and jest, and games and dances,
The days go by in joy that sense entrances.

                                    Ibid. stanzas 21 *et seq.*

A different form of temptation assails Gradasso, and
proves equally irresistible to his particular weakness.
His fortunes are recounted as follows:

Gradasso had remained within the wood,
 Nor found or track or pathway to win through,
And 'mid the trees his passage that withstood,
 A feathery ash was ever first in view,
And as he hewed it with his broadsword good,
 Lo ! a great war-horse clove the trunk in two,
With shining coat of roan and sorrel blended,
Dame Nature ne'er had made a steed so splendid.

The bridle in his mouth was massy gold,
 His harness rich with pearls and stones so rare,
That for vast treasure it had well been sold.
 Gradasso takes no thought and has no care,
That all is wrought in false enchantment's mould,
 But he with courage high approaching there,
The broidered rein doth seize on undisputed,
And leaps into the saddle agile-footed.

Then straight the charger bounded into air,
 Nor stooped again to earth, but through the sky
Did soar aloft and swiftly onward fare,
 As one in dreams doth sometimes think to fly ;
No battle or assault in arms did e'er
 Inspire with dread Gradasso's spirit high,
But here, I grant you, fear his breast assaulted
To see himself to such great height exalted.

For lo ! a hundred paces high and more
 The phantom creature through the air did fly,
The Baron looked below, but still did soar,
 On this strange ladder, as to scale the sky.
Good space of heaven they thus had traversed o'er
 When 'neath them was the river seen to lie,
The beast enchanted then to earth descended,
And diving in the fount, its roamings ended.

Thus 'neath the wave Gradasso plunged amain,
 While to the surface swam the mighty steed,
And hied him to the forest back again,
 As swiftly as though wings his hoofs did speed ;

But 'neath the water did the knight remain,
　His heart within him changed in very deed,
And while all memory of the past forsook him
To sporting with the Naiads he betook him.

To sound of trump they trode a measure gay,
　Unknown on earth its woven steps of glee,
And in each pass and pause they kissed alway,
　With melting lips that never closed might be ;
And in such act all memory swooned away,
　In lapse that easy pardon wins from me,
Who hold that such sweet kiss from lips so parted,
Converts with luscious touch the hardest hearted.

Ibid. stanzas 24 *et seq.*

There now remains but a single knight to effect the deliverance of his comrades, and the subtle allegorical meaning underlying the whole passage is emphasised in the fact that it is by the assistance of his own true love that he is enabled to resist the spells of the alluring nymphs. Brandimarte is here the type of constancy, and is therefore alone worthy to be victorious in the struggle with the enchantments that assail that virtue. He owes his triumph to the aid of Fleur de Lys, and it is achieved in the following fashion :

Of shrubs and trees he felled above a score,
　And saw from each a novel task unfold,
Now giant birds that painted feathers wore,
　Now fairy palaces, now heaps of gold ;
But all soon faded and were seen no more,
　For Brandimart with front secure and bold,
No heed doth pay but left them all behind him,
And thus at last did near the river find him.

But when the Baron came upon the shore,
　His face flushed over with a lively red,
And changed in mind, he by a longing sore
　To plunge into the amorous wave was led ;

To stress of strong enchantment given o'er,
  Thought of Orlando and all else was fled,
And he had headlong flung himself demented,
If Fleur de Lys had not the act prevented.

For she with magic artifice had wound
  Four wreaths or coronals of blossoms rare,
With herbs in strange and distant places found,
  That freed from magic spell whoso should wear;
With one now Brandimarte's head she crowned,
  Then did from point to point his mind prepare,
With ordered plan, when in the enchanted river,
Orlando from its magic to deliver.

The gallant knight, when she her mind had spoke,
  Incontinent his lady's hest obeyed,
And plunged into the river 'mid those folk
  Who all around him danced, and sang, and played :
But not like them with mind distraught and broke,
  Saved by the garland Fleur de Lys had laid
Upon his brow, where it secure reposes,
Wove by her magic of enchanted roses.

As through those halls of revelry he strayed,
  In the fair palace gold and crystalline,
On the Count's brows one coronal he laid,
  And did forthwith the other two assign
Unto his comrades twain, then was displayed
  To all the four at once the spell malign,
They left the ladies and their joys sad-hearted,
And from the stream reluctantly departed.

Like hollow gourds they floated where on high
  Each martial crest did first to sight appear,
The helmets next and shoulders met the eye,
  And then with ease they to the bank drew near,
Where swept aloft like airy butterfly,
  That circles round the flame it holds so dear,
They by a mighty blast in air uplifted,
Were in a flash from out the forest drifted.

Ibid. stanzas 31 *et seq.*

Thus, in Boiardo's last water witchery, the true love-spell has conquered the false, and in the progress of the idea through his pages from the original fetish faith in a water philtre, through the classical shadow-myth of Narcissus, we have reached its ultimate phase in the mediæval phantom-fable, with its underlying moral and allegorical significance.   Here the old elemental beliefs practically vanish from Renaissance poetry, for Ariosto, in taking up the unfinished theme left him by his predecessor, does so in a thoroughly modern spirit, and either abandons or burlesques all the fantastic creations of the wonder-world into which the elder bard transports us. A materialist at heart, he craves for no super-sensuous elysium, and sees no shadowy background to the world of physical facts so vividly present to him.   Love, in his creed, needs no extraneous aid to reinforce its own witcheries, and the siren-snares of fount and stream so conspicuously paraded in the " Orlando Innamorato " are superseded in its sequel by the personal charms of the witch-woman herself.   Merlin's Fount only appears to introduce a series of tableaux from Italian history, with no hint of its magical attributes, and no gnome or nixie beckons from its brim to tempt the traveller to sip its lethal wave.   The   illusory   brain-phantasms   of   the Middle Ages, the sylvan semi-humanities of the elder world, vanish like ghosts at cock-crow, before the search-light of that mocking genius by whom the haunting presences of primeval nature are exorcised for ever from the domain of modern song.

But Boiardo's water-spells were not exhausted by those suggested by older fable or tradition, for the closing cantos of his work contain the most marvellous series of enchantments found throughout its pages, to

which the wandering champion is introduced by a
Fountain Fay's instrumentality. Mandricardo, who here
makes his first appearance, is the hero of this adventure,
for a fresh set of actors take their places on the stage at
the opening of each book, and as Agramante, Rodamonte, Ruggiero, and all the other African chiefs present themselves in the initial chapter of the Second
Book, so Mandricardo, the fierce King of Tartary or
Scythia, sets out at the beginning of the Third to avenge
his father, Agricane, on his slayer, Orlando. Vowing to
take neither arms nor steed, but to win both on the way,
he starts, unarmed and unattended, on his enterprise,
and is met on its threshold by the following experience:

> Thus wandering all alone had he passed through
>   Armenia's land, and many countries wide,
> Till he one day did from a hillock view
>   A fair pavilion by a fountain side.
> And with the thought straight bent his steps thereto
>   That if he horse or armour there descried,
> By methods fair or foul would he endeavour,
> To seize, nor would depart without them ever.
>
> So when upon the level plain he trode,
>   He passed inside the curtains without fear.
> Nor far or near a human creature showed
>   To guard the fair pavilion and its gear.
> A voice alone from where the fountain flowed,
>   Low gurgling 'mid its water tinkling clear,
> Said : Cavalier, ye by excess of daring
> Are prisoner made, and stayed from farther faring.
>
> But whether he heard not or gave no heed,
>   He to the words gave little thought or care,
> But the pavilion searched to help his need,
>   If horse or armour he might chance on there ;
> And arms upon a carpet spread indeed,
>   He saw, with all befitting knightly wear :

And to a pine-tree by the fountain's eddy,
Saw hitched a steed caparisoned and ready.

That gallant Baron, without heed or thought,
   Did in that harness swiftly him array,
And took the steed, but when to go he sought,
   A fire before him kindled was straightway.
The pine-tree first the conflagration caught,
   And burned was to the roots without delay;
The fire spread round about, on all things gaining,
The tent and fount alone untouched remaining.

Trees, grass, and stones, that place contained were swept
   By flames devouring, in confusion dire,
While stretching wide the blaze advancing crept,
   Till round the knight it closed in circling spire,
And on him last, the fire enchanted leapt,
   And helm and shield and all his mailed attire,
The shirt of steel and chain and plate together,
Burned on his back, like straw in scorching weather.

In circumstance so strange the cavalier
   Did of his usual courage nought abate,
But from his horse that lofty soul sprang clear,
   And dashed right through the fire so passing great.
When to the fountain come in his career,
   In leaped he, to the bottom diving straight;
No other hope of safety was there left him,
Since of his very shirt the flames bereft him.
          Idem, book iii. canto i. stanzas 15 *et seq.*

Here he finds himself a prisoner to the Fountain Fay,
who has in her keeping the arms of Hector, brought
hither and bestowed on her by Eneas in gratitude for a
service she has rendered him. The sword alone is missing, for it has passed into the possession of Orlando, and
is no other than the celebrated Durindana, which the
winner of the rest of the trophy is bound to recover in
order to complete it. An extraordinary series of com-

bats and enchantments then begin, in all of which Mandricardo is victorious. The story is worked out with
amazing verve and vividness, but some of the stanzas of
the closing scene must serve as specimens of the brilliant
descriptive passages with which the episode abounds :

> The serpent slain, straight looked the cavalier
>   On the dark grotto, overhead and round ;
> A carbuncle gleamed there as chandelier,
>   And like the sun by day, shone underground.
> The tomb was from a single stone cut clear,
>   And so o'erlaid and with adornments crowned,
> Of polished silver, coral, lucid amber,
> A finger's breadth of rock showed not the chamber.
>
> A lofty throne was in its midst upreared,
>   Of whitest ivory without a stain,
> And on an azure cloth gold-starred and sphered,
>   Like altar-cloth or pall draped o'er it plain,
> A knight all panoplied to sit appeared,
>   Who, as in rest, unheeding did remain,
> Appeared, I say, not did so, be it noted,
> The empty arms no human figure coated.
>
> These arms those of the doughty knight had been,
>   Who is through all the world so much renowned ;
> Of Hector, I would say, who, well I ween,
>   With every virtue prized on earth was crowned.
> His panoply, whereof to speak I mean,
>   Without the sword, without the shield was found,
> Where was the shield my verse above declareth,
> The sword, hight Durindan, Orlando weareth.
>
> The burnished plates shone dazzling to the sight,
>   Which scarcely suffered they on them to rest,
> With gold inlaid and priceless jewels bright,
>   Great emeralds, rubies, pearls, all of the best,
> Wild longing Mandricardo's heart filled quite.
>   A thousand years it seemed till in them drest,

The hauberk and each piece he weighed appraising,
But most upon the ornate helm kept gazing.

Upon its crest a lion ramped in gold,
  Whose paw held out a scroll of silver fine,
Beneath it, golden, too, the casque's close mould,
  With six-and-twenty clasps of one design ;
But its full front the carbuncle did hold,
  Which like a lamp illumed that dreary mine,
And as its nature is, shed radiance sparkling
Through every corner of the cavern darkling.

While still the knight stood gazing, as in awe,
  Upon the arms, well worthy of such gaze,
He heard a clang behind, as who should draw
  An iron gate aside, whose hinges graze,
And turning, many ladies enter saw,
  Who moved in numbers through the dance's maze ;
Clad in strange garb and new, the ranks assigned them
They took, while pipes and shells rang shrill behind them.

And gambolling all round, they pirouetted,
  And bounded vertically high in air,
And dancing thus, began a song that fretted,
  On high notes, in shrill unison voiced there,
The strain, than starlings' keener, passion-whetted,
  Through the lone vault resounded everywhere ;
Then in the end they ceased in hush unanimous,
And knelt down all before the knight magnanimous.
                    Ibid. canto iii. stanzas 25 *et seq.*

This adventure was directed to the glorification of the
house of Este, since Hector's arms and shield with their
cognizance, a white eagle on a blue field, were intended
to pass eventually into their possession. But this piece
of courtly flattery, which the poet's death cut short at the
stage here reached, was part of the treasure bequeathed
by him to the genius of his successor.

CHAPTER VIII

Lyrics of Boiardo

FEW literary masterpieces have had so strange a history as Boiardo's "Orlando Innamorato." Forgotten for over three centuries in the land that gave it birth, while reproduced in the disguise of a paraphrase, on the title-page of which its original author's name did not even appear, it was once more restored and brought to light in a splendid modern edition, with exhaustive notes and introduction, published in London in 1831 by Sir Anthony Panizzi of the British Museum.

The first complete edition of the original text, published at Scandiano in 1494, a year after the poet's death, by his son, Camillo, was followed by fifteen others, of which the last appeared in Venice in 1545. It was entirely superseded, sixty years after its author's death, by the "rifacimento," or adaptation of Francesco Berni, a facile and humorous poet with a great command of the Tuscan vernacular. He takes many liberties with the original, altering, omitting, and transforming according to his own humour, and treating the subject as far as possible from that comic point of view which was so much his specialty that the adjective Bernesque has been coined from his name to describe this jocose vein in poetry. Thus Boiardo's poem fell into complete oblivion, and ceased to be reprinted, a neglect which Signor Rajna attributes to " the pedantry of language which has been so fatal to Italian literature from the fifteenth century onwards." It is, no doubt, full of archaisms of language, solecisms in grammar, and antiquated or local phrases ostracised by the fastidiousness of the purists, but it has, nevertheless, a freshness of spirit, and an intimate sense of immediate inspiration which have evaporated in the more polished medium to which it was transferred by its remodeller. The tyranny of the Tuscan tongue could alone have had power to relegate so great a work to the limbo of literary fossils.

It bears, however, every appearance of imperfect transcription in the first instance, and perhaps even of having been taken down in parts from oral renderings current among the Lombard people, since Boiardo was himself a man of high scholarly attainments and a master of classical expression. Like all Italian poets of his age, he made his *début* in Latin, and only as his powers developed found utterance in his native tongue. But in the lyric poems we have a specimen of his use of the latter which seems more studied and has less of the character of an improvisation than the " Orlando," and which we therefore presume, though not published until 1499, five years after his death, to have been left by him in a complete and revised form ready for the press. Here, though the language is not free from the antiquated forms then current in districts where it was only in process of adaptation to polite use, it has none of the slipshod colloquialisms which occasionally crop up in the great narrative poem. This volume, entitled "Sonetti e Canzone del Poeta clarissimo Matteo Maria Boiardo,

Conte di Scandiano," had also slipped out of sight under the dust of ages, and only reached, as far as is known, a second edition, published in 1501, within two years of its first appearance. From this obscurity it was rescued by the same indefatigable editor who had done so much for the memory of its author, and a splendid edition of only fifty copies was printed by Sir Anthony Panizzi for private circulation in 1835. It is now very rare, and can only be had when a copy accidentally happens to come into the market.

A selection of fifty-four of the pieces contained in it had, indeed, been given to the world by Venturi in 1820, but in this mutilated form much of its original sense and meaning is obscured. The lyrics consist entirely of love poems addressed, in the poetical fashion of the day, to a lady whose identity is shrouded in mystery, though conjectured on the evidence of two acrostics to have been Antonia Caprara, born in Reggio in 1451. The poet's attachment to her, if not entirely imaginary, is supposed to have lasted through the years 1471 and 1472, and hints in the poems suggest that she was married, and died young. The volume is divided into three books. In the first the poet celebrates the charms of his lady, and his own passion; in the second he reproaches her with her coldness and cruelty; and in the third there is a mixture of both themes, and her indifference and beauty are alternately sung.

The opening sonnet seems to imply that the lyrics were composed long after the emotion that elicited them had evaporated, and they must thus be regarded rather as records of a past than as utterances of a present sentiment. It runs as follows :

Love, from whose own fair sun some rays I caught,
   In the sweet days when life put forth its flowers,
   Invites me to call up from memory's bowers
What then with joy, but now with dole is fraught.

Thus have I gathered what my mind distraught
   Spake in the season of Love's rapturous hours,
   When with voice glad, but hindered in its powers,
To syllable fond words 'mid sighs I sought.

Now with embitted faith, by falsehood sweet
   Consumed, my soul not merely lays aside,
But flies in scorn the error of its youth.

Yet surely, he who without glow or heat
   Of love, doth pass the years of life's spring-tide,
May live, but bears no living heart in sooth.

The tenour of this sonnet seems inconsistent with the
theory that Antonia Caprara was the lady to whom the
lyrics are addressed, since it certainly implies that the
passion they portray was experienced in youth or early
manhood. This in her case was impossible, as she was
seventeen years the writer's junior, and his attachment to
her is conjectured to have begun only in his thirty-seventh
year, an age which to an Italian seems very serious if not
almost venerable, and one to which he would never apply
the term *età fiorita*, used here in the second line to
describe the date of this phase of his life. The whole
context certainly presents an obstacle to the acceptance
of the received theory, if it be not absolutely fatal to it.
For my part, I should be inclined to put back the
date of Boiardo's romance to a much earlier period than
that usually assigned to it, or to conjecture that his lyrics
have a more general character than that suggested by a
mere superficial interpretation of them, and that they

sum up what the poet may have experienced at different times and for different objects of his adoration.

The first Canzone is, like most of its companion pieces, strictly impersonal, expressive of a form of admiration equally applicable to any lady.

I.

Who shall find voice and words commensurate
  With utterance of what in my heart doth lie?
Who to my thought lend wings, the high and great
  Desire I feel, to track in flight on high?
Unless it soar elate,
  And my poor speech attain
  Where I would bid it fly,
Who of my star shall sing in fitting strain?
Of fair things she is fairest I maintain,
  Nor thought can e'er her beauty fitly tell,
Since Heaven to hide it from man's sight is fain,
  And doth forbid the height where it doth dwell.
Unless Love's aid to us be shown
  In order that the spell
Of its bright realm by us be felt and known.

II.

Lend aid, O Love, lest my weak spirit fail
  To gauge the height of that embellishment
Which to adorn this time doth so avail
  Its shining glory to our age is lent.
If brighter shines, when pale
  The fires of day around,
  Amid stars thinly sprent,
The moon, with purest silvery radiance crowned,
And all with flames her pallid face is bound,
  And light her horns doth fill resplendently,
On her alone our eyes intent are found,
  Since light from her alone they now may see,
Thus shines this luminary here on earth,
  And sole containeth she,
All beauty, grace, nobility and worth.

III.

As in the night-sky liquid and serene,
  The Star of Love comes forth before the day,
With golden beams and such effulgence sheen,
  The whole horizon shimmers with its ray.
And she doth lead, I ween,
  The lesser stars in queue,
  Who round her all give way,
And yield the sky, and lowly homage do;
And then, distilling showers of precious dew,
  From her damp tresses, which in moisture steep
The herbage green and flowers of varied hue,
  She soaks the land with pearls that she doth weep;
My Lady thus from all the prize doth gain,
  Since Love doth with her keep,
And all the charms of others render vain.

IV.

Whoso hath seen dawn breaking in the skies,
  With rose and jacinth crowned, and so bedight
That ere from out the deep the day doth rise,
  All heaven is painted with its flush of light;
And deeper grow the dyes
  Of rose incarnadine,
  Beside which quenched outright
Were all our hues that like to it are seen;
And the rude shepherd marvels much, I ween,
  At the red Orient's vermilion glow,
Which slowly spreads o'er all the sky its sheen,
  And as he looks more lucent still doth grow,
Thus shows the angelic visage in like guise,
  If any dare I trow
To look her in the face with steadfast eyes.

V.

As when with fiery rays from out the main,
  The sun to meet the dawn of day doth leap,
And as though hung 'twixt sky and watery plain,
  Doth trembling tread the pavement of the deep,

And when he grasps the rein
  His fiery team to steer,
  And with gold wheels the steep
Of heaven ascends in luminous career ;
No eye may dare to fix his radiance clear
  Since gold and crimson mingle in its blaze,
Whose splendour our dull sight doth dim and blear,
  And blunt our human vision with its daze ;
Such is the aspect of this visage bright,
  Which, since it met my gaze,
Hath ta'en from it all other power of sight.

VI.

O sweetest thought that doth with Love a flight
  So lofty take, and sing the visage fair,
The thought whereof doth melt my heart outright,
  Remembering its form and semblance rare ;
Give over enterprise so bold and high
  Since so far may not dare
The powers that in our human nature lie.

The breaks and pauses in this measure, as in all the
Petrarchian lyrics, had a meaning in their own day that
they have lost in ours, since they were adapted to some
form of musical notation. The names "Sonetto" and
"Canzone" were not the mere metaphorical applications of
the terms of one art to another so much in vogue in
modern parlance, but had a literal significance descriptive
of the metrical arrangements they described. Sir Anthony
Panizzi writes an interesting disquisition upon this branch
of the subject in his essay on Boiardo, prefixed to the
edition of his chief work. "Boiardo's poetry," he says,
"though in the manner of Petrarch, has all the marks of
originality. His imagery and style, as well as his diction,
are his own, and he resembles more the character of
the predecessors of the bard of Laura than that of his

successors.   His poetry was not written to be read, but to
be sung, and was subject to those musical as well as
metrical laws by which that of Petrarch had been
governed.   In his days music was still subject to poetry,
and the inanimate instruments were designed to support,
not to drown, the human voice.   Hence it is that lyrical
compositions written since that period, and not intended
to be accompanied by such music, are no longer possessed
of the same melodious harmony.   The lines of Petrarch,
with those of Dante, Cavalcanti, and a few others of the
same stamp, as well as those of Boiardo, breathe a strain
of sweet, majestic, rich, and glowing melody which has
seldom, if ever, been seized by even the happiest imitators
of Petrarch."

Dr. Garnett remarks, in referring to this passage, that
"Panizzi seems to consider Boiardo the last of the truly
melodious lyrists of Italy, though it is just to point out
that his remark respecting the predominance of the instrument over the voice did not become applicable until
the seventeenth century, and that he elsewhere seems to
confine the decay of Italian melody to the centuries
immediately preceding his own time (1830)."

The divorce between the higher forms of poetry and
music had, however, set in much earlier, and Metastasio
is the only recent Italian poet of any eminence who has
sought to reunite them.   As to the effects of the change
on lyrical poetry, Panizzi goes on : "The distribution
of accents or pauses in the lines of the old bards was
determined by the musical time, and when the sister art
ceased to be the inseparable companion of poetry, a
spurious and artificial jingle was affected, whilst pure
melody was no longer one of the principal elements in
poetry.   Hence it is as difficult to understand by what

means the lyrical effusions of the ancient poets read so peculiarly and at the same time so simply musical, as it is impossible to emulate their exquisite beauty in this respect. We may safely affirm that there has not been in Italy, during the past two centuries, a man capable of writing one single *canzone* possessing the melody of those which were left by the poets of the fourteenth and fifteenth centuries."

But we moderns, in thinking of

Music married to immortal verse,

must carefully clear our minds of all ideas of operatic strains or even of the more ancient cadences of national airs. The notation prescribed for Italian lyric poetry was, we may be assured, of a much more severely formalised character than our lightly moving measures, and the phrases to which sonnets and *canzoni* were written survive, if anywhere, in some of the old church chants with their constantly reiterated closes. They were, no doubt, traditional, and would sound strangely remote and outlandish to our ears, accustomed to such infinitely varied modulations. As in the chanting of the psalms, a number of words would be sung on a single note, with a rise or fall of tone for the closes.

The only survival at the present day of what we may suppose to have been a form of this very ancient declamatory music is the extraordinary chant to which the Tuscan peasant dramas, called *Maggi*, are sung. These plays, which turn on classical or religious subjects, such as the story of Cyrus, of the Conte Ugolino, of Saul and David, or some legendary saint, are invariably written in rhyming quatrains, each recited to the same phrase of melody, closing with a prolonged note like a cry, and repeated without change or variation throughout the entire piece. Thus, as it is always in the same pitch, the characters must be exclusively represented either by men or women, since the voices must all sing the same notes in the same key. A similar chant is still used by the Sicilian and Calabrian mountaineers for the recitation of popular poetry, each class of song having its special measure traditionally prescribed.

The chants of the more polished lyric bards must, however, have been subdued to more harmony with the words than this primitive voice of the hills and woods, which sounds like an echo of an older world.

It is obvious that a totally different standard of criticism must have been applied to poetry when it had to conform to a musical canon whose laws are entirely unknown to us, from any prevailing at the present day, when it is generally taken in by the eye alone. Whether owing to these rhythmical limitations on his genius or not, Boiardo is much more grave and restrained in his lyrics than in his octaves. The *Canzone* just quoted is evidence of this difference, in its emulation with the great masters of his art. Its series of images for his lady's beauty take the form of a stately procession through the hours of night and dawn, to the splendid pæan of sunrise, which touches the highest note of lyrical ecstasy. It is noteworthy as an illustration of the author's exceptional endowment with the colour sense so apparent in many of the descriptive passages throughout his works and forming one of the points where he seems to come into touch with the modern world.

The passionate love of flowers, which is another of his characteristics, is apparent in Sonnet xxx., written in one

of the moments when the writer's star of love was supposed
to be in the ascendant :

> Give rose and lily with full hands to me,
>   And pinks and fairest blossoms strew around,
>   All who to weep my woes with me were found
> Now of my joy and gladness sharers be.
>
> Give blossoms white and vermeil, fair to see,
>   To match this day bright colours should abound,
>   With luscious perfume sprinkled be the ground,
> That all the place may with my mood agree.
>
> Pardon doth grant, and peace to me hath given
>   My gentle foe, nor doth my death desire,
> She whose sole boast is mercy and not hate.
>
> Then wonder not if I am all on fire,
>   But wonder rather that not spent and riven
> Is my poor heart in bliss and joy so great.

No poet, ancient or modern, has associated nature more
intimately with all his moods and feelings than Boiardo,
who, in his transports of joy or woe, seems to feel as
though love were immanent in the universe. His eyes
are ever, too, fixed on heaven, and he unrolls before us a
marvellous series of sky-scapes, in which all the pageantry
of day and night are painted in few words, and as though
with a brush loaded with colour. But his favourite hour,
as we can easily see, was the dawn, which he never tires
of imaging forth in its summer glory of crocus and carna-
tion. It has, indeed, a special charm in Italy, as in all
southern countries where the sun rises to near mid-heaven
at noon. Under the shortened shadows the high relief
of morning is lost, and the landscape becomes flat and
featureless in the almost total absence of chiaroscuro.
In the evening its beauty is restored, but the heated air

has lost some of its transparency, and only with the freshness of the dawn recovers its full magic as a scene-painter.
Boiardo felt this instinctively, and while his sunrise effects
are amongst those most frequently recurred to, he has
seldom, if ever, described a sunset with anything like the
same vivid glow.   The following Sonnet, No. xix., opens,
as do many of his songs, like an aubade :

> The hour of day that doth to love invite
>   Contentment to my inmost soul doth bring,
> As dawn I see come forth in rose hues bright,
>   And from soft shade hear Philomena sing.
>
> The morning star such fulness hath of light
>   All others fade where she her ray doth fling,
> As Sol she leads behind her in his might,
>   In her own beauty proudly triumphing.
>
> To all I hear or see of sweet and rare
>   The love-lit face I liken in my mind,
> And ever see its perfect semblance there.
>
> And in the dewy mead her image fair
>   By turns in rose and lily now I find,
> And now to both together her compare.

The sonnet preceding this is remarkable for its embodiment in the third line of a well-known phrase of Dante's
"Il tremolar della marina," showing how great was the
influence which the elder poet, though so remote from
him in style and subject, had over Boiardo's mind.   He
has reproduced the same idea, though in his own language,
in one of the initial stanzas in the "Orlando":

> No fairer heaven doth sparkle to our sight,
>   All gemmed with orbs to which Night homage pays,
>   Nor the deep all aquiver 'neath the rays
> Of rising sun in calm expanse of light.

Nor e'en those stars which from supernal height
   Distil the dews of morn on arid ways,
   Nor shining ice, nor rime whereon the blaze
Of sunlight in resplendence glitters bright.

Nor aught unto our mortal gaze doth show,
   How lovely, or how sweet so'er it be,
That shines on heaven or breathes on earth below,

So fair as the mild glance's radiancy
   Of those bright eyes that Love doth guide, I trow,
And who believes not dares not look to see.

Bad weather has so rarely been a source of inspiration to
the Muse, that we subjoin Sonnet xxxix. as an instance
of Boiardo's indentification of himself with all the moods
of nature :

What envious rain and wind of blusterous might
   Doth Fortune to my onward way oppose !
   And buffet me about with frozen snows,
That me she may detain from my delight.

But nought the frowning sky doth me affright,
   Since true good will no evil weather knows,
   And such a fire within my bosom glows
That plashing rain and cold unfelt are quite.

Since I with Love walk in close company,
   He warns me from the false and crooked path,
And makes the straight and level highway clear.

White flowers and roses white now seem to me
   The driving flakes whirled down by heaven in wrath,
While thinking on live Sun which I draw near.

Boiardo is less happy in those reproaches to his lady
which seem to have been in his day part of the prescribed
ritual of the lover's worship. The reiteration of this
phase of love, with its constant deaths invoked and
martyrdoms undergone, has always an artificial ring in

the ears of the modern reader, who is apt to discount them in accordance with the prosaic standard of a utilitarian age. But in the best of these pieces, in which the author expresses his love for nature at least as strongly as his passion for his innamorata, he rises to a level sufficiently high to entitle him to rank with the great lyrists of his time.

CHAPTER IX

Verse Letters of Ariosto

THE two opposite currents of tradition, so strangely fused in the Italian literary revival, are traceable in the dual aspect of Ariosto's works. While as the singer of Orlando he is but a courtier and man of letters masquerading as a popular minnesinger, he adopts in his other writings the mannerisms snd standards prescribed by the later fashion of a reversion to antique models. The most inimitable of imitators, he infuses life into the closest copy by the exuberance of his own nature, and breathes into his most trivial utterances a meaning and vitality which are totally absent from the pseudo-classicalism of the later and debased Renaissance.

Horace, whose character and career offered some close parallels to his own, was in an especial degree the object of his sympathy and study, so much so that whatever success he achieved in Rome during the Pontificate of Leo X. was due rather to his skill in the interpretation of his Roman prototype than to his own poetical merits. The versified epistle, a style of composition of which Horace was the great exemplar, if not the absolute inventor, was seized upon accordingly by his kindred genius as a vehicle for that semi-moralising, semi-introspective vein of thought in which he showed the way to so much of our latter-day prose. Half sympathy, half egotism, the letter, in the form of a *tête-à-tête* on paper, takes the whole world into the confidence of the writer, and is addressed to humanity at large under cover to a single individual. There is no such effectual method of self-revelation, since it mirrors forth for us the man either as he is, or as he elects to appear, a scarcely less valuable index to character. Ariosto, too strongly moulded for mental posturing, is carelessly or cynically sincere in self-delineation, and his poetical epistles have the stamp of the portrait of a master painted by himself.

His life coincided with that " golden prime " of culture in Italy when the long-sown seed of the past ripened suddenly to a harvest. The forty years between his birth and Boiardo's (1434–1474) formed an interval which separated the working lives of the two singers of Orlando by the difference between one epoch of human progress and another. The fruit of the Tree of Knowledge had been plucked, for good or ill, before the younger poet came of age.

He was of a noble family established in Ferrara since 1300, whose patronymic was derived from a place called Riosto. From his mother, Daria Maleguzzi, he inherited the poetic ability of her father, Gabriele. In 1503 he entered the service of Cardinal Ippolito d'Este, the patron to whom his letters so frequently refer. The date was a fateful one for him, since in the same year, having finally abandoned Latin for vernacular poetry, he began the " Orlando Furioso," his constant task during the next thirteen years. In 1513, when he was thirty-nine, the only serious attachment of his life began in a meeting in Florence with the fair widow, Alessandra Benucci, to whom his love songs are addressed. He is believed to have married her, but never acknowledged her as his wife, from the fear, it is supposed, of losing some ecclesiastical preferments held conditionally on celibacy. A coolness between him and his patron, traceable in the letters, began with his refusal to comply with the desire of the latter that he should take Orders, and he eventually transferred his services to the Duke of Ferrara, from whom he received an allowance. In 1522 he was appointed Governor of the Garfagnana, where, under circumstances of great difficulty, as we shall see from the letters, he played his part most honourably and well. "While I am in power I will have no friend but justice," was his official motto, and the saying shows that his cynicism veiled a power of rising to a conception of public duty rare in an age of unblushing self-seeking. The duties of the post were most irksome to him, and the Duke failed to support his authority as he desired. Recalled at the end of three years of exile, he returned to Ferrara in June 1525, built himself a small house, and devoted the remaining eight years of his life to revising his poem and constantly remodelling his garden, his official duties being limited to the superintendence of Court pageants and theatricals. He lived to complete the final edition of the "Orlando Furioso," which was published in 1532, and died on Christmas Day of the ensuing year of the sudden aggravation of an old complaint, anæmia, probably due to weakness of the heart.

On many of these phases of his life, as well as on the manners and events of his time, his letters throw a flood of light.

Seven in number, these satires, as the poet has styled them, using the word in its classical sense as signifying a

discussion or dissertation, not necessarily in the vein
which we moderns have agreed to call satirical, are more
truly letters than either the Satires or Epistles of
Horace, inasmuch as they are more exclusively personal
either to the writer or his correspondent. They contain
none of the keen-edged social parables and studies from
life so prominent in their classical prototypes, and are
altogether of a more intimately autobiographical character.
Ariosto, indeed, had little taste for subtle discrimination
of the half-tones in portraiture, and his grasp of human
nature is limited to the appreciation of passions and
foibles common to all. Hence he gives us no types
from the Court of Ferrara or from the suite of the
Cardinal of Este in any degree corresponding to the
sketches of Tigellius, the singer, Ummidius, the miser,
or Maenius, the parasite, outlined for us by the sharp-
pointed stylus of the Augustan bard. His private
worries, his dealings with his patron, his health, his
regimen, his pecuniary affairs, are his principal themes,
the treatment of which is illuminated by touches of hard-
bitten shrewdness and gleams of caustic humour scattered
at random here and there.

   These everyday topics are descanted on in the measure
consecrated by Dante, with its endless chain of linked
triplets, and closes long deferred to the end of letter or
canto. The unbroken sequence of this form of versification gives an apparent abruptness to the style, every
transition of idea coming like a sudden check amid the
ceaseless flow of the metre. Indeed, it is not always easy
to follow the poet in his rapid plunges of thought through
the pauseless cadences of his triple chimes, which leave
no break for change of subject or style. Varying in
length from some 500 to 800 lines, the Satires, written in

the ten years from 1517 to 1527, cover the busiest period of the poet's life. The first, addressed to his brother Galasso, contains the most minute and housewifely directions for the lodging which he desires to have taken for him in Rome, whence he passes on to explain the motive of his journey.

> Galasso, near the temple that doth win
>   Its name from that bold priest, who Malchus' ear
> So deftly shore away from hair and skin,
>   Lodging provide me for four beasts and gear,
> Reckoning a room apiece for me and Jack ;
>   My mule and one old jade be stabled near.
> Where'er I lodge, in room or attic back,
>   Be few the stairs and much the light, I pray,
> Nor place for fire and chimney let it lack ;
>   Nor for the steeds less thought and care display,
> Since quarters fine would serve them not a pin
>   If wanting in due store of straw and hay.
> A wool or cotton mattress (not too thin)
>   My ribs to flatter, in my couch be laid,
> So that for sleep I need not seek the inn.
>   Of dry and seasoned firewood store be made,
> That one accustomed homely fare to dress,
>   May cook plain beef or mutton by its aid ;
> I want not one to furnish forth a mess
>   So spiced as e'en death's palate to provoke
> And the grave's inmates rouse to fresh excess.
>   Let Ser Vorano—born the earth to soak
> With dripping fat—in such one's spits and pans
>   Up to the ears his greasy muzzle poke ;
> Who hunger for food's sake desires and fans—
>   Not food for hunger's—may on viands brood,
> And for such dainty meals lay all his plans.
>   By my new valet be a bond made good
> By earnest money, with a cook home-fed
>   On bread and garlic, with his brethren chewed,
> Fresh from their spades, while he the oxen led ;
>   Who now doth sigh for pheasant, pigeon, quail,

And tires of sameness in his daily bread ;
And who can tell the difference without fail
'Twixt flesh of goat or boar, when mountain-bred,
And that which fattened in th' Elysian vale.

The second Satire is written to his brother Alessandro
and another friend, Lodovico da Bagno, both in the suite
of the Cardinal of Este in Hungary, and deals with the
much-vexed question of his own refusal to accompany
that princely prelate on his journey thither. He paid
the forfeit in the loss of the favour of his patron, whose
anger, fanned by envious and malicious courtiers, caused
the poet's dismissal after fifteen years' service and
flattery. Let us hear how he gives voice to his heart-
burnings and recriminations in his self-imposed banishment.

Fain would I, Alexander, brother mine,
    And gossip Bagno, news from ye obtain,
If courtly memories to us incline.
    If still my lord accuse me, and complain,
And if some plead my cause, and say whereto,
    Whilst others leave this place, I here remain.
Of if all trained to adulation's cue
    (The art to which we most observance pay),
Ye help him to my blame with reasons new.
    A fool is he who doth his lord gainsay,
Although he should aver he hath espied
    The sun at midnight, or the stars by day.
And if he choose to praise or to deride
    An absent one—then tuned to the same key,
A chorus loud is heard on every side.
    And he who dares not through humility
His mouth unclose, applauds with pliant face,
    And says with every feature, I agree.

He goes on to enumerate all his reasons for refusing
to accompany his patron, alleging the prohibition of

physicians, who judged the northern winter dangerous for his health, and his horror of the suffocation of the stoves and the unwholesomeness of the food as the main obstacles.

> And heady wine, to me forbid by all
> >As worse than poison, at your feasts is quaffed,
> And sacrilege 'tis held to shirk the call.
> >On all their meats strange savours they engraft,
> Where pepper, cardamoms, and spices blend,
> >To me marked baneful by the leech's craft.
> Here you may tell me that I could depend
> >On finding for my seat some ingle nook,
> Where no foul exhalations could offend.
> >And that my viands as I pleased, the cook
> Should dress apart, my wine I could dilute,
> >Drink nought or little as my taste should brook.
> Then while you feasted, I must dull and mute
> >Sole in my cell from morn to eve abide,
> At lonely board that might Carthusian suit.
> >With pots and dishes I must be supplied,
> From kitchen and from parlour, and with store
> >Of household goods endowed like new-made bride.

In the following passage his financial position and relations to his patron are portrayed in phrases which have all the ring of sincerity in their bitterly reproachful strain.

> You might say next—Then let your victuals straight
> >By your own man at your own cost be ta'en,
> And eat your fowl cooked at your private grate.
> >But my poor service doth not yet obtain
> Such guerdon from the Cardinal in fee
> >As might a hostelry in court maintain.
> To thee no thanks, Apollo—nor to thee
> >Fair college of the Muses—not the stuff
> To make a mantle have I earned through ye.
> >—Oh yes, my lord has giv'n you—Yes enough
> For mantles more than one—I grant 'tis true,
> >But not for love of ye one frill or ruff.

If to his praise my verse attuned hath been,
  He says 'tis pleasant idling, and more grace
I should have done him in his following seen.
  And if in Milan's Chancery a place
Is mine, where with Constabili I share
  A third of not'ry's fees in every case.
'Tis but because as courier swift I fare,
  And changing beasts and guides, ride spur and boot,
O'er rock and mount, and death and peril dare.

Marriage is the subject of the third Satire, written to his cousin, Annibale Maleguccio, on his betrothal, and containing precepts based on that shrewd practical wisdom of which the poet had so large a store at the service of his friends. The habits of fine ladyhood, in those days evidently the same as in ours, the abuse of rouge and cosmetics, extremes either of feminine piety or dissipation, form in turn the subject of his pungent diatribes, while his recommendation of a medium share of good looks, avoiding the opposite poles of beauty and ugliness, forms an amusing contrast to his rapturous laudations elsewhere of the charms of Alessandra Benucci, the fair widow, believed to have been his unacknowledged wife. He begins by expressing his disappointment at having been left to hear from outsiders the news of the coming event in the following very simple and natural terms :

All other friends, dear Hannibal, save thee,
  Give me the news that thou a bride hast won,
Thy silence wounds—the fact doth gladden me.
  Perchance thou hid'st it, lest I counter run
To thy desire, as one to censure led
  The act in others he hath left undone.
But much thou errest, if thou thus hast said,
  For I, though single, find no cause for blame,
If Jack and Peter, Paul and Martin wed.
  Nay, rather my condition mourn, and claim

Indulgence, if by varying chances still,
    Are ever thwarted my intent and aim.
For I have ever held, and ever will
    That save with woman at his side to tame,
His better nature man cannot fulfil.

Coz, thou dost well to marry, but give ear,
    Think well on't first, for later spoken " no,"
Serves not to change a " yes " once uttered here.
    In this my counsel I would clearly show,
Though univited to such part by thee,
    What thou should'st seek, what fly from and forego.
Thou laugh'st at me, perchance, and dost not see
    How I can guide thee, who did never own
Such chain on neck or foot from shackles free.
    But hast thou—when two play at cards, ne'er known
That who looks on takes of the game a view
    More just than his by whom the stakes are thrown ?
If my advice then hit the target true,
    Or go anear—be by its guidance led,
If not—to it and me give folly's due.
    But ere I further go, one word be said,
If thou dost marry urged by love's decrees,
    Thine impulse follow, and undoubting wed.
All virtues hers, so she thy fancy please,
    And well I know no orator, in Greek
Or Latin, could dissuade thee by his pleas.

The poet's motives for remaining in the service of the Duke of Este are discussed in the fourth of these epistles, addressed like its predecessor to Annibale Maleguccio. His office, entered on in April 1518, was that of cameriere or famigliare, with a monthly salary of eight gold scudi, or twenty-one lire (about fifty-two francs), in addition to allowances for rations and forage for a horse. Its regular duties of superintendent and organiser of court spectacles and dramatic entertainments were varied by occasional missions to the other Italian capitals, as

L

the bearer of letters of condolence or congratulation to
their respective sovereigns. His position had doubtless
its drawbacks, and he complains of it as follows, in his
usual grumbling tone of philosophic contempt for his
surroundings, though these were not on the whole un-
congenial to him.

> With most men here I know I disagree,
> Who life at Court a grand one deem alway,
> Which seems instead dire servitude to me.
> With all my heart let whoso likes it stay,
> To leave it I myself will not be slack,
> If Maia's son but smile on me one day.
> One load or saddle fits not every back,
> What one may bear with scarce a thought will gauge
> Another's tender points, and gall and rack.
> Ill can the nightingale endure the cage,
> Goldfinch and linnet less of prison tire,
> But in one day the swallow dies of rage.
> Let who doth meed of hat or spur desire
> Serve King or Cardinal, or Pope or Duke,
> To nothing of all this do I aspire.
> Sweeter the turnip in my ingle nook
> I dress myself, and on a skewer impale,
> Then peel, with vinegar and must to cook,
> Than at another's table flesh of quail
> Or boar or thrush. My sleep 'neath drugget rude
> Is sound as though 'neath gold and silken veil.
> And more I love to rest in lazy mood
> My limbs, than boast that they have travelled been
> 'Mid Scythians, Indians, or the Ethiop brood.

A very much more onerous charge was conferred upon
the facile-tempered, ease-loving court poet in his appoint-
ment in February 1822, to the Governorship of the
Garfagnana, a turbulent outlying province of the Ferrarese
dominion. In this exile—for so he regarded it—he passed
more than three years, with the title of Ducal Commis-

sary, and the duty of restoring some semblance of order among a people of banditti. Despite his reluctance to fill a position apparently so incongruous, he discharged its functions admirably, and this episode of his life is the one that gives the highest idea of his character and powers.

The mountain-locked Valley of the Serchio, straitened between the Modenese Apennine on the one side, and the Apuan Alps or Carrara Mountains on the other, was a debatable land constantly disputed between Florence, Ferrara, and Lucca, whose frontiers met on its border. Conquered by the Florentines during the reign of Leo X., its inhabitants, on the death of that Pontiff in 1521, had revolted in favour of the House of Este. On December 7 of that year the Citadel of Castelnuovo was captured by the townspeople from the Florentine Governor, Bernardino Ruffo, an event still commemorated in a piece of sculpture over the gate of the tiny capital, representing an eagle holding a lion in its claws. In one impregnable eyrie, that of the Verrucole, the flag of Este had been upheld throughout the Florentine occupation by a garrison of banditti, who naturally claimed and received an amnesty in reward for their fidelity. Other malefactors, though without such title to pardon, were able to secure equal immunity by crossing the mountain borderland, everywhere easily accessible, into the adjoining territory of Florence or Lucca. The legendary brigand, Filippo Pacchione, was one of these, though some doubt is now cast on his capture and release of the author of the " Orlando Furioso." Each petty magnate was at feud with his neighbour, and the year 1521 had witnessed the murder of the Count of San Donnino, shortly followed by that of his widow and son, in their own castle, by the bravoes of a rival chieftain, Pier Maddalena.

A guard of ten mounted crossbow-men was the military force with which the ex-court-playwright was expected to trample out these live embers of faction and revolution. Yet the indolent poet laureate of Ferrara proved an energetic and capable governor, who, though he generally shrank from inflicting the extreme penalty of the law, and was described by his turbulent subjects as "too good," succeeded, by the enforcement of severe edicts against brigandage and its abettors, in pacifying his province and extirpating some of its worst disorders.

The Fifth Satire, giving his own impressions of this striking phase of his life, is the most interesting, and illustrates, moreover, the strange difference between the earlier and later mind in its attitude towards natural scenery. Unmitigated abhorrence is the sentiment with which a country, now ranking amongst the most beautiful in Italy, is regarded in Ariosto's pages. The rich valley, opening a golden highway between the ramparts of its flanking mountains, unrolls an ever-changing panorama of loveliness, with its shifting perspective of ravine and gorge, and ridge and hanging forest, crowned by the phantom Alps of Carrara, lifting to heaven the ethereal pallor of their marble cliffs. Miniature fortresses, their walls formed by a ring of houses facing inwards, hang as cornices on every crag, and command each its own vision of unsurpassable loveliness. We shall see how the beauties of this enchanted valley were viewed by the great singer of the Renaissance, who preludes, by way of contrast, with a description of the tamer scenery of his home :

Sweet promptings the blank page with words to fill
    Our Reggio's beautous scenes erst breathed in me,
My native nest too did like mood instil.
    Thy fair Mauritian home in dreams I see,
And that bright spot swift Rodano beside
    With shady seat, fit scene for Naiad's glee.
The fishpond with whose clear pellucid tide
    The garden girds itself, the brook whose rapid flow
The sward doth furrow, to the mill to glide.
    Nor doth my memory lose the vines that grow
In fields where bounteous Bacchus doth preside,
    Or hill and glen the high-set tower below.

Was ever dwelling less than this of mine
    For sacred studies fit? Of all delight
More void? More full of dreariness malign?
    'Twixt east and south the Pania's naked height*
Doth gird me in—elsewhere the jagged chine
    A pilgrim's fame makes glorious hems the sight.†
Deep in a ditch I dwell, and if I pine
    To move a foot, must climb with rude essay
The savage spurs of woody Apennine.

The social condition of his district and his own consequent troubles are next descanted on, in a passage which
is one of the most instructive presentments of the condition of Italy at the time:

If forth I walk or in my castle stay
    Complaints and cries and brawls salute my ear,
Thefts, murders, hates, and ires attend my way.
    So that with brow now clouded and now clear,
Some I must e'en entreat, some threat and blame.
    One there condemn, absolve another here.
Whole sheets I daily write—despatches frame—
    Succour or counsel craving from the Duke,

---

  * Pania alla Croce, one of the Apuan Alps.
  † Monte Pellegrino, in the Modenese Apennine.

The robbers round about to chase and tame.
  For know, the licence of this land doth brook
No curb, since first the panther in its hold
  Clutched it, the lion's rending claws then took.
Assassins roam abroad in gangs so bold
  Whoso is sent to capture them must hide
Stuffed in a bag, his flag, nor dare unfold.
  Most wise who near the castle doth abide.
To him the business touches still in vain
  I write, but fitting answer is denied.
Each little town lifts up its horns amain,
  They number eighty-three, divided all
By fell sedition that therein doth reign.
  Think if Apollo, when on him I call,
Will to these caves from classic Delphi haste,
  To hear unceasing noise of strife and brawl.
What drove me here? inquire full well thou may'st,
  From studies sweet, companionship most dear,
To hide me in this drear and trackless waste.
  Know that not avarice of mine was here
In fault, for ever well content was I
  With stipend from Ferrara drawn each year.
But thou know'st not, perchance, as time went by,
  And war broke out, how slow leaked forth the store,
And how the Duke then wished the charge should die.
  While raged the war, unmurmuring this I bore,
I murmured only when that time past through,
  The hand then shut unclosed to me no more.
While worse 'twas that my place in Milan too
  Where law was hushed 'mid war's tumultuous din,
Left me my stipend in arrear to rue.
  I hasten to the Duke and thus begin,
My want relieve, or let it irk you not
  That I should go elsewhere my bread to win.
The Garfagnana people, then red-hot
  From their revolt, which chased Marzocco out
To seek another pasture ground, I wot,
  With heralds, and with letters most devout
To leave them not, the Duke full loudly prayed,
  Their wonted chiefs and honours still without.

Of me was improvised election made,
    Perchance because the time was over brief
For choice more fitting to be duly weighed,
    Or else, that on my liege's mind the grief
Of these his subjects lighter sate than mine,
    And duly thankful I for such relief,
Thankful, in sooth, for the intent benign,
    Rather than for the gift, great though it be,
Yet foreign to my wishes and design.
Now if you ask this people touching me,
    Harshness, not mercy, they with one consent,
Will say would with their wicked works agree.
    And they perchance with me are ill content,
As I with them, and like the fool am I,
    Who knew not how to prize the gem chance sent.

He goes on to illustrate his meaning in the prevailing
fashion of the time, by a wealth of more or less apposite
similitudes, of which the subjoined may serve as a
specimen :

Like him of Venice in the days gone by,
    On whom the king of Portugal bestowed
A Moorish barb of value rare and high.
    Who straight his sense of gift so royal showed
(Unmindful that to different trades pertain
    Rudder and reins, each used in different mode)
By leaping on the steed, when he was fain
    With hands the saddle—spurs the flanks to clutch.
" Ye shall not throw me ! " then he cried amain,
    The horse leaps upward, goaded overmuch,
And the good sailor deeper in his side
    Clasps the keen spurs, more sharp than lance's touch.
With blood his mouth and bridle both are dyed,
    Nor knows the steed which mandate to obey,
Since this doth check, that urge to forward stride.
    But with a bound or two cuts short delay,
While to the earth is flung the cavalier,
    Head, ribs, and shoulder bruised from his essay.

When white from head to foot with dust and fear,
　　He rose at last, small thanks the King had won,
For he with plaints pursued the royal ear.
　　Far better he—far better I had done,
He for the steed, and for the province I,
　　To say, Hereto, Lord, fitness have I none,
Another grace with gift so rare and high.

The poet still held the governorship of the Garfagnana,
when the proposal that he should go as ambassador to
Clement VIII. elicited a letter to Buonaventura Pistofilo,
Secretary to the Duke. In this Satire, the sixth of the
series, he moralises in a strain which modern taste might
deprecate as trite and obvious on the insufficiency of
ambition to satisfy its votaries, illustrating the fate of the
over-aspiring by the following pretty fable.

A gourd there was, which once so high did sprawl
　　That in a few brief days its shoots o'erlaid
A neighb'ring pear-tree's topmost branches tall.
　　The pear one morning oped its eyes dismayed,
From sleep prolonged—and saw the garland fair
　　Of fruitage new upon its crown displayed.
And said: Who art thou? How hast clambered there?
　　And where wast thou, ere I alas! gave o'er
These wretched eyes to slumber unaware?
　　Her name she told, the spot showed where of yore
She had been planted—whence in three months' time
　　With swift ascent she to such height did soar.
And I (rejoined the tree) did scarcely climb
　　So high, when frost and heat I had defied,
And all the winds, for thirty years of time.
　　But thou, who in a trice to heaven dost stride,
Be sure, that rapid as has been thy growth
　　Decay as swift shall overthrow thy pride.

A purely personal matter forms the subject of the Seventh
Satire, addressed to Cardinal Bembo, probably between

1526 and 1528, and recommending to him the poet's son, Virginio, for whom he desired to find a suitable tutor while studying at the University of Padua. The difficulty, as he explains, lay in the disreputable character of the scholars of the time, a phenomenon due to the paganising tendency of their studies. The Satires, of which this is the last, cover a relatively small portion of Ariosto's life, in the later part of which he abandoned this style of composition. Invaluable as a luminous exposition of the inner workings of his mind, they furnish also a vivid reflected image of the society in which he moved, and it is scarcely too much to say that we learn more about the Renaissance from these semi-jocular epistles than from any other single set of writings handed down to us. Their very homeliness is a guarantee of their fidelity, as it shows that nothing is either added or omitted for effect. No incident is too minute, no detail too prosaic, to be worked into the heterogeneous mosaic of their triple rhymes, and they thus serve to show that the versatile Muse of the writer was equally at home in the real and the fabulous, the familiar and the remote.

CHAPTER X

Italian Folk Songs

THE seeming anomaly that the highest order of poetry is the product of an early stage of civilisation is easily explained if we remember that only in that phase of society has it a genuine function to fulfil. It is then not an ornamental or conventional form of diction, but the only mode of speech possible to a mind charged with ideas never expressed, and incapable of expression in the ordinary language in use around it. It is the struggle for utterance of thoughts which must be conveyed in figures and metaphors, because primitive speech, dealing only with material facts, has no ready-made symbols for them. The poet is, in short, the man whose mind is ahead of his language; the pioneer of thought into hitherto unexplored fields of conquest ; and his powerful imagination, thus forging the instrument with which it works, stamps it with his own creative impress, giving it a directness and vitality of which all later graces of diction are but insipid adulterations. Only in the early youth of an idiom could the Psalms of David, the Iliad of Homer, or the Divine Comedy of Dante have been produced.

All primitive peoples use the language of poetry when they seek to convey abstract ideas, uncoined as yet into the common currency of speech. The Zulu, for instance, who has no words for describing qualities apart from the objects possessing them, can only do so by comparisons. If a thing is round he says "it is like a ball"; if a man is straight, "he is like an assegai." A particular kind of spotted cotton is known amongst them as "the Pleiades," and gradations of colour are distinguished by the names of different sorts of beads forming the currency of the country. When Cetewayo, in answer to a deputation, said that "to introduce spirits into a country was to steal the brains of the people," he used the language of Shakespeare, and was a poet without intending it.

The Irish peasant, in similar fashion, uses terms of expression in speaking his own rude language which might be transferred to an epic poem. The grandfather of the writer, having lost his way among the mountains of Killarney, was directed to the right path by a peasant in an Irish sentence of which the subjoined line is a literal translation:

Where yonder mountain's brow the drop from heaven divides.

Even when rendered into English, the Irish turns of thought and imagery are often singularly forcible and impressive, like the phrase of a roadside blind beggar in the south of Ireland, who solicited the alms of passers-by "for a poor blind man under a lonesome cloud of darkness." A sightless person is always described by the Irish as "dark," so that "the dark girl" means the blind girl, not a brunette as in ordinary English.

It is the spontaneousness and sincerity of whatever supplies a genuine want in contradistinction to the artificial coinages of eclecticism that gives to popular poetry its special value as an index to national character.

Italian song is peculiarly suggestive in this respect, since it has remained almost entirely the pure tradition of the people, little, if at all, affected by external or literary influences. It thus faithfully mirrors the tastes and tendencies of the different populations inhabiting the Peninsula, who may be roughly divided into two classes, typified by the Tuscan and the Piedmontese, while Sicily, from the peculiar vicissitudes of its history, is, in respect of poetry, the meeting ground of both.

The broad line of demarcation between the races on the hither and farther shores of the Po is strongly marked in the popular poetry of those two sections of the country. The songs in the sub-alpine districts, in their greater rapidity of thought, definiteness of subject, and simplicity of diction, reflect a type of character practical, resolute, energetic, closely akin to that of northern peoples, while in the mid-Italian lyrics, with their limitation of idea, generally to a single aspect of the theme, their delicate analysis of feeling, and inexhaustible fertility in decorative language, we can trace the subtler genius and more reflective temperament of a southern race. Classed respectively as songs of action and of emotion, the one may be held to express energy, the other sensibility in the people from whom they spring.

The folk-songs of Piedmont are almost exclusively of a dramatic character, narrating historical or legendary incidents in brief, condensed language—very frequently in the form of dialogue. Now, of this narrative poetry there is not a trace elsewhere from the Alps to the Faro, in the living lore of the people, though that it once existed amongst them and has died out is proved by the copies of old poems of this character still extant in libraries and museums. As Signor Rubieri says, speaking of historical poetry, "while the sub-alpine wrote nothing but remembered much, the Tuscans wrote much, but remembered nothing."

In Tuscany we have narrative entirely replaced by introspective poetry, describing the poet's own state of mind or external things in relation to it, the beloved object transfigured by his fancy, or some aspect of nature reflecting his mood at the moment. In Sicily alone do the two classes of poetry exist to any considerable extent side by side, for while it has, like Piedmont, a large stock of legendary and historical verse, it has, in common with Tuscany, an equally rich supply of canzoni, or detached emotional stanzas. But while the latter are the early and spontaneous growth of the soil, the former are obviously of later, and probably foreign origin. Their presence is perhaps due to Provençal influence, which, felt in Piedmont from geographical contiguity, was exercised in Sicily through the sway of a foreign dynasty, of which one sovereign, Frederick II., was himself a trouveur of no mean order. Thus, through the entire of the peninsula of Italy, it is only at the foot of the Alps that we find the versified narrative, or ballad, so dear to northern taste.

The most remarkable of these ballads is one which, widely diffused under the title of "Donna Lombarda," recounts the end of the tragic-fated Rosamond, captive and consort of Alboin, king of the Italian Lombards. Compelled by her tyrant-spouse to drink from the cup made from the skull of her father, the king of the Gepidæ, slain in battle, she avenged herself for the outrage by her husband's murder, concerted with his shield-bearer, Helmichus or Elmegiso, with whom she

fled to Ravenna, taking with her a quantity of jewels
and treasure.   Here her beauty and wealth excited the
cupidity of the Byzantine prefect, Longinus, who per-
suaded her to rid herself of Helmichus by a cup of poison
presented to him on leaving the bath.

Helmichus drank, but, suspecting the nature of the
draught before finishing it, compelled the traitress to drain
the remainder.   It is this closing episode in the career of
the fatal " Lombard Woman " that the ballad narrates :

> Lovest thou me, Lombard woman,
>   Lovest thou me, lovest thou me?
> What must I do? to a husband
>   Wedded I be, wedded I be.
> Perish thy mate, Lombard woman!
>   Slain and by thee, slain and by thee.
> What must I do that he perish?
>   Slain and by me, slain and by me?
> Listen and learn in what manner
>   Slain he shall be, slain he shall be.
> Close by the house in the garden
>   Hideth a snake, hideth a snake.
> Take thou its head and to powder
>   Grind it and break, grind it and break.
> In the black wine then infuse it,
>   Fill the cup high, fill the cup high.
> Your husband will come home from hunting
>   Thirsty and dry, thirsty and dry.
> Pour me some wine, Lombard woman,
>   With thirst I pine, with thirst I pine,
> What hast thou done, Lombard woman?
>   Turbid the wine, turbid the wine.
> 'Twas but the sea-wind at even
>   Stirred the lees up, stirred the lees up.
> Drink then thyself, Lombard woman,
>   Drain thou the cup, drain thou the cup.
> What must I do since this moment
>   No thirst have I, no thirst have I?

By my sword's point thou shalt drink it,
　　Drain the cup dry, drain the cup dry.
One drop from the goblet she hath ta'en—
　　Pale grows the Lombard woman's cheek.
A second drop hath she drunk amain—
　　The Lombard woman a priest must seek.
A third drop drinks she, and help were vain—
　　Let the Lombard woman her grave bespeak.

Count Nigra, who has made this ballad a subject of special study,* believes it to date from the same epoch as the event it chronicles—that is, the sixth century. As the Italian language did not then exist, his conjecture is that the song was transformed with the development of the idiom, in its oral transmission from lip to lip.

Notwithstanding its archaic style and the rudeness of the dialects in which it is preserved, it is a fine remnant of early popular poetry, not without an element of tragic power in the swiftness with which the action hurries to the close. It exists, with very trifling variations, in the principal dialects of North Italy, the above translation being from the version current in the Canavese district, where Count Nigra describes it as sung to a most lugubrious chant, probably as old as the words.

Clotilda, the daughter of Clovis, is the heroine of another historical ballad, which narrates her ill-treatment at the hands of her husband, Amalaric, king of the Visigoths, and the vengeance wreaked on him by her three brothers; but the North Italian version of the tale is apparently nothing more than a transcript of the Provençal rendering of the same subject.

The military spirit of the Piedmontese is very conspicuous in their ballad literature, in which the incidents

* "Canti Popolari Piemontesi." Conte Costantino Nigra.

and the vicissitudes of a soldier's life make a large figure, as in the following specimen from the Monferrino dialect : *

THE RETURN.

Speak, fair youth, I prithee say,
　　From what land dost tidings bring?
In the wars I've been away,
　　In the wars a-soldiering.

Prithee tell me, oh fair youth,
　　My true lover did you see?
Yes, I've seen him in good sooth,
　　Though his face was strange to me.

Gentle youth, pray tell me where
　　Thou didst see him and with whom?
At the Abbey of St. Clare,
　　Where they bore him to the tomb.

Prithee, oh fair youth, declare,
　　What his garments' tint and hue?
White and russet was his wear,
　　Like an emperor to view.

O fair youth, I prithee say,
　　Was he honoured by his peers?
Fifty torches led the way,
　　And as many cymbaleers.

To the earth she sinks tear-laden,
　　Sinks to earth in grief and woe.
Cheer ye, cheer ye, pretty maiden,
　　And in me your lover know.

A common phase of Italian domestic life is illustrated by ballads like the following, expressive of the grievances of the son's wife under the roof of his parents :

* " Canti e Racconti."   Domenico Comparetti.

THE DAUGHTER-IN-LAW.

When I lived in my father's dwelling,
  Good macaroni was my food.
Now I am married, there's no telling
  If macaroni's bad or good.

When in my mother's house I tarried,
  On finest paste I used to dine,
I scarcely know since I am married,
  Whether the paste be coarse or fine.

And while the mistress and her daughter
  The macaroni all devour,
The son's poor wife, with pail and water,
  Stays in the corner pots to scour.

And while the daughter and her mother
  May drink good wine and have their fling,
The son's poor wife can drink no other
  Than water from the nearest spring.

And while the mistress and her daughter
  May go to balls and dance and play,
The son's poor wife must have it taught her
  To rock the babe the livelong day.

Matrimony, from whatever point of view, does not seem
to be regarded with much favour by Piedmontese lasses,
if the following stanzas may be taken as representative of
their feelings towards it :

Sing merrily, all ye maidens,
  Who are unmarried still,
For other thoughts when wedded
  And cares, your minds will fill.

Your husband's father and mother,
  And husband you'll have to please;
Must handle distaff and spindle,
  And needle for broideries.

M

> You'll have your hand on the table,
>   To cut the paste alway;
> You'll have your foot on the cradle,
>   To rock the babe all day.

The spirit of the French *chanson* is echoed in these Piedmontese ballads, which have the same incisiveness of style in their brief narratives, often in the form of dialogue. It is strange, as marking a wide divergence in national character, that the love-ditty proper, the staple of central and southern Italian song, should not exist at all in Piedmontese, and in the other sub-alpine dialects, only as an obvious imitation. In Venice and Istria it has a stamp of spontaneity, as it is seasoned with a dash of *espièglerie* characteristic of the vivacious natives of the lagoons. Here is, for instance, a Venetian serenade with its sentiment thus qualified with a touch of ironical self-ridicule :

> False traitress! Couldst thou but a notion form
>   Of all the pains I've borne for love of thee!
> Whilst thou wast in thy chamber close and warm,
>   Outside among the shrubs poor I would be ;
> Rosewater then appeared the rain and storm,
>   The lightnings love's own signals seemed to me ;
> The tempest rude a zephyr 'mid the leaves,
>   While I was there outside beneath thy eaves.
> Outside beneath thy eaves I made my bed,
>   As coverlet the sky above me spread.
> The doorstep as a pillow 'neath my head,
>   Alack, poor me! how hard the life I led !

A cradle song, or *Ninna Nanna*, from the Istrian dialect may serve as a specimen of a class of compositions generally consisting of rhymes with little or no meaning, evidently intended only to vocalise some sing-song lullaby :

> I told you before and I tell you so still,
> My baby will soon go to sleep, yes, he will.
> Little by little off he'll go,
> Like wood that's green by a fire that's low,
> The green wood never in flames doth start,
> Core of his father's and mother's heart ;
> The green wood never sends sparks on high,
> Sleep my heart, sleep my hope, hush a bye.

But it is in Tuscany that we find the characteristic spirit of Italian folk-verse typified and concentrated. The poetry of this race, who "lisp in numbers," consists of endless variations on the inexhaustible theme of love, all constructed on a prescribed model and cast in a traditional mould. It is the utterance of generations of youthful hearts, ranging through infinite gradations of tenderness rather than of passion, that meets us in these exquisite word-harmonies, all tuned to the same key and inspired by the same dominant motive. The Tuscan " Rispetti," or love-greetings, are almost invariably cast in an octave stanza composed of two pairs of alternate and two of consecutive rhymes, the latter prettily styled "rime baciate" (kissing rhymes). In the closing quatrain, the idea expressed in the two first lines is invariably repeated in the two last, but with an inversion of the phrase, in the following fashion :

> With thy fair mien and ways, speech fairer still,
> Thou raisest me to life and then dost kill,
> With thy fair speech, and fairer mien and ways,
> Thou killest me, and then to life dost raise.

The antiquity of this form of versification is proved by the direction appended to one of the old lauds published in 1485, "to be sung like the Rispetti," that is to the same melody or chant. Every phase of the tender

passion is expressed in these stanzas; nor need quarrel-
some lovers be at a loss for a vehicle for their feelings,
since there are "Dispetti" ready-made to hand for the
purpose, to say nothing of "Disperate," "Contra-dis-
perate," and "Scampanate."   Here is an example of the
mildly reproachful strain, addressed by a maiden to a
fickle swain :

> Light youth, you do as does the changeful leaf
>   That yields and turns to every passing breeze,
> Or like the serpent, when her vesture brief
>   She sheds, to deck her in fresh liveries.
> And like the serpent of the earth you be,
> To others kind, but venomous to me,
> And like the serpent of the earth you are,
> At peace with others, but with me at war.

The language of hyperbolical compliment is common to
lovers in all climates, but surely golden tresses have
never been more daintily commended than in the subjoined apostrophe of the Tuscan peasant :

> Would'st see thy servant die of love straightway,
>   Dress not in curls those shining locks of thine,
> But down along thy shoulders let them stray,
>   Where they seem skeins of gold from out the mine.
> Where they seem skeins of finely-threaded gold,
> Fair are the locks and fair the head they fold ;
> When they seem skeins of gold and silk most rare,
> Fair are the locks, and she who combs them fair.

The tender inconsistencies of a lover's fancy are expressed
in the following stanza, in which the epic octave is substituted for the rustic form :

> Oh flower of beauty that dost ever blow,
>   Unchanged through all the seasons of the year,
> Who looks on thee, and doth thy sweetness know,
>   Hath a perennial spring for ever near ;

> Oh, flower of beauty, midst the people go,
> And learn how fair to all thou dost appear;
> Oh, flower of beauty, rather hide apart,
> For I alone would know how fair thou art.

A quaint conceit of a kind much in vogue with the elder *minnesingers* of all countries, is embodied in the following :

> Now would to Heav'n that love were judged by weight,
>   And who were short of love should pain endure,
> For that such sentence ne'er should be my fate—
>   Unless the scales were false—I then were sure.
> Unless the scales were false, and gave no sign,
> Unto which side the balance should incline ;
> Unless the scales were false and crooked quite,
> And none should know how love to weigh aright.

Another example is a variation on the common type from having an extra pair of lines—ten instead of eight :

> Did I but think my love could list to me,
>   With lusty voice then would I shout and sing,
> But sundered by hills, vales, and mounts are we,
>   Nor can my voice to such far distance ring.
> We're sundered by the leaves of corn-fields green,
> He cannot hear me with such space between ;
> We're sundered by the leaves of trailing vine,
> He cannot hear me from his house to mine ;
> We're sundered by the leaves of poplars tall,
> He cannot hear me, he is out of call.

The form of the Rispetti is used for improvisation upon all subjects, as in the subjoined stanza, in which Beatrice di Pian degli Ontani, the shepherdess-improvvisatrice of the Abetone, replied to a question about her education :

> My lads and lasses, prithee wonder not,
>   If my rude song in faulty verses flow,
> For to my house no teachers came, I wot,
>   Far less to schools for learning did I go ;

And would ye know the school I did frequent,
'Twas round these hills in hail and rain I went,
And would ye know the study that I made,
'Twas fetching wood and digging with the spade.

The "Strambotto" is generally more rude and fragmentary than the "Rispetto," seldom completely reproducing the epic stanza on which it was originally modelled.
"Stornelli," or "Fiori," are ejaculations in song, beginning
with the invocation of a flower, and sung to the dance-
music of the saltarello.   Here is an example of what may
at first have been intended as a sort of game played while
dancing :

Oh flower of rye,
From a glad heart now let me sing for joy,
Once more at peace with my true love am I.

The singular chant that echoes among the hills of
Tuscany, as from valley to valley and from slope to slope
the peasants converse with each other in its far-heard
rhythm, is not the music to which any of their popular
songs are set.   It is the versified peasant dramas called
"Maggi," as was pointed out in a previous chapter, that are
sung to these wild, weird notes, the whole dialogue being
sustained on a single musical phrase of a few bars, reiterated through a performance that frequently lasts for
hours.   This traditional phrase, with its long-drawn
recurring cry, is the favourite vehicle for popular prose
utterance throughout Tuscany, and to its wailing cadence
the peasants in the long summer evenings may be heard
recounting, by the hour together, their joys and sorrows,
deaths or other incidents of family life, either to an
audience or in soliloquy.   May not Horace and Tibullus
have heard the same notes in the rude rhythm in which
they describe the peasants of Latium as exchanging

vituperative epithets or singing behind the plough? Horace, indeed, speaks of this primitive Saturnian metre as having been supplanted by the introduction of Greek culture, but it is at least possible that it may still linger in these highlands amid a people who have seen more revolutions and been less affected by them than any other race on earth.

The poetry of the Marches is almost identical with that of Tuscany, as may be seen in the example of two Rispetti, spoken by a youth and maiden respectively:

> With what a grace, sweet maiden, dost thou move,
>   How fair thou art with that bright head of thine;
> Earth thrills beneath thy foot her joy to prove,
>   And trees break into flower and blossoms shine.
> Thy graceful step doth call the blossoms out,
> Like roses that in April blush and pout;
> Thy beauteous mien doth bid the flowers appear,
> Like roses when the summer months are here.

> Now look ye what misfortune hath been mine!
>   To have a tongue, and yet perforce be mute,
> To pass my own true lad and give no sign,
>   To see him—and be powerless to salute,
> I greeted him, indeed, in thought and heart,
> Though thou, poor tongue, of speech hadst lost the art,
> I greeted him, indeed, in heart and thought,
> Though thou, poor tongue of mine, couldst utter nought.

In Umbria and Latium the octave stanza is lengthened —in the latter by repeating the two opening lines again at the close—in the former by extra variations on the Ritornelli, as follows:

> I go, my love, to roam from thee so far,
>   That news of me can scarce come back to thee,
> But as a sign, I leave behind a star;
>   When it no longer shines, weep, love for me.

When night or day it shines no more on high,
Weep, pretty love, for I am like to die.
When day or night it shines on high no more,
Weep, pretty love, for I am at death's door.

When the bright star no longer shineth clear,
Weep, pretty love, for I am on my bier.
When the bright star no more on high is found,
Weep, pretty love, for I am underground.

In Naples, where an element of the grotesque enters into southern passion, the songs which are so prominent a feature of popular life are principally in burlesque vein. Produced for public competition on the festival of Piedigrotta (September 8), the one then chosen by public acclamation as the queen-song of the year attains universal celebrity.

The popular wit is apparent in the trade songs or street cries of Naples like this, " Zuoccolaro, zuoccolé," in which the dealer in clogs or wooden shoes advertises his wares :

Wooden shoes, who'll buy, who'll buy !
  Wooden shoes, who wants a pair ?
Though the price is none too high,
  I'll abate it to the fair,
Who her charms hereby renews—
Wooden-shoe-man, wooden shoes !

Some there are so small and neat,
  Fashioned with especial care,
Made express for dainty feet,
  Meant alone for such to wear,
That their beauty nought may lose—
Wooden-shoe-man, wooden shoes

As each nail I hammered straight,
  I began to sigh amain,
Thinking what a precious weight
  Would the senseless wood sustain.

Wishing I such lot might choose—
Wooden-shoe-man, wooden shoes!

Many a heart with love on fire,
   Will your fate with envy see,
Many a lover will desire
   Such a pair of clogs to be.
Then poor me will they abuse—
Wooden-shoe-man, wooden shoes!

If among you one is found
   Who doth love—I prithee take
These, which make no creaking sound,
   Mamma's suspicions to awake,
Fear not if my wares you use—
Wooden-shoe-man, wooden shoes!

Ever honest with the fair,
   I ne'er wrangle o'er the price,
For all difference to square,
   A few honeyed words suffice.
Thus their favour ne'er I lose—
Wooden-shoe-man, wooden shoes!

The cry of the laundresses of the Vomero, "Jesce sole!"
(Out sun!) is thus amplified in verse:

Out sun! shine out! and hide no more,
   Nor leave us here to sigh in vain,
See how to pray you o'er and o'er,
   So humbly we poor girls are fain.
To burn our faces black, indeed,
In hottest haste you come full speed,
To bleach our sheets when we implore,
   On crutches must you limp amain,
Out sun! shine out! and hide no more,
   Nor leave us here to sigh in vain.

The remaining stanzas are in the same spirit, which also
animates the Song of the Grinder or Arrotino:

> Women, here comes the grinder,
>   Women who wants to whet?
> Come quick at this reminder,
>   To have your scissors set.
> I keep the grindstone turning,
>   With a whirli whirligo,
> 'Tis a pleasant way of earning,
>   That our merry trade doth show.

From Calabria comes the following stanza to a lady of the name of Anna, with a play on the word *Anno*, the year:

> Anna, thy name is borrowed from the year,
>   And all the beauties of the year are thine,
> Thou bear'st high summer in thy glances clear,
>   While on thy flesh the snows of winter shine.
> Ripe fruits of autumn thy warm lips appear,
>   Thy face of very spring-tide is the sign,
> And if I e'er should lose thee, sweetheart dear,
>   My whole year gone, what day should then be mine?

The character of Sicilian song is variously ascribed to Arab and Provençal influences, but Signor Vigo,* the most exhaustive writer on the subject, would trace it still further back to the old Greek culture of the island. But these are speculative theories, while the identity of character of its earliest traditional form with that of Tuscany is a palpable fact. Cast, too, in the octave stanza, though of slightly different structure, and similarly expressive of various phases of feeling—love, hatred, jealousy, or anger—these emotions are clothed in that larger amplitude of exaggeration and hyperbole derived from contact with an Eastern race. Other forms of poetry, approaching more nearly to the ballad type, are of modern growth on a soil where verse is the spontaneous

* "Canti Popolari Siciliani."   Leonardo Vigo.

utterance of the people. Their taste seems to demand uniformity rather than variety of sound, as the form of octave stanza, the use of which among them can be traced back to the fifteenth century, is constructed on a single pair of rhymes alternated throughout, while for these they prefer a certain amount of assonance, generally produced by the inversion of the vowels, as in *via* and *vai*. The following specimen of the Sicilian octave is formed, all except the closing lines, of cynical proverbs dovetailed together in evident bitterness of spirit :

> To fallen tree, the axe, the axe straightway !
>   To man in prison, death without debate,
> Unlucky who relations' help doth pray,
>   He who hath nought should lean upon the great.
> A wife is never a true friend, they say,
>   Who hath a mother 'scapes the worst of fate,
> When beat of drum broke on the public way,*
>   My best friend played the hangman for me straight.

The next example recalls Petrarch's sonnet, " Vago Augelletto " :

> Oh turtle-dove, who of thy gentle mate,
>   The lost companionship dost aye deplore,
> Who mak'st thy moan in places desolate,
>   And with thy tears the way dost moisten o'er,
> Come hither, and to me thy woes narrate,
>   And I will tell what makes my heart so sore ;
> Thou thy dead love dost weep disconsolate,
>   I mourn her living still, but mine no more.

Its intimate association with the life of the people gives a peculiar interest to the national poetry of Sicily. It is here that at harvest-time and other festive seasons the village streets may be heard echoing to those contests in

---

* The police or soldiers to arrest rioters.

song which the memory of the peasants enables them to sustain, sometimes for hours together, an exercise which they call *cantar lu Ruggiero*. A man and woman, for instance, will answer each other in appropriate stanzas on a given subject, such as censure and praise of the fair sex, from house to house, or from threshing-floor to threshing floor, until one or other is beaten off the field from the exhaustion of his repertory. Their stock is often a very extensive one, and a village weaver-girl is said to have known by heart 600 canzoni, or 4800 lines of verse. The retentiveness of the popular memory thus exercised is illustrated by an incident witnessed by Signor Salamone-Marino, who assisted at what he calls the popularisation of a poem at Borgetto in 1867. The piece happened to hit the public fancy from the local allusions and biting sarcasms on well-known characters, with which the author (a countryman of the name of Salvatore d'Arrigo) had seasoned the traditional panegyric on the saint whose feast was being celebrated. The people flocked round to listen, and, after two or three recitals, were able to repeat, without missing a syllable, the entire poem of thirty-one octave stanzas, which in a few days thus attained a wide circulation.

Each class of poem, such as drinking songs or love ditties, has its special traditional musical measure, and among them is the chant of the Tuscan Maggi, whose wild stave is believed to be of Arab origin. The voice is generally accompanied by some stringed instrument— violin, lute, or guitar—and singing and dancing are combined in " La Ruggiera," defined as a pantomimic song-dance. Two couples go through the figure with much gesticulation, pausing for the vocal part of the performance, which consists of words chosen at discretion, sung to a prescribed melody, accompanied by guitars and violins. The name recalls that of "Sir Roger de Coverley," but it is scarcely likely that the English country-dance is called after Sicilian Roger.

Stefano La Sala, one of the principal popular poets of Sicily, a poor and hard-working nailsmith of Palermo, is described by Signor Vigo, who visited him in his humble forge, as chanting poems and stories in all metres to the monotonous beat of the hammer on the anvil — a Harmonious Blacksmith indeed.

The blind minstrels of Palermo form a regular guild, constituted under legal sanction in 1661, possessing diplomas which they keep religiously guarded from profane eye under triple key, and bound to certain religious observances, among them the annual production of a song in honour of the Madonna for her Feast on December 8. On this anniversary Signor Vigo says it is interesting to see them competing for public favour, each rehearsing in turn the new song and new words, while their boy-guides congregate together and amuse themselves with childish sports. The society consists of thirty members, all singers and players, some inventors of new rhymes (trovatori), others rhapsodists, repeating from memory only. Having acquired a prescriptive right to hold their weekly meeting in the portico of the Jesuit convent, they were at perpetual feud with the Order, which vainly sought to dislodge them.

The public competitions between rival bards in classical Greece are recalled by those which take place between the Sicilian improvvisatori as described by Signor Vigo:

"Among the most pleasing and novel spectacles are the *tenzoni* (contests). Fairs are held in Sicily to which different poets repair, singing and accompanying themselves like the early troubadours, and each followed by a crowd who applaud and pay him. Disputes then arise between the admirers of this one or that, leading to competitions between the poets, either brought together by their respective partisans, or meeting accidentally under a tree or in a booth or tavern, it matters not where, provided there be plenty of wine from capacious jars to moisten contentious throats. The combatants are debarred the use of prose, and forbidden weapons, for which they are searched before the duel begins. They exchange salutations, challenges, and questions in verse, and generally proceed after the first greetings to proposing intricate questions which must be answered impromptu; then as the contest becomes more animated, they pass on to witticisms or sarcasms, and woe to whichever falters or has not his rhymes at command— woe to the vanquished! His defeat mortifies his adherents, and he retires sometimes followed by hisses, but boasting of former triumphs and challenging the victor to fresh combat at another fair; the latter meantime empties his flask, joyously twanging the lute, viol, or psaltery, whose tinkle is still heard in some remote villages. Sometimes, and indeed this is the usual end of the contest, the defeated party rushes at his conqueror to make an end of him, and force scarcely avails to keep them apart, until the priest intervenes, and makes them exchange a fraternal embrace. These formal contests resemble duels to the death, but in the more peaceful competitions the poets eulogise the saint whose feast is being held, answering each other impromptu, and this takes place, for instance, at San Giovanni di Galerno on June 24 every year."

The author narrates as follows the proceedings at this feast in 1852:

"In presence of five or six thousand spectators the image of the saint was brought out and placed upon the car, on which ascended five poets, Antonino Russo, aged six, led by his father, Salvatore a smith, Giovanni Pagano, farmer, Andrea Pappalardo, shoemaker, and Salvatore da Misterbianco, farmer. The poets celebrated in turns the life and miracles of the saint, and then came to a tournament amongst themselves; all used the Sicilian octave except Pappalardo, who used the sestine with the last two lines rhyming together; none withdrew from the field, all were facile and imaginative improvvisatori, and if one were to bear off the palm, I should assign it to the smith, as endowed with the greatest play of fancy. All five were judged worthy of prizes. The people applauded or were silent, though on other occasions they sometimes make the poet descend from the platform if he fails to give satisfaction, hesitates or stops, and they took such pleasure in the performance as to stay scorching in the sun for over two hours. None know how or when this contest was instituted, but all agree that it is very ancient."

Of Sicilian ballad literature the most remarkable relic is the "Baronessa di Carini," reconstructed piecemeal from the lips of the people by Signor Salvatore Salamone-Marino, and published by him with a commentary.* The subject is the fate of Caterina La Grua, murdered

* "La Baronessa di Carini" and "La Storia nei Canti Popolari Siciliani," Salvatore Salamone-Marino. Among the principal collectors of Italian folk-songs, besides those already cited, are Giuseppe Tigri, "Canti Popolari Toscani": Niccolo Tommaseo, "Canti Popolar iGreci, Illirici, Corsi e Toscani"; Angelo

by her father on December 4, 1563, in his rage at the
discovery of a love affair carried on in his absence. To
this tragedy, probably historical, legend has appended
the descent of her lover to the infernal regions to visit
her shade, resulting in his conversion and subsequent
life of penance. At the old castle of Carini, opposite
the island of Ustica, on the northern coast of Sicily,
the impress of a blood-stained hand on the wall
is still shown as that made by the ill-starred heroine
in her fall. An extract descriptive of the sunrise on
the morning of her death may serve as a specimen of
the ballad :

> Incarnadine descends the morning light
>   On Ustica's gaunt spine and on the sea,
> The swallow soars aloft on pinions light,
>   To greet the sun with matin song of glee ;
> But lo, the sparrow-hawk doth bar her flight,
>   With greedy eyes the fluttering bird that see,
> Back to her nest she hies her in affright,
>   And scarce escapes the peril she doth flee.
> Nor dares look forth, but hides in fear of capture,
> Hushed and forgot her wonted song of rapture.

The popularity of this ballad is attested by the existence
of fragments in various parts of Italy ; and the lament of
the lover is recognisable by some characteristic features
in the Neapolitan song " Fenesta che luciva." The feats
of celebrated brigands form the theme of several Sicilian
ballads, which, however, do not treat them from the
sympathetic point of view generally accorded to such
heroes in popular literature.

Dalmedico, "Canti del Popolo Veneziano"; Giuseppe Pitré,
"Sui Canti Popolari Siciliani"; Giuseppe Morosi, "Studi sui
Dialetti Greci"; Achille Canali, "Canti Popolari Calabresi."

The tenacity of race distinction on Italian soil is illustrated by the survival in Sicily of two foreign nationalities, whose identity centuries of residence have not sufficed to merge in that of the native population of their adopted country. Of these the Albanians, planted in the sixteenth century, are the most numerous, reckoned at 85,000 between Sicily and Calabria. Here they form separate village communities, retaining their own customs and religious rites, and speaking a language known as Greco-Albanese, Latin, as they term that of their neighbours, being little understood by them. At the ecclesiastical seminary, founded for their priests in the eighteenth century, the Athenian dramas are acted by the students on gala occasions. They still regard Greece as their native country, and from some of their settlements in Sicily go in pilgrimage to the top of a mountain before dawn on June 24, and, with their faces turned to the East, address the following invocation to the Morea:

> Oh fair Morea,
> Since leaving thee I ne'er have seen thee more,
>   There is my sire,
>   There doth my mother dwell,
> I left my brothers' graves upon thy shore,
>   Oh fair Morea,
> Since leaving thee I ne'er have seen thee more.

Although the Siculo-Albanians have imitated the Sicilian stanza in some of their recent poetry, their primitive songs are of a totally different character, always unrhymed, very irregular in metre, and of a more fantastic and Eastern cast of thought. In the subjoined specimen, rhyme has been substituted in the translation for the sonorous rhythm of the original, which cannot be reproduced in English:

N

Haste to the garden now
　　Thou bright and merry maiden,
Cull there an olive bough,
　　With the black olives laden.
Black as the maiden's eyes of night,
Oh, maiden mine snow-white,
Maiden, my heart's delight.

Run to the garden quick,
　　Oh bright and merry maiden,
The quince's branch there pick,
　　With the white quinces laden.
Like the fair maiden's brow of light,
Oh, maiden mine snow-white,
Maiden, my heart's delight.

Speed on the garden way,
　　Oh bright and merry maiden,
Pluck a pomegranate spray,
　　With its red fruitage laden.
Like the fair maiden's blushes bright,
Oh, maiden mine snow-white,
Maiden, my heart's delight.

Haste to the garden now,
　　Thou bright and merry maiden,
Break there an apple bough,
　　With the sweet apples laden.
Like the maiden's form so round, so slight,
Oh, maiden mine snow-white,
Maiden, my heart's delight.

A still earlier immigration is represented in Sicily by
50,000 Lombards, descended from soldiers of that
nation who accompanied the first Norman conquerors
into the island. After the lapse of more than seven
centuries they still form a distinct element in the population, and speak a Lombard dialect, adulterated, not
with Sicilian idiom, but with the Norman-French of their

early brothers-in-arms. They, too, have their songs modelled on the Sicilian stanza, but with a strain of burlesque more in harmony with German taste, recalling the fact that this race came of Teutonic stock.

While the influence of all the various elements in the Italian population is distinctly traceable in the poetry of the nation, its two most strongly contrasted types are embodied in that of the Arno Basin and of the Subalpine Slope. In the one we have the utterances of a self-reflective mood, centred on a single theme, and set, as it were, to minor keys of thought; in the other, an unimpassioned chronicle of facts, told in verse often rude and bald, but animated with dramatic spirit, and moving with the brusque vivacity of a military quick step. In the preponderance in the one of feeling, in the other of action, we see portrayed with curious distinctness those two opposite but complementary types of national character which made Piedmont the sword, as Tuscany is the brain of Italy.

CHAPTER XI

The Tuscan Béranger

No man since he who first sung of the other world in a tongue previously despised in this has exercised so powerful an influence on the Italian language as the modern satirist of the Tuscan hills. What Dante effected for the spoken vernacular of his own day, raising it to be the model of classical diction, Giuseppe Giusti did for the rural idiom of his native mountains, rendering it the ideal standard of speech, and that, too, at the very time when the national aspirations for political unity rendered some such common standard a necessity for Italy.

Born of a family of provincial gentry in the little town of Monsummano, perched high above the green amphitheatre of the Val di Nievole, he made it his recreation from boyhood to wander on foot among the encircling Apennines, there gathering from the lips of the peasantry those pungent touches of wit and pathos, keen-whetted as by the sharp air of the uplands, with which he has enriched modern Italian. Like the mediæval craftsman, who elaborated from the homeliest types of nature the exquisite ornamentation of his foliated shafts, Giusti has wrought into his polished lines with consummate effect the shrewd proverbs interchanged in fence and foil of rustic wit by the hardy mountaineers of Pistoia or the rude shepherds of the Maremma. So entirely, indeed, is his vocabulary drawn from the dialect of his rural fellow-countrymen, that while it is regarded as the purest ideal of Italian Attic, it has been found necessary to publish a specially annotated edition of his poems for the use of non-Tuscan readers.

The present prevailing fashion in Italian literature tends, it must be confessed, to an exaggeration of the peculiarities of Giusti's style, and the reaction led by him against pseudo-classicalism threatens, like all reactions, to carry public taste into an opposite extreme, that of giving literary currency to all the familiar colloquialisms of Fiorentine street slang. The idiom of the Mercato Nuovo may be a very quaint and forcible vehicle for popular wit and eloquence, yet at the same time quite incapable of giving utterance to all the ideas of a higher plane of culture.

The name of Béranger, borrowed by Giusti's compatriots for their favourite lyrist, refers in reality to but one aspect of his character, that of a poet of the people. The sunny singer of Parisian Bohemianism has no chord on his lyre that vibrates to those minors in which the Italian satirist sounds the notes of a deeper pathos—a sterner moral. Not a lyre, indeed, but a violin is his instrument, capable of those penetrating poignancies that pierce to the quick of human nature. In the Tuscan character, through all classes and degrees, a keen and caustic sense of humour is associated with a profound sensibility to melancholy impressions. This dual nature, in which the sources of laughter and tears are placed close together, was reproduced in Giusti in its most intensified form, and he repeatedly analyses it in his writings. Thus in the lines to Gino Capponi he describes himself as expressing,

> This smile whose seeming mirth is grief defied.
> (Questo che par sorriso ed é dolore),

while to Girolamo Tommasi he writes in the same strain :

> But ah! a laugh that echoes not within,
> For like the starving mountebank am I,
> Who, gnawed by want, to please the crowd must try
> With gibe and grin.

It is this tragic sense of the incongruities of life that gives its trenchant incisiveness to Giusti's verse, sharpened, like a two-edged sword, with the double keenness of ridicule and wrath; the vehicle, now of denunciation, trumpet-tongued as the blast of an accusing angel, now of pungent raillery levelled at injustice or abuse with the seemingly unconscious pleasantry of Pulcinella. Half harlequin, half Mephistopheles, he launches jests or sneers indifferently, and is either grim or jocose as the humour takes him, but ever with such unfailing mastery of his weapons that neither jest nor sneer fails to cut to the bone.

No kindred spirit to Béranger, with the bubble and sparkle of French vivacity in his effervescing verse, have we in this scathed and scathing moralist, whose airiest lines suggest such deeper meanings as though the frowning gaze of the genius of Tragedy were fixed on us from beneath the hollow comic mask, and whose cap and bells crown the grisly protagonist of the Dance of Death. Rather among a people resembling the Tuscan in their shrewd sense and keen humour will English readers seek a parallel to the Italian poet, and in Giusti's habitual turn of mind and thought find a curious faraway kinship to those of Robert Burns. Giusti, like Burns, wrote in a rustic idiom, though with a polish of style that fitted it to classical use; like Burns, he lived much among the people and was the interpreter of their feelings; like Burns, he contemned and scorned the flimsy shams of society, and recognised with the same intensity the common stamp of universal humanity which they ignore. Both natures were perhaps originally compounded of the same metal, but moulded by circumstances and surroundings to uses and capabilities as different as are those of a finely-tempered Italian rapier from those of a stout and serviceable Scottish dirk.

The active part of Giusti's life was coincident with that incipient phase of the Italian revolution when an ever-growing sense of exasperation in men's minds, a feeling of bitter wrong and burning humiliation, was undermining the structure of foreign domination as surely and silently as the gradual operations of nature sap the foundations of a ruin. All the vital forces of the country were engaged in preparing the national renovation; all its intellectual and moral strength was bent to the same purpose; and art and literature were either pressed into the service of patriotism or neglected altogether. Thus Giusti, born a poet, was developed into a political satirist by the conditions of the society in which he moved, concentrating its seething passions into that series of epigrams which were not the least among the myriad forces all working to the same result of national liberation. He belonged to that unfortunate generation of Italians who sowed in blood and tears the harvest which their descendants were to reap in joy; and who by a succession of abortive conspiracies and insurrections drew down upon their country and themselves all the

miseries of repression. The poet saw the machinery of
mediæval statecraft in full operation around him—the
scaffold and the dungeon the familiar allies of authority;
the official spy and paid informer the vile tools of
tyranny; exile and proscription the wages of patriotic
aspiration; and his heart burned within him, and wrath
armed his pen with that concentrated energy of diction
which made his epigrams resemble, not squibs, but
thunderbolts.

He was not, however, a mere political lampooner, but
a social satirist as well, who has held up to opprobrium
the most characteristic vices of his age and country in a
series of personifications which resemble Hogarth's cari-
catures in their vigour and fidelity. A gallery of odious
types, all more or less products of political profligacy, are
made to pass before us like the slides of a magic lantern,
revealed in their native hideousness by the focussed light
of his withering power of epithet. Thus the venal
alliance between money and birth is the theme of "La
Scritta" (The Contract), descriptive of the nuptials of a
worthless and impoverished patrician with a usurer's
daughter; the vulgar ambition of the rich tradesman,
that of "La Vestizione" (The Investiture), in which
Becero, the ex-grocer, is decorated with the insignia and
title of "Cavaliere." The base arts of a career in which
conscience, honour, and self-respect are sacrificed to
worldly advancement are flagellated in "Gingillino";
the contemptible figure of the political weathercock
is pilloried in the "Brindisi di Girella"; fashionable
frivolity and aristocratic inanity are satirised in "Il
Ballo" and "Il Giovinetto"; while the demoralising
effects of the Government lottery on the rural classes are
portrayed in "Il Sortilegio" and the "Apologia del

Lotto." So universally recognised were the types he has thus depicted, that the names affixed to them have passed into the language as contumelious epithets to stigmatise similar characters. Personal satire, however, he held in the greatest abhorrence, and nothing so roused his ire as the attempt to identify his typical abstractions with particular individuals.

Giusti's genius was somewhat late in maturing, and his early years gave no special promise of ability. Born in 1809, he was sent, after a somewhat desultory preliminary training, to the University of Pisa, then rather a school of revolutionary principles and juvenile dissipation than of learning or morals. The youthful poet graduated much more brilliantly in the former than in the latter course of education, and his father was so disgusted with his conduct that he recalled him from the University at the end of three years and kept him at home for an equal lapse of time. In 1832 he returned to Pisa, having in the interval begun to try his prentice-hand at verse-making, and after eighteen months more of the old student life of idleness and folly took his degree in Jurispudence in June 1834, having devoted fifteen days to reading for his examination. That it did not require a very profound course of preparation may be inferred from the fact that one of the students about the same time enlivened the dulness of his legal studies by versifying a great portion of the Canon Law, and sent up at his examination, on the theme " De Pallio," a paper in rhyming couplets, for which the professors, quite unconscious of the poetical nature of the composition, gave him most favourable marks. This University life, with its friendships and follies, its political enthusiasms and reckless defiance of discipline and order, had a lasting influence on Giusti's

character, and to " The Memories of Pisa " he consecrated the poem which he himself preferred among all
his productions, in which he recalls with undisguised
exultation that he was ever found in the ranks of the
most illustrious scapegraces.

Having taken his degree, he established himself in
Florence under pretence of practising as a lawyer, but
continued the same round of amusement, alternating
with desultory reading, passing his subsequent life between the Tuscan capital and the parental roof at
Montecatini. In 1835 he wrote the verses which first
made him known as a political satirist, under the form of
a mock lament for the death of the Emperor Francis I.
of Austria. In the autumn of the same year he suffered
the most bitter sorrow of his life, caused by the faithlessness of a lady for whom he felt his first and only serious
attachment. To her was addressed the exquisite love-
poem, " All' Amica Lontana," in a brief absence at the
seaside, during which the poet was superseded in her
fickle affections. He went through months of despairing
grief, and was so far inconsolable that he was never
again, according to his own repeated declarations,
capable of the same depth of feeling, and that any subsequent wound to his heart was, in comparison, but a mere
graze.

He was next to experience all the terrors of physical
suffering, for a long and painful malady of the digestive
organs attacked him in 1843 in consequence of a series
of nervous shocks acting powerfully on his sensitive fibre.
The first was the conflagration of his writing-table under
his eyes, owing to the burning down of a candle, incautiously left lighted while he slept, an accident which
cost him the fruits of years of labour in notes and memo-

randa ; the second a protracted attendance on the death-
bed of an uncle to whom he was much attached ; and
the third an encounter in the streets of Florence with an
infuriated cat, which flew at him unprovoked, and attacked
him with teeth and claws. The fear of hydrophobia,
induced by this singular mischance, so preyed on his
mind as to cause a total disarrangement of the digestive
functions, producing not only acute pain but also total
apathy of mind and incapacity for mental exertion.   His
letters at this period gave a sad picture of his state, and
in one of them he replies to the would-be consolatory
reflection of a friend, that suffering is always the lot of
genius, by saying that "when under the pincers one
would bid adieu to the brain of Galileo."

Travelling was tried as a remedy, and in 1844 he took
a trip to Rome and Naples in company with his mother,
renewing old and contracting new friendships on the
way, and, among other notabilities, meeting on intimate
terms the brothers Poerio.   The return journey was
signalised by a pleasant little incident.   At a village
hotel at Sant' Agata, between Capua and Gaeta, the
company discovering, in the course of conversation, that
our travellers came from Pescia, began to cross-examine
them about "the famous poet Giusti," and the truth was
finally revealed by the mother's embarrassed silence and
conscious glance at her son when asked if the subject of
discourse was handsome.

The distractions of travel procured Giusti a short
respite from suffering, but in the ensuing autumn he had
so severe a relapse that he believed his death imminent,
and wrote a paper containing his testamentary disposi-
tions in regard to his works, as well as a skeleton auto-
biography, to form a groundwork for the history of his

life by one of his friends.   He, however, recovered, and
was able in 1845, with the assistance of his friend Mayer,
to edit the first edition of his poems for the press, urged
to undertake the task by the publication of a pirated
edition at Lugano, in which they appeared mutilated and
distorted.

Perhaps the most agreeable phase of his life was that
which followed, during which the friendship of Manzoni
and Grossi opened to him a new range of sympathies and
affections.   It began through the happy accident of
having accompanied his friend Giorgini in a trip to
Spezzia, where the Marchesa d'Azeglio and Vittorina
Manzoni (afterwards the wife of Giorgini) were taking
the baths.   These ladies being about to return home the
following day, Giusti and Giorgini, starting in a little carriage to escort them as far as Genoa, finally accompanied
them all the way back to Milan, where Giusti, during a
month spent under Manzoni's roof, won all hearts by his
graces of mind and manner.

This episode occurred in the autumn of 1845, and the
correspondence which followed shows the close and
tender friendship which bound him for the remainder of
his life to Manzoni and Grossi, as well as to d'Azeglio
and to Gino Capponi, at whose house he always stayed
when in Florence.   These men were linked together by
the noble aim they had in common in all their labours,
the political and moral regeneration of their country.

Manzoni's letters to Giusti breathe, like everything
that came from his pen, the most exquisite and lovable
soul that ever accompanied so high an order of genius ;
a soul whose intellectual and moral attributes were not,
as too often happens, in direct antagonism but in
harmonious combination, the one forming the perfect

complement of the other. He winds up one letter of such playfulness as only he could have written with the touching request: "And you, my dear and good Geppino, make haste to love me, for I am old, and there is no time to be lost about it." In another he addresses a grave though affectionate rebuke to Giusti for having, as was reported, allowed himself to be led away into ridicule of religion, as well as into personal satire; from which accusations the poet writes in all humility to exculpate himself. For the first he excuses himself on the plea of inadvertence and want of reflection, but meets the second with a point-blank denial, save in the case of public and historical personages. The incident shows how the influence of a character like Manzoni's may keep up the whole moral standard of a nation. The Lombard novelist, who devoted ten years to rewriting his great work in order to assimilate its language to the purer Tuscan, frequently applied to Giusti, the master of that idiom, for advice and assistance, and many of his letters are dissertations on the meaning of popular phrases and turns of expression.

It may be imagined how the revolutionary movement of 1848 was hailed by these votaries of Italian liberty. Giusti raised a company in his native place which formed part of the heroic band of Tuscan volunteers slain at Curtatone and Montanara. He regretted that the state of his health did not permit him to share the glory and peril of the campaign, but he entered the ranks of the National Guard, and underwent drill and discipline as a private before rising to the rank of Major. Under the new constitution of Tuscany he was returned as deputy to the Assembly, and took part in its debates, maintaining as firm an attitude of opposition to the extremes

of liberal as he formerly had to those of despotic government.   The fall of the Ridolfi Ministry, under the
repeated attacks of the minority of the Chamber, elicited
his witty sonnet on " Majorities," beginning *Che i più
tirano i meno*, and directed against the apathetic attitude
of the more numerous party.   Its pungent satire is quite
as applicable to Italian politics in our day as it was
in his.

Giusti did not long survive the public misfortunes following on the brief dream of national emancipation; his
health had been declining for some time, and in the
autumn of 1849 he was attacked with a severe miliary
fever, from which he recovered, indeed, but with the fatal
germs of tubercular consumption in his system.   To the
last he continued his literary labours, and his sick-room
in the Palazzo Capponi was lined with books, and the
bed, from which he was to rise no more, strewn with
papers and memoranda.   The disease made rapid
progress, and death came suddenly in the end.   On
March 31, 1850, in his forty-first year, he was suffocated
by the bursting of a blood-vessel, and died before the
aid of science or religion could reach him.   He lies
buried in the church of San Miniato, on the cypress-
studded height overlooking Florence, and the inscription
on his monument records that from the graces of the living
idiom of his country he created a form of poetry never
before attempted, and used it for the castigation of vice
without derogating from the belief in virtue.

Giusti's life and character are illustrated by a mass of
letters, which are among the greatest models of epistolary style extant in any language, and are invariably recommended to students of Italian as the *ne plus ultra* of
vivacity and purity of diction.   They give the impression

of the most unstudied spontaneity, and seem to reflect the mood of the writer at the moment, now witty now tender, exalted with the most lofty sentiments of wisdom or morality, bitter with cynical irony, or tragic with the terrible eloquence of suffering. Here is a portion of one addressed to the Marchesa d'Azeglio in October 1844 :

"MY DEAR FRIEND,—I write to you from Colle in Val d'Elsa, a little village which by courtesy is called a town. The air of these districts is good ; the people in the main as good as the air ; and Poldo Orlandini, who has received me into his house, is own brother to that Checco Orlandini whom you saw at the Mayers', and who, in that process of mutual friction that we call social intercourse, has kept his primitive stamp, a shade rough to one accustomed to everything polished, but of sound metal. The touch of these pavements was like the pouring of fresh oil on a dying lamp to my health ; but after eight or ten days' breathing space I am not going to be such an ass as to be caught by the bait of hope that has been dangled before me so long. The un- tempered air of Leghorn plays the very mischief with a man whose nerves are strained like the strings of a violin. Up here the winds arrive, I might almost say, watered, and even that accursed African blast, after the exertion required for reaching these heights, is so changed that it seems as if it were almost a native of them.

"I mount a pony every morning that seems scarcely bigger than a pigeon, and which, being accustomed to carry the doctor, tries to turn down every lane and stop at every door like the tinker's donkey. These peasants, who look no higher than the beast's legs, call out to me from all sides, 'Oh, doctor, is that you?' Indeed, a

few days ago a woman brought her child out to me to
the road to be physicked, and it was no easy matter to
persuade her that I had nothing of the doctor but the
mount.   From the very first the animal and I had made
a pact of mutual forbearance, and after going five or six
miles at a pace suited to my invalid pulse, we return
straight home as pleases heaven.   The natives of Colle,
whose eyes are not trained to a certain harmony between
the horse and rider (only think how indispensable in our
Cascine, or your ramparts !), see nothing extraordinary in
the discrepancy between my Florentine surtout and the
Maremman saddle, but unlucky me, if I were to stumble
upon some summer visitor accustomed to breathe the
unadulterated air of the capital!   If I ever wished to
split myself in two after the fashion of St. Anthony it
would be now, and I would give anything to be able to
dismount from the saddle in spirit, while I remained
there in the flesh, to see the figure I cut.   Not being
equal to that, I study myself as best I can in my shadow,
and sigh for the pencil of him who drew the vignettes
to Don Quixote."

Here is an extract from another written to a friend,
Luigi Alberti, in which he analyses his physical sufferings, and after some preliminary description continues :

" When in bed it seems as if the time to get up would
never come ; when up, every hour before going to bed
seems a thousand ; in the house, I feel a mania to go
out ; when out of doors a passion to rush back to the
house ; when standing I long to sit down, when sitting
to stand up, and so on in everything.   Add to this, now
the most burning desire for life and health, now a weary
longing to have done with it once for all; on one side,

the dearest memories, the best loved faces, with all the follies, hopes, and seductions of youth crowding on my mind ; on the other, the future, now glowing with light, now gloomy with silence and darkness; now imaged as a place of rest, now as an interminable and unknown track, or again as a black and fathomless abyss. Days of calm that hold me in suspense like a soul in Limbo, and in which my complaints

> Sound not as wild laments but gentle sighs;

and then again a spasm which has no defined name or locality, which, without being a distinct pain or a recognised affection, mimics and includes all the tortures of a hospital ; resembling in this some of those fashionable phrases which say nothing but suggest everything. A red-hot pincers rending the vitals—a garment of flax-carding machines—a strait-waistcoat which cramps and racks me from head to foot—are feeble comparisons for this class of tribulation. There are sluggard troubles which delight in sticking close to you in bed ; there are others which have the noble ambition of keeping you company at table, out walking, at the theatre, and even at the ball; granting you a sort of *habeas corpus* which never releases your mind from the wretched feeling of having a prosecution hanging over you. Mine is one of those maladies of vagrant tendency which are little believed in until they go so far as to set half-a-dozen chemists hard at work, four doctors in commotion, and to strew sand before the door."

Giusti's was doubtless one of those obscure maladies in which mind and body act and react upon each other in a series of mutual jars, and the sensitive organisation of genius had to discount thus in bodily pain its exalted

intellectual privileges. In these letters the poet's dis-
position and character are seen under their best aspect,
and there are some, such as the letter of advice to a boy
entering college, and of consolation to a young cousin
afflicted with lameness, which for their combination of
practical wisdom and admirable sentiment deserve to be
written in letters of gold.

Few artists have left so clear and minute an analysis
of their creative impulses as Giusti, who had the power
of dissecting and detailing, like an indifferent spectator,
all the wayward vagaries of inspiration in his own mind.
He describes how in the first frenzy of working out an
idea he would sit at his desk for hours, writing, erasing,
sketching out, recasting, in a fever of activity and
creation ; then, disgusted with the futility of his attempts
at expression, would fling aside his papers in disgust, and
abandon all mental exertion for a phase of wild gaiety
and social distraction.   Then, after an interval, his glance
would light accidentally on the notes he had been at
work on, and he would find that the fancied failure contained all the elements of completion, and only required
in reality a little arrangement and reconstruction to be
a presentable addition to his literary offspring.   His
biographer, Signor Frassi, tells us that when the first idea
of a subject kindled in his brain he began to cast it into
shape, whatever the place or circumstances in which he
chanced to find himself; while walking or in society,
listening to conversation or making himself agreeable to
a lady, however otherwise engaged, the rhymes and verses
went on forming themselves in his mind.   As soon as
the plan was thus blocked out, he would read the rough
draft to his friends, to ladies, servants, or any audience
he could get, judging of its effect not so much from their

words as from the expression of their faces, or some involuntary gesture of dissent or approbation.   Then modi-
fying and changing whatever had seemed to fall flat or
be unintelligible, he would lay it by for some time
until he had forgotten it, and could judge of it from some
fresh point of view, when he would put it through another
process of reconstruction.   He was not less prompt in
adopting and assimilating the ideas of others than in
taking corrections and suggestions from them, so that
his mind, always on the alert, gathered materials everywhere.

The insight his life gives into his method of working
is an additional instance of the unwearied patience of
genius in pursuing its ideal ; for we find that these playful
trifles, apparently spontaneous and facile as though
written impromptu, were in reality the result of infinite
thought and pains.   Each was kept by him for months,
during which it received day by day the last finishing touches of perfection from his fastidious taste ;
attaining by the substitution, here, of a more concisely
forcible phrase, there of a more felicitous epithet, that
consummate degree of polish in which it was finally given
to the world.   The facsimiles of the manuscripts prefixed
to the editions of his works are embroidered with erasures
and corrections, in which it is apparent how laboriously
the final thought struggles into luminous expression.

It was not through the ordinary channels of publicity
that Giusti's poems reached their readers, for the rigorous
censorship of the press made it impossible to make use
of it for their circulation.   It was in manuscript form that
they left their author's hands, then passed eagerly from
one to another, they were copied, recopied, multiplied and
reproduced, until they attained in this primitive fashion

a diffusion as great as if they had issued from the press in several editions. Signor Carducci, who has written a brief memoir prefixed to one edition of these poems, relates how when a boy he was dragged from one remote village to another to transcribe and recite them. Thus it came to pass that Giusti, by a fate singular if not unique in modern letters, was a famous poet before a line of his had been printed. It was, indeed, only by the surreptitious publication of his works by others that he was at last induced to edit them for the press.

The working on his mind of the society in which he lived, and the forcible impressions he received from its abuses, are vividly portrayed in some of his pieces, which give thus an analysis of the poet's methods from his own point of view. They sum up in his own condensed phrases the story of the evolution of his genius, and show how it was bent or warped to satire by bitterness of spirit inspired by the circumstances around him. The poem addressed to Gino Capponi is of this introspective character, and is interesting as an example of his graver style. The metre he has here chosen is, as he says in a note, an old one, which notwithstanding its great difficulty he desired to restore, as the additional line lends greater dignity and weight to the tripping octave stanza.

As one who mid the torrent's rush doth guide
   His bark, while angry currents stem the way,
Seems to stand motionless, while past him glide
   Shores, hills, and distant woods in shifting play;
So doth my mind amid the eddying tide
   Of human destinies bewildered stray,
And while the varied scene doth pass before it
Of universal life, feels coming o'er it
   Dull stupor, that no utterance dare essay.

Till with the dizzy tumult wearied quite
  The secret forces of my soul I feel,
And gaze and think, and fail to grasp aright
  What to mine eyes intent those sights reveal,
Nor feel within me of such verse the might
  As should respond to that wild clarion peal.
So hurried by the stir and hum around me,
I dream and rave, and in its whirl confound me,
  Like the dead leaf the wind doth drift and wheel,

But when from men afar, I meditate
  Some task of subtle fancy breathing warm,
And in the mind's sweet toil would recreate
  The heart that weary travail doth inform ;
Lo! to assail me come importunate
  As though of insects vile a buzzing swarm,
Past memories clothed in jeers to mock and flout me,
Like spectres armed with scoffs, all crowd about me,
  Till they and I in combat strive and storm.

Thus to her room withdrawn, the maiden fair
  In glad intoxication brief and light,
That, left by dance and music lingering there
  Nor sleep nor weariness can put to flight,
Still seems to hear the hushed and vacant air
  Thrill to the festive clamour of delight,
Till the impressions left by loving glances,
The lights, the whirl, the vortex of the dances,
  Change to a troublous vision of the night.

The poet then goes on to describe his mental questionings,
as, in moments when inspiration flagged, he seemed to
doubt the genuineness of his vocation as a satirist, and
almost to loathe the darker view it compelled him to
take of life.

Then o'er this sea, whose perils thou dost brave
  With sail so feeble and with bark so slight,
Doth storm-cloud ever lower and tempest rave,
  And plaints of wretches drowned the hearing smite ?

Nor e'er doth laugh the sky, or pause the wave?
　And doth the sun in clouds aye veil its light?
And in this dust much burdened and much daring,
Which on the road to heaven with thee is faring,
　Is nought but vice apparent to thy sight?

And who art thou with scourge so prompt to smite,
　Who the harsh truth so harshly dost proclaim?
And stinting praise to what is fair and bright,
　Dost tune thy acrid verse to wrath and blame?
Hast thou, thy standard following aright,
　Learned Art's true ministry and secret aim?
And hast thou first from thine own heart uprooted
Vain pride and folly to thy part unsuited—
　Thou, whose rebuke would others' feet reclaim?

Then, stung with grief, I breathe a sigh of care,
　And curb my vagrant thoughts to musing slow.
As calling back the how, the when, the where,
　My brief life-record o'er and o'er I go.
Ah! thus the past retracing, I cull there
　'Mid thousand thorns, but one poor flower ablow.
With error wroth—with error stained—now soaring
With the great few supernal heights exploring—
　Now sunk to raving with the vulgar low.

Sad theme of wrath that solely fires me still,
　How is my heart by thee opprest and tried!
Oh butterfly, who in glad flight at will
　From flower to flower along thy path dost glide,
And thou, sad nightingale, whose voice doth fill
　With love songs all the woods at eventide,
Compared with your sweet tasks how sore doth fret me,
The strife of soul in which doth ever set me
　This seeming mirth which is but grief defied.

The strange duality of genius, by which it seems to
override with irresistible compulsion the choice and will
of its possessor, has seldom been more vividly portrayed
than in this elaborate piece of mental self-dissection.

Similar phases of mind are analysed in the poet's more ordinary vein of grim humour in his lines to Girolamo Tommasi, while one of his common moods of satirical morality expresses itself in the following four stanzas, narrating a characteristic incident, and entitled "An Involuntary Salute." The metre is one extensively used by him, as it lends itself to the fierce bite of his verse:

> Emilio smiled, because as once we fared
> Together, through the maniac's dread abode,
> Awed by the dreadful spectacle it showed,
>   My head I bared.

> But if he would in churlish mood go past
> Without salute, all who are short of brain,
> His hat upon his brows well might remain
>   Nailed firm and fast.

> My wont it is to do misfortune grace,
> And without varnish of the Pharisee,
> To trace the working of divine decree
>   In misery's case.

> Before the illustrious dunce whom wait upon
> Obsequious greetings of the servile mass,
> Before fools aping wisdom's mien, I pass
>   Contemptuous on.

In the same metre are the lines addressed to a popular singer, satirising with condensed bitterness the social homage paid him, and the comparative neglect of learning and scholarship. The concluding stanza sums up the ironical lesson of the preceding ones:

> Boys, learning is in vogue, but how insane
> Who money to your schooling would devote.
> 'Tis throat and ear are wanted—ear and throat—
>   Plague take the brain!

One of the most brilliant of Giusti's political satires was

that entitled " King Log," in whom his compatriots had
no difficulty in recognising his own sovereign, the reigning
Grand Duke of Tuscany :

> To King Log the Supine,
>   Who our Frog-land rules over,
> My knees I incline
>   And my head I uncover;
> To him from heav'n lighted
> This ode is indited ;
> Oh sweet and benign
>   Is King Log the Supine.
>
> On his wat'ry estates
>   He crashed down with a spatter,
> For you know wooden pates
>   Ever make the most clatter.
> But soon the noise ended
> And mutely extended,
> For derision a sign,
> Lay King Log the Supine.
>
> But this sight roused the fen
>   To a pitch of distraction,
> " And is this the end then
>   Of a monarch of action ? "
> [Of language with glib use
> Croaked chorus amphibious.]
> " To be hissed from the bog
> Why such fuss, O King Log ?
>
> " Shall a trunk from the grove
>   Be thus crowned to degrade us ?
> 'Tis a blunder of Jove, ·
>   Or a hoax he hath played us ;
> Pack off without fracas
> This Most Serene jackass,
> And dismiss from our bog
> His Inertia, King Log."

The Tuscan Béranger

Hush, hush, all ye fools
   Who declaim with such vigour ;
To reign o'er your pools
   Leave this royal lay-figure.
To empty your purses
Or silence your verses,
To butcher or flog
Is no part of King Log.

The sport of each shift
   Of the currents and breezes,
In his palace adrift,
   He just floats as chance pleases,
The deep leaves unsounded
In statecraft well grounded,
Oh wise and expert
Is King Log the Inert!

For a moment decoyed
   If his head he submerges,
By its lightness up-buoyed,
   See how quick it emerges
In safe high and dryness !
He well is styled Highness,
For the title doth square
With King Log to a hair.

Do ye pine for the lash
   Of a serpent to rouse ye ?
Sleep contented to plash
   In the mud that doth house ye.
O impotent blockheads,
For your toothless sockets
Seems created express
Good King Log's Supineness !

For a nation that teems
   With good things so abundant,
Common sense were it seems
   But a virtue redundant.

> O people discreetest !
> O Prince for them meetest !
> What a pattern fine
> Is King Log the Supine !

The interest of many of Giusti's political satires was necessarily ephemeral, and it is matter of regret that the circumstances of his time should have led him to expend so much of his most brilliant verse on subjects more or less remote from the sympathies of posterity. The piece in which, under the title of "The Boot," he gives an allegorical sketch of the fortunes of his native country, has more historical interest, and we append the first six stanzas as a sample of his lighter vein of sarcasm :

> I am not made of common vulgar leather
>   A hob-nailed boot for rustic sole to press,
> And though I seem rough-hewn and pieced together,
>   Who wrought me was no cobbler ne'ertheless,
> With double sole and uppers stout to aid me
> Through wood and stream, fit for all use he made me.

> Though round me, down from calf to heel doth eddy
>   The humid wave, I spoil not, nor decay,
> Good at the chase, I with the spur am ready,
>   As many and many an ass full well can say.
> A row of thick-set stitching guards and hedges
> My ridgy middle seam and upper edges,

> To draw me on is no light undertaking,
>   Nor every dolt and fool can compass it,
> Indeed a weakly leg I cramp to breaking,
>   And for most limbs am but a sad misfit ;
> None in good sooth is able long to bear me,
> And turn and turn about they mostly wear me.

> I spare you here the wearisome recital
>   Of those who in desire of me have vied,
> But of the few more famous ones, a title
>   Will pick out here and there as chance may guide ;

And tell how upside down and topside under,
They turned me, passed from thief to thief as plunder.

It seems incredible, but once the notion
  I took to gallop off, I know not how,
And coursed with loosened rein o'er earth and ocean,
  But having overdone the pace, I trow,
My balance lost, by my own mass o'erweighted
I toppled o'er, and lay full length prostrated.

Torn by a mighty scrimmage, then I found me,
  And a vast human deluge supervened;
Of tribes come from a thousand miles around me,
  By counsel of a priest, or the foul fiend,
At leg and tassel all made furious snatches,
And cried aloud, "Good luck to whoso catches!"

The poet runs on through twenty-eight stanzas in the
same sportive vein, ending with an aspiration for some
sturdy wearer to appropriate the tattered boot, repair its
damages, and remove the patches that disfigure it.   Thus
the invariable moral of Italian patriotism closes the satire,
pointing its significance as a thinly-veiled protest against
foreign domination.   This piece, in common with many
of his productions, illustrates Giusti's preference for the
homeliest similitudes to point his meaning, or, in his own
language, for "donning the rustic blouse instead of a full-
dress coat to write in, unlike so many others who deck
themselves in a suit of gold lace for the purpose."

  "The rustic blouse," for instance, was donned when
he in the following gay stanzas, called "The Snail,"
celebrated the homely virtues embodied in a type in
which they had never been sung before:

    Here's a health to the Snail!
     Heaven prosper a creature
    Which for merit and modesty
     Might be our teacher.

Star-gazers and builders
   The staircase and spy-glass
Adopted from her,
   For her horns form an eye-glass,
While her shell's corkscrew gyral
Suggested the spiral.
   Here's a health to the Snail!
Whom I bid you admire all.

Content with the comforts
   The gods have provided,
With Diogenes' view
   She has long coincided.
To breathe the fresh air
   From her shell she ne'er issues
Convinced that to gad
   Of her time were a misuse;
Thus shunning diseases
Like snuffles and sneezes.
   Here's a health to the Snail!
Whom her dwelling so pleases.

Leave foreign comestibles
   Of pungent savour
To tickle digestions
   Long dead to home flavour.
She, feeling her organs
   In good working order,
In search of provisions
   Ne'er crosses the border.
But munches in quiet
The herbage close by it.
   Here's a health to the Snail!
Beast of regular diet.

Of conduct and manners
   Few hold the calm tenor,
And more than one ass
   Apes the lion's demeanour:

But she, though a mollusc,
   From nature's own law
Learns in every dilemma
   Her horns to withdraw.
Nor threatens terrific,
But frizzles pacific.
   Here's a health to the Snail!
Of all beasts least horrific.

Dame Nature, with prodigies
   Furnished not sparely,
This privileged creature
   Has gifted most rarely.
Because (executioners
   Listen and wonder)
A new head she grows
   If the old head you sunder.
Fact strange in narration,
But past refutation.
   Here's a health to the Snail
The most blest of creation.

Ye owls stuffed with learning,
   Who set up as preachers,
Though it seems not your fellows
   Learn much from such teachers;
Ye vagabond rovers,
   Bon vivants, scapegraces
Ye masters enraged,
   And ye servants sans places,
I pray sing in chorus,
This refrain sonorous,
   Here's a health to the Snail!
Whose example's before us.

Hatred of artificial disguise was the keynote of Giusti's
character, and his writings are little more than protests in
various forms against all phases of affectation and hypo-
crisy.   His constant aim was that absolute artistic sincerity

which is one of the notes of genius, since it is only to strong
natures that complete power of self-revelation is given,
and the disguises of feebler souls are worn like a pauper's
uniform, rather from poverty than from choice. So in
Greek sculpture gods and heroes stand undraped, while
lesser mortals are clothed in convention and garbed in
formality.   This directness of aim in Giusti is clearly put
in the lines to Girolamo Tommasi, which are throughout
a denunciation of the petty falsities of art :

> My mood 'twixt grave and gay, dear friend, this vein
>   Of semi-serious piebald verse hath caught,
>   Nor can I plane the rough-hewn bark of thought
>   Nor mute remain.
>
> I, too, mistook my cue, and in the heats
>   Of youth, with glance inspired and fervid lip,
>   Paid toll to Petrarch in a noviceship
>   Of amorous bleats.
>
> But on my ear at every instant smote
>   A secret voice from conscience' deep recess,
>   In accents low, but with emphatic stress,
>   " Alter thy note ;
>
> Why fear to show thy form without disguise,
>   And cramp its outlines in a borrowed suit ?
>   Shunning thine image as the senseless brute
>   Its shadow flies.
>
> Ideas which thy thine inner self should gauge
>   Passed thus distorted through the prism of art
>   Faint reflex hues at second hand impart
>   To the dull page."

And farther on he again expounds his motives in adopting
the line marked out for him by the consciousness of his
powers and the necessities of the time :

How blest were I my soul to tranquillise
    If e'er o' o'er softer themes my thoughts might range,
    To scatter flowers and feelings interchange
            In tender guise.

Perish each venal fraud and selfish aim,
    Though with them die my pen's rebuking sneer,
    For my soul sickens at applause bought dear
            By public shame.

But while our necks beneath this yoke are bowed,
    Be our tongues armed with every stinging phrase
    Of savage scorn, 'gainst infamy to raise
            Their protest loud.

I ne'er will pen, so far as I can judge
    Phrases, or feigned, or false, or worldly-wise,
    Or seek as public censure to disguise
            One private grudge.

But farces of our time, things as they are,
    Describing when my pen is in the vein,
    With heaven's good help, my yarn I'll spin in plain
            Vernacular.

Praised be the man who to the end doth wear
    His proper garb, although he may have died
    A very dunce, if his lip ne'er hath lied,
            Oh dunce most rare !

That Giusti's command of the language of tenderness
was not less complete than his mastery of that of satire
is sufficiently proved by the beauty of the lines addressed
to the lady whose faithlessness exercised so baneful an
influence over his life. To this disappointment, as well
as to the increasing development of the satirical side of
his genius, is doubtless due the absence from his works
of a greater number of such effusions.

Little as there is in his writings to recall those of Dante,
he himself ascribes the development of his poetic faculty

to his early and incessant study of the father of Italian
song. One of his first infantine tasks was learning by
heart the story of Ugolino, and the last work that occupied
him up to the hour of his death was a Commentary on
the " Divina Commedia." This essay, though left in a
fragmentary state, ought, if carefully edited and arranged,
to be of considerable literary interest.

It would be difficult to sum up Giusti's career as a whole
better than he himself has done in the sonnet addressed
to Tommaso Grossi in 1841, embodying the epitaph
which he would have chosen for himself, and to which
the unvarying consistency of his life fairly entitles him :

> Behold me, Grossi, aged thirty-five,
>   With my wild oats at last entirely sown,
>   And on my head these strands of silver strown,
> To temper the few follies that survive.
>
> At a less stormy age I now arrive,
>   Half prose, half poetry—to thought now prone,
>   And now to sober mirth.—In part alone
> 'Twill pass, in part amid the human hive.
>
> So downward, at this pace habitual grown,
>   Still humouring the crowd with jest and brag
> Till death shall come to still each word and tone.
>
> Too happy if the long and weary fag
>   Of life's highroad have earned my grave a stone,
> With the inscription, " Faithful to his Flag."

CHAPTER XII

Manzoni and Modern Romanticism

WHEN Alessandro Manzoni died in Milan on May 22, 1873, full of years and honours, the world was momentarily thrilled with the consciousness of having lost the greatest literary figure that had been still a living presence to the existing generation. The last survivor of that race of giants whose task had been to bring literature into harmony with the change in thought effected by the French Revolution, he belonged in truth to an era long past ere the close of his life of eighty-eight years, and was the property of that generation which had seen the Romantic movement inaugurated in Germany by its twin luminaries, Goethe and Schiller, and carried to its culminating-point in English letters by the genius of Walter Scott. But unlike those great leaders, each of whom was but the precursor of a whole army of followers, Manzoni, the founder of Romanticism in Italy, may be said to have epitomised in himself the movement which he headed, and to have created a school comprised in one man, as that man is summed up in one work. The story of that work, as we shall later try to show, throws some light on this unique phenomenon in the history of letters.

While it would be a task of no little nicety to assign to

P

Manzoni his own special niche in the universal temple of fame, that which he occupies in the imaginative literature of his own country is at least easily discernible. Here he is *facile princeps* of all who have appeared since the great cycle opened by Dante was closed on one line of development by Tasso with his great Christian epic, and on another by Ariosto with that other Comedy, which is no longer Divine but Human. And between the humanity of Ariosto, represented, or rather travestied in the aristocracy of knights and ladies, and that of Manzoni, incarnated in the idealised peasant type of Lombardy, yawns a gulf marking the whole interval between mediæval and modern thought, the step from feudalism to democracy. This gap is bridged, indeed, in Italian letters by two strong individualities which loom across it, the one in the guise of an antique Tragic Mask, the other in that of Venetian Harlequin, inspired by the Muse of Comedy. But while Alfieri was the latest avatar of the genius of classicalism, Goldoni, who stripped the conventional mask from the stereotyped quartet of the Italian stage to give free play to the undisguised human features of his actors, symbolised and heralded the era of Romantic literature. In " Le Barufe Chiozote " and his other Venetian comedies, we find for the first time that full sympathy with the lower classes which is the predominant feeling in " I Promessi Sposi." But Italian Romanticism, which thus appealed straight to the heart of the people, drooped and languished, because it commanded no truly national idiom in which to address them.

The problem of Manzoni's career, the half century of silence that followed its splendid fruition, must be referred to the same cause, of which he was himself fully conscious as fettering the free play of his powers. He did not possess by birthright a literary language, and this disability reduced him to artistic dumbness for the latter half of his life.   This was the key at once to the barrenness with which his genius was stricken, and to the scantiness of the Italian contribution to Romantic literature down to the present time.

Like most great artists, he received in early childhood the impressions most vividly stamped upon his future work.   Racy of the soil he sprang from, foreign culture could never efface or supersede the ineffaceable memories of rural Lombardy in which his mind was steeped. Descended from a family of old but untitled provincial nobility, he had among his own ancestors, the lords of Barzio in the Valsassina, types of those petty tyrants whose misdeeds he has held up to execration for all time.   A local proverb compares their turbulence to that of the mountain torrent, and Massimo d'Azeglio, when travelling in the district, learned a trait that might have been added to the portrait of Don Rodrigo himself. It seems that the code of Barzio required that the chieftain's dog should share in the homage paid to the family, and the peasants were expected humbly to doff their hats to him with the formula, "Reverissi scior cà," "Your servant, Mister dog."

The only child of an ill-assorted marriage, Manzoni was born when his father, Don Pietro, was about fifty. His mother, Giulia, daughter of Cesare Beccaria, the well-known economist and author, was considerably younger, and no sympathy in tastes counterbalanced the disparity in years.   The dissensions of the pair ended in a virtual separation, Donna Giulia making Auteuil, near Paris, he rprincipal abode, and resumingher maiden name.

At the time of the poet's birth, on March 7, 1785,

the family had long been settled at Lecco on Lake Como, where his father owned a good deal of property, including the beautiful villa of Il Caleotto, his usual summer residence.   In Alessandro Manzoni's features the peasant type of Lecco was so exactly reproduced, that his friends, walking through its streets in later years, were often disposed to stop and exclaim at the likenesses of him they met.   He received his earliest impressions of life in the house of a peasant, where, in accordance with the custom of the time, he was put out to nurse.   Here in the farmhouse of La Costa, one of those rambling buildings with tiled roofs and small windows which stud the maize fields of Lombardy, the poet, amid the hills round Como, so familiar to his readers, imbibed that sympathy with outdoor life and rustic nature which is the dominant motive of his romance.   His foster-mother, Caterina, wife of Carlo Spreafico, a lively little brunette, is generally supposed to have been the original model of Lucia, but many separate impressions probably converged in that ideal type of simple womanhood.   Caterina was a good story-teller, and in the dusk of winter evenings would often entertain her small audience, including her baby charge, "Lisandrino," with many a tale of peasant lore.

The next picture of our poet is as a very small boy, sobbing inconsolably in the corridor of a monastery, where the unexpected disappearance of his mother left him alone among strangers.   Thus at six years old, in sore tribulation of heart, he began his school life at the College of the Somaschi Fathers at Merate.   His impressions of this, and of other schools where he was sent later, were none of the pleasantest; he had little appetite for books and much for food, and the provision was far more ample for satisfying the former than the latter. The cravings of an organism destined to last in working order for close on ninety years were doubtless exorbitant, for even in his father's house "Lisandro" often found the fare insufficient, and the good-natured cook, Antonio, would sometimes supplement the regular meals to which Don Pietro restricted his son's appetite with contraband snacks of bread and cheese at odd moments. His vacations at Il Caleotto were bright spots in his school life, and his days passed pleasantly in quail-netting among the hills or in setting miniature water-wheels in the streams. One memorable walk in company with a servant deserves to be recorded, for the man took him to the Capuchin Convent of Pescarènico, the same which his readers know so well as the residence of Fra Cristoforo. The place and scene sunk deep into the boy's imagination, for the convent chapel was full of music and lights for the afternoon service, and one of the friars singled out their young visitor to take part in their devotions by giving him a taper to hold, little dreaming how long that trifling incident would be remembered.

Meantime the brain that was so busy storing up raw material for the imagination to work on was sluggish in other exercises, and the boy was often in disgrace with his teachers for idleness or stupidity. On one occasion while doing public penance in the middle of the room he saw a companion taking advantage of his misfortune to rifle his desk, and was detected in an attempt at mute protest against the invasion of his property by a series of grimaces and contortions. A sharp box on the ear from the master brought him to a sense of his position, and taught a truth illustrated later in his novel, that authority, while often remiss in protecting the rights of the unfortunate, is never behindhand in repressing their efforts at self-redress. Some of Renzo's experiences of the law and its interpreters may have had their germ in this incident of schoolboy life.

Released from the restraints of school at fifteen, and turned loose on the temptations of city life, he was saved only by the interposition of a friend from being ensnared by them in one of their most alluring forms. He was in the habit of frequenting the Ridotto, or public gaming-table, and here the elder poet, Vincenzo Monti, found him one evening absorbed in play. His remonstrance proved efficacious, and the boy having promised to eschew the fatal habit, went home to tell his mother of his resolution. She applauded it, and proposed a trip to Paris to facilitate adherence to it. "No," he said, "I should deserve no credit in that case, for I should not have conquered myself. On the contrary, I will go to the Ridotto every evening and look on without playing." He did so, and at the end of a month came triumphantly out of the perilous ordeal, cured for life of the fatal passion which had so nearly drawn him into its vortex.

A great historic pageant, Napoleon's triumphal entry into Milan, was witnessed by the boy-poet in 1800. He assisted, too, at the state performance in his honour at La Scala in the box of a lady, the Countess Cicognara, who had made herself conspicuous by her denunciations of the French. The First Consul, well aware of this, focussed the lightnings of his eyes on her through the evening as though he wished to fulminate her. The unnoted schoolboy in the back of the box watched, wondered, remembered, till, when, after the lapse of twenty years the victor of Marengo died as the solitary exile of St. Helena he concentrated the impressions of that evening into one line of immortal verse. "What eyes that man had!" he exclaimed once as he recalled the incident towards the close of his life, and on another occasion he acknowledged that it had inspired the celebrated line in his ode.

The next scene of Manzoni's life was laid at Auteuil, where he went to reside on his father's death in 1805. Here mother and son moved in the small but select literary clique of philosophers modelled on those of the eighteenth century, and contemptuously styled by Napoleon the "Idéologues." It comprised such men as Volney the sceptic, Cabanis the materialist-doctor, and Claude Fauriel, who, despite his own fame as a philologist and critic, will be best known to posterity from his share in forming the mind of the young Milanese, with whom he formed a lifelong friendship.

Manzoni's courtship, at twenty-two, of Henriette Blondel, the sixteen-year old, blue-eyed daughter of a Genevese banker, inaugurated his happy married life of twenty-five years. His marriage in February 1808 was in more ways than one the turning-point of his mental history, since it led unexpectedly to his conversion to the Catholic faith, which he and his mother had abandoned for the sceptical opinions held by the set they moved in. The first impulse came from his newly-wedded bride, who, coming under Catholic influences in Paris on her wedding trip, was converted to that faith from the Reformed Evangelical creed in which she had been brought up. All her efforts were then directed to winning her husband from infidelity, and some biographers assert that she even threatened to leave him if he remained unconvinced. A painful struggle then arose in his mind, which, after months of anxious perplexity, resulted in his full and entire adoption of the Catholic faith. On the subject of this momentous change he always maintained a strict reserve, and its history was never revealed by him to any one. A profound sense of humility was the principal moral residuum of his phase of scepticism, and he was once heard to declare that he believed his life to have been exceptionally prolonged in order that he might continue to acknowledge and deplore the errors of his youth. It is remarkable that "I Promessi Sposi" contains two instances of sudden conversion, those of "Fra Cristoforo" and the "Innominato," no doubt in some degree suggested by his own experience.

His religious and artistic convictions were arrived at simultaneously, for from the same period of his life dates his definitive abandonment of the principles of classicalism for those of the Romantic school. With the bent of his mind thus formed and settled he left Paris in 1810, and took up his abode at Brusuglio, a villa belonging to his mother, where his life for many ensuing years was a domestic idyll, diversified by family interests and country pursuits. Financial embarrassments, due to the malversations of a dishonest agent, were found in 1818 to have necessitated the sale of his father's property, with the villa of Il Caleotto, associated with the memories of his boyhood. It was in accordance with his unfailing sympathy with the lower orders that, on finding his peasants hopelessly indebted to the estate, he drew his pen through the accounts and wiped out all arrears by a universal act of grace.

The period of his literary activity was comprised in the six years from 1819 to 1825, the thirty-fourth and fortieth of his age. The remainder of his life was that of a quiet country gentleman, much occupied with rural pursuits, the rearing of silkworms, and grafting of olive and mulberry trees.   Although never a conspirator himself against Austrian rule, he was on terms of intimate friendship with those who were, and narrowly escaped being implicated in the movement of 1821, through the imprudence of one of its leaders in offering him a place in the provisional government.   On the incorporation of Lombardy with the newly formed kingdom of Italy in 1859 he was nominated Senator, but never took any active part in politics.

The latter half of his life was saddened by a series of domestic misfortunes, beginning with the loss of his wife on Christmas Day 1833.   The death in the ensuing year of his eldest daughter, Giulia, married to Massimo d'Azeglio, was followed by that of his mother and another daughter in 1841, and out of nine children born to him only two survived him.   Among his most intimate friends was Tommaso Grossi, his fellow-poet and novelist, who lived under his roof for years, and held the place of a younger brother in his affections.   When Grossi's marriage dissolved this close companionship, Manzoni filled the blank in his life by a second marriage to Donna Teresa Stampa, a widow with a grown-up son, who made him an attached and devoted wife, while her son, Count Stefano Stampa, was unremitting in his attentions to his step-father, who thenceforward spent most of his time at the beautiful villa of Lesa on the Lago Maggiore.

The brilliant verses of Giusti had early attracted the attention of the Lombard poet, who saw in them " a new glory for Italy," and he was drawn into intimate personal relations with him in 1845, through the Tuscan poet's meeting with Vittorina Manzoni in company with his friend Giorgini, who afterwards married her. A life-long friendship resulted from his stay of a month under Manzoni's hospitable roof at this time.

The inevitable solitariness of old age came upon Manzoni in the successive deaths of friends and rela-tives. Giusti died in 1851, Grossi in 1853, and he was left for the second time a widower in 1861. Yet even after so many griefs it was reserved for him to die of a broken heart at eighty-eight, and taste a crowning sorrow on the verge of the grave. On April 28, 1873, his eldest son, Pier Luigi, his constant companion, counsellor, and caretaker, who had filled the place of so many dear ones lost, died at the age of sixty. A sad picture is that presented by biographers after his death, of the bereaved old man, wandering through his desolate house, calling vainly for his son, or holding imaginary conversations with him, unable to realise his loss. Weakened by a fall coming out of church during the previous winter, he rapidly succumbed under the added strain of mental suffering, and died of cerebral meningitis within a month of his son, on Ascension Day, May 22, 1873.

The almost regal obsequies in which the national grief and veneration found expression formed a strange contrast to the simple life of the unpretending poet. Florence would have claimed his dust, to lay with that of her illustrious dead in Santa Croce, but his family preferred that it should rest in the cemetery of his native city. The remains, after lying in state for two days in the Municipal Palace, visited by thousands of his fellow-citizens, were escorted to the grave by a magnificent *cortège*, comprising the Princes of the Royal House, the great officers of State, and delegations from the Italian municipalities. But the most fitting tribute to his memory was Verdi's Requiem Mass, the splendid homage of art to art, of genius to its fellow.

In Manzoni's character we find no trace of the strange moral dualism, the perplexing discord between the author's life and his works, which so often startles us in the records of literature. He wrote loftily because he felt nobly, and there is no note, through the whole gamut of emotion struck in his works, that had not been sounded in his own heart. Manzoni may be called the laureate of justice, which is the protagonist of his muse, as love is of that of other poets. The strongest motive force in his nature was the hatred of injustice, and though the most pacific of men, he was capable, at sight of it, of being roused to something like a paroxysm of fury. "Porci di sciori!" [Pigs of gentry!] he once exclaimed with flashing eyes, in language of untranslatable vituperation, when walking in his old age through the streets of Milan, he saw a carriage nearly drive over an old woman, covering her with mud as it passed. His great romance, though, like all true art, it points its moral without obtruding it, is from title-page to finish a protest against the oppression of the weak by the strong, of the helpless by the tyrannical great.

His three larger works form a trilogy, each hinging on a leading idea, referable to so many stages of Italian history. "Il Conte di Carmagnola" is directed against civil discords, the curse of Italy in the past; "Adelchi" against foreign domination, her bane in his own time; while in "I Promessi Sposi" looms up more dimly the question of the future, not for Italy alone, but for the world—the aspirations of the masses for enfranchisement and equality. Thus drama is ever with him the vehicle for social speculation. In the two first works, the author's protest is spoken by a chorus of the people, while in the third it finds no distinct articulate utterance, but forms the motive underlying the whole plot. In the former there is a conflict of sympathy, as the sentiment thus conveyed jars with the direct action, and runs counter to the interest centred in the main actors.

Francesco Bussano, the principal figure of the first piece, produced in 1819, is an historical character, who, born at Carmagnola in 1390, in the condition of a shepherd-boy, rose to eminence as a soldier of fortune in the service of Filippo Maria Visconti. This prince, whose power he was mainly instrumental in consolidating, became jealous of him for that very reason, and by a variety of affronts disgusted him with his service, and drove him to enter that of Venice. The tragedy opens with the war against his former employer, in which he is at first victorious. His clemency in releasing the prisoners and his slackness in pursuit of the foe excite suspicions of double dealing, and after a series of intrigues he is inveigled to Venice and executed as a traitor by order of the suspicious government of the Republic. The drama follows literally the historical facts save in deciding in favour of its hero the doubtful point of his innocence. Its subject recalls that of "Wallenstein," which may have suggested it. Despite two fine scenes, in one of which Carmagnola orders the release of the prisoners in defiance of the Venetian commissioners, and in the other takes leave of his wife and daughter on the eve of his execution, the drama is deficient in interest as a whole. It wants the organic vitality derived from a culminating point of action, and resembles too nearly narrative in dialogue.

The chorus, interpolated at the end of the second act and put into the mouths of supposed spectators of the battle, traverses the general current of the action, which has a soldier of fortune as its chief exponent.   Fine as a lyric, it is dramatically irrelevant, and contrasts in this respect with Max Piccolomini's splendid panegyric on peace in "Wallenstein," where, as springing from his newly-born love for Thekla, it is artistically justified by its connection with the main thread of the plot.   The writer of an article on "Italian Tragedy" in the *Quarterly Review* for December 1820, though generally unfavourable to the author, calls this chorus "the most noble piece of Italian lyric poetry which the present day has produced," and subjoins a translation of it *in extenso*.

The subject of "Adelchi" is likewise taken from Italian history, and is furnished by the invasion of Charlemagne and overthrow of the Lombard monarchy in 772–74. Adelchi, or Adalgiso, is a Lombard prince who performs prodigies of valour in defending the kingdom of his father, Desiderio, holding the invaders at bay at Le Chiuse, a line of impregnable fortifications stretching across the head of the Val di Susa.   The Franks are on the point of abandoning the enterprise in despair, when an emissary of the Pope arrives in their camp by untrodden paths over the mountains, and leads them by the same route to the rear of the Lombard position. The feelings of the enslaved Latins on witnessing the subsequent rout of their oppressors are described in the chorus, which is thus open to the same criticism as that in "Carmagnola" of awaking a strain of sympathy opposed to that felt for the hero, Adelchi.   Its effect in the original depends very much on the rhythm, difficult to reproduce in English, and suggestive at once of weight

and swiftness, like the moving thunder of galloping
horse : *

> From moss-covered arches of ruins commanding,
> From woods, from loud forges in ashes now standing,
>> From the furrow bedewed with the sweat of the slave,
> A people dispersed doth arouse and awaken,
> With senses all straining and pulses all shaken,
>> At a sound of strange clamour that swells like a wave.

> In visages pallid and eyes of dull seeming,
> Like sunlight through cloud masses suddenly gleaming,
>> The might of their fathers a moment is seen ;
> In eyes and in visages doubtfully blending,
> The shame of the present seems struggling, contending,
>> With pride in the thought of a past that hath been.

> 'Tis the lost Latin race, that by barbarous numbers
> Subdued and defeated, the soil still encumbers
>> Where triumphed their fathers ; and helpless and weak,
> As a flock given o'er to each spoiler voracious,
> By the pitiless Goth to the Herule rapacious,
>> To the wandering Lombard is left by the Greek.

> Now they gather in hope, to disperse panic-stricken,
> And by tortuous paths their pace slacken or quicken,
>> As, 'twixt longing and fear, they advance or stand still,
> Gazing once and again, where despairing and shattered,
> The host of their tyrants flies broken and scattered
>> The wrath of the swords that are drinking their fill.

> But hark ye ! those brave ones their leaguer thus holding,
> And from hope of escape your oppressors enfolding,
>> By paths steep and rugged have come from afar ;
> Forsaking the scenes of their festive carousing,
> From downy repose of soft couches arousing,
>> In haste to obey the shrill summons of war.

---

* A translation of this chorus, in which Dr. Garnett colla-
borated, has been published in his " Italian Literature," but it is
taken from a different version, and some of the stanzas here given
are omitted.

In their castles they left their fair wives broken-hearted,
Who, while striving to part, still refused to be parted
  'Mid repeated farewells choked by tears as they flowed ;
With war-dinted helmets on brows closely fitted,
In haste their dark chargers they saddled and bitted,
  And rushed o'er the drawbridge that clanged as they rode.

And deem ye, oh fools! that the meed and the guerdon
These warriors hope, is to lighten the burden,
  The woes of a people to soothe and allay ?
If such the desire with these heroes that pleaded,
This pompous array and these toils were unneeded,
  Unneeded the perils and pains of the way.

For they too are lords of a people degraded,
Condemned to the soil by their victors invaded,
  Or crowded in dens of the cities they've lost ;
Had the lip of the victor one word only spoken,
The yoke of those slaves had been riven and broken,
  The lip of the victor that word ne'er hath crost.

Then turn ye again to your ruins yet stately,
To peaceable toil in the workshops quenched lately,
  To the furrow bedewed with the sweat of the slave ;
Draw closer ye yoke-fellows bound in one tether,
And speak of your hopes in hushed whispers together,
  Sleep happy in error, in dreams fondly rave.

To-morrow ye'll learn, to fresh sorrow awaking,
That the victors, their rage 'gainst the vanquished forsaking
  Have granted a peace which your tyrants doth save ;
That both reign in common, the booty dividing,
Clasp hands and pledge faith, while unchanged and abiding
  In name and condition are master and slave.

The treachery of the Lombard chiefs during the sieges of
Pavia and Verona occupy the succeeding acts, working
up to the conclusion of the tragedy in the captivity of
Desiderio and death of Adelchi, who in reality escaped
to Constantinople. The woes of his sister Ermengarda,

divorced by Charlemagne and dying of a broken heart,
interweave an element of romance with the historical
events, but are almost extraneous to the rest of the
action. Her delirious ravings on hearing of his marriage
with her rival Ildegarda end with the following lines :

> Oh, were it but a dream ! which in the dawn
> Should melt in mist, whence, drowned in troubled tears,
> I might awake to find my Charles still near,
> And hear him ask the cause, and with a smile,
> For lack of faith upbraid me.

Despite many fine passages, the interest of the drama is
marred by its want of concentration, the action being
prolonged over a battle and two sieges. Manzoni's
dramatic power was far inferior to his lyrical gift, but it
is his prose that has made him immortal. Here he has
perhaps never been surpassed in his power of calling up
by a few simple words pictures that live in the reader's
memory for ever, like fragments of his own actual experience. The pages of " I Promessi Sposi" are strewn
with such vignettes, where a whole scene is suggested by
a few touches ; now landscapes, like Renzo's overgrown
and deserted vineyard, or the village sleeping in the
moonlight ; now interiors, like Don Ferrante's library or
the convent parlour at Monza. Amid these minor gems
of genre painting, great tragic scenes, such as the plague-
stricken city, the Lazzaretto of Milan, or the castle of the
" Innominato," stand out in solemn perspective like the
larger features of a landscape overshadowing the minute
details of the foreground.

In his character-drawing Manzoni has a like equality
of touch, and the slight sketches of the minor personages
of his tale have the same masterly finish relatively to
scale as the great historical portraits of Cardinal

Borromeo and the "Innominato," in right of which he may take rank as the Titian of literature. The very supernumeraries of the piece, represented in other works by the veriest lay figures, never flit across his stage without leaving some trace of their individuality; and even the garrulous convent porter, who only speaks once as he opens the door for Lucia's mother, is as vital as the noble figure of Fra Cristoforo himself. Yet Manzoni's detail is never trivial, nor his homeliness vulgar, for we have in him the true artistic discrimination whose end is always so perfectly attained as to justify its means, however ordinary.

We have seen how he rises to his highest rhetorical level in his tragedies when interpreting in lyrical form the feelings of a multitude, and in his romance this power is more fully displayed in his manipulation of masses of men, swayed by a common impulse, yet composed of discordant and incongruous element. On these separate units he never loses his grasp, and while combining them in single action, puts before us that multiple personality of a crowd whose corporate volition is the incalculable sum of many varying individual motives. The aimless surging of the human tide, stirred by contrary currents of opinion, the power of blind caprices working on many minds in common, the compound potentialities of a multitude, have never been so thoroughly realised as in the description of the bread-riot at Milan and the mob-siege of the Forno alle Grucce.

On the tumultuous background of this angry multitude Manzoni paints with masterly touches the portrait of the old courtier, Antonio Ferrer, as he shows at his carriage window "that face of humble, complaisant, obsequious benignity which he had hitherto reserved for those

Q

occasions on which he found himself in the presence of his master, Don Philip IV., but was now obliged to expend in propitiating the furious mob of Milan."

The helpless and bewildered crowd of villagers roused by the night alarm, the gathering knots in the streets of Milan, "like the scattered clouds which, chasing across the sky after a storm, make people look up and shake their heads, saying, 'The weather is not settled,'" all such aggregations of human atoms are described by him with like vivacity and force, while they never unduly distract the attention from the main action and the principal personages. This power of grouping masses of men seems to be a typical characteristic of Manzoni's genius, and was doubtless derived from that philosophical tendency of his mind which balanced his poetic temperament and gave him the power of regarding humanity in its social as well as in its individual aspects.

Manzoni's first lyrical productions were a collection of " Inni Sacri," or hymns for the various feasts of the ecclesiastical year, composed during that phase of his life following his marriage when all his writings were religious, as a reparation for his period of apostasy. They were surpassed in fame by his great ode " Il Cinque Maggio," written on learning the news of the death of Napoleon at St. Helena on May 5, 1821. It ranks as the most popular lyric in Italy, and justifies the dictum of Goethe in a preface to an edition of Manzoni's works published at Jena in 1827, that lyrical poetry is the highest form of rhetoric, and that he knew of no modern poet so qualified to excel in it as this author. Translated into German by Goethe and Paul Heyse, and imitated in French by Lamartine, this tribute to a hero's memory has tempted the greatest masters of other countries to essay its reproduction, which is rendered difficult by the dependence of the original for its effect on the interchange of the three different forms of accentuation in Italian, in which it is placed on the ultimate, penultimate, and antepenultimate syllables as in città, dolore, and trèmolo. For these rhythmical effects a greater frequency of rhyme is perhaps the best English substitute, which, with the retention of the form of the stanza, may give the effect of the versification. A German critic, Herr Sauer, compares the opening phrase, "Ei fu," to the initial bars of a great symphony preluding the solemnity of its strain.

> He was—and is not—without sign
>   Its latest breathings heaved,
> Lies the once mighty clay supine
>   Of such a soul bereaved.
> While earth as pulseless, stricken dumb,
>   The tidings hath received,
> And muses on the latest hour
>   Of him—the man of fate—
> Nor knows if to the blood-stained power
>   Of mortal tread as great.
> In all the ages yet to come
>   Her dust shall palpitate.
>
> Glitt'ring in royal state—adored—
>   I saw him—and was mute ;
> Next with swift change o'erthrown—restored—
>   Last trampled under foot :
> While thousand-voiced acclaimed the throng,
>   My Muse spake no salute,
> By servile praise and cow'rdly taunt
>   That fallen glory strips
> Alike unstained, she wakes to chant
>   So bright a star's eclipse,
> And to his urn one deathless song
>   Now pours from virgin lips.

The Alps and Pyramids alike,
  The Tagus and the Rhine,
Have seen his bolts of thunder strike,
  His lurid lightnings shine,
He burst where Don and Scylla roll,
  And blazed from brine to brine ;
Was this true glory—wherefore ask ?
  To after ages leave
The arduous sentence—ours the task
  The image to perceive,
Whereof the Maker willed his soul
  Should largest stamp receive.

The stormy nature's rapturous thrill
  In great designs conceived —
The heart's unrest that nought could still
  Till empire was achieved ;
And grasped the prize in which before
  But madness had believed.
All—all he tasted—boast of fame
  Enhanced as danger's prize—
The victor's crown—flight's bitter shame—
  The throne—the exile's sighs—
Twice o er to dust abased—twice o'er
  Exalted to the skies.

His name was heard when armed for strife
  Two warring centuries,
Clashed in a jar with discords rife,
  Yet hung on his decrees,
As arbiter he spoke their fate,
  And hushed them at his knees.
He fell—to wear out empty days—
  Hedged by a narrow isle ;
A mark for envy's rabid gaze—
  Compassion's pitying smile—
For inextinguishable hate,
  And love nought could beguile.

As o'er some shipwrecked wretch the surge
    Sweeps with o'erwhelming might,
In waves which late from verge to verge
    He scanned with straining sight,
Still hoping in the futile quest
    On distant shores to light ;
So on that soul with gathered weight
    Did tides of memory roll,
And oft he purposed to narrate
    His deeds—and oft the scroll
To all futurity addrest
    From his tired fingers stole.

And oft, as to still twilight paled
    Day's apathetic rest,
He stood, his meteor glances veiled,
    Arms folded on his breast,
By crowding memories assailed
    Of all that life held best ;
Rehearsing how the tents rose fair,
    'Mid echoing vales and meads,
The gleam of arms in serried square,
    The surge of charging steeds,
And swift commands to which ne'er failed
    Fulfilment of swift deeds.

Ah ! by such bitter grief unmanned,
    His spirit had been driven
To dark despair, had not a hand
    In mercy stretched from Heaven.
Shown regions where to wing its way
    To the soul's flight is given ;
And led him on to pathways bright
    With hope that never ends,
Through fields eternal, to delight
    That all desire transcends ;
Where darkling dies the fleeting ray
    That earthly glory sends.

Oh Faith! immortal, blest, benign,
   Proclaim thy triumphs loud,
Add to their record one more line,
   For never soul so proud
To the mysterious shame divine
   Of Golgotha hath bowed.
Nor let reproach for earthly fault
   His weary dust offend,
The God who humbles to exalt—
   Chastises to befriend—
Did to his dying couch incline
   To bless his lonely end.

The fame attained by these spirited stanzas, which, written off in the emotion of the moment, have all the verve of improvisation, astonished no one more than their author, who declared long afterwards that he was quite unprepared " for the hit made by that ode, full of Gallicisms and Latinisms." It established him at once in the position of the first lyric poet in Italy, yet was followed by no other effort in the same line.

But the debt of Italian literature to Manzoni cannot be measured by the mass, nor even by the merit of his work. It lay in the fact that he first, by a stupendous effort, moulded the language in which he wrote to what was practically a new creation of Italian prose in a form adapted to the exigencies of modern letters. For it must be borne in mind that from the fourteenth to the nineteenth century it had been written by but one master, Machiavelli, while in fiction it had been untried from the " Decameron " to " I Promessi Sposi." The novel, which in England and France had had a long pedigree, and a gradual progress to perfection, sprung in Italy full grown from the brain of Manzoni, in a masterpiece un-approached by his successors. He thus produced an absolutely new form of literature in what was practically a new language, written by an extraordinary *tour de force*, and coined as he went along.

For it had been the fate of the idiom of his country to be used in letters as an artificial convention, from the time of fourteenth-century writers, by whom it was first forged as an instrument of culture out of the raw material of the spoken dialect, through the long line of their followers, who, aiming at imitating them, kept it in a state of pupilage, cut off from its vital spring in the life of the people. Deprived thus of all power of growth or expansion, it was reduced to a mere literary *argot*, a fit vehicle for the utterances of scholiasts and pedants, but not for the expression of human emotion. The laws by which its bondage were enforced were of a puerility inconceivable to foreigners, while their violation was punished by literary ostracism. Meanwhile in Tuscany alone was it spoken in a familiar form, while throughout the rest of Italy provincial dialects were the means of oral communication even among the educated classes. The literary language, indeed, was and is learned by the cultured as matter of education, but remains scarcely less remote from their daily thoughts than Latin from those of an accomplished Englishman.

Down to Manzoni's time, the principal staples of literature, poetry and drama, abstract treatises and historical works, were of a nature to be written with more or less difficulty out of dictionaries and vocabularies. With a novel, the principal creation of Romanticism, the case is different, since, dealing with everyday life in its familiar aspect, it requires the command of familiar expression such as is learned, in Giusti's phrase, " only from the living dictionary on two legs." How in Italian to attain such a form of utterance was the problem which occupied Manzoni's thoughts all through his career. He sought to solve it by grafting the dead branch of literary convention on the growing trunk of the spoken idiom of Tuscany, substituting the *uso fiorentino*, the living custom of Florence, for all the rules of grammars and vocabularies as the highest standard of philological fitness. This linguistic revolution was the main work of his life, carried out at such cost of pains and labour as I shall endeavour to show. And if his followers have gone to too great lengths in the same direction, adopting into the written language all manner of *fiorentinerie*, the very slang of the Florentine hucksters, the Billingsgate of the Mercato Nuovo, it is no more than has befallen the work of all reformers, social, political, and literary alike. How early the problem of language presented itself to Manzoni's mind, may be gathered from the following passage in Sainte-Beuve describing his discussions with Fauriel when about one-and-twenty :

" But the latter [Manzoni] amid his hopes felt some bitterness of heart. Well aware that poetry can only correspond to its original aim when rooted in social and popular life, he readily perceived that Italy, from many causes, was here excluded from her natural destiny. Her political subdivisions, the want of a common centre, inertia, ignorance, local pretensions, had created a profound discrepancy between the spoken and written tongue. The latter had, by deliberate choice of those who used it, become a dead language, and could not appeal to the different populations with direct and immediate efficacy. And thus, by a singular contradiction, the first condition of the existence of a pure and simple language of poetry

in Italy was that it should found itself upon artifice.
Manzoni was early alive to the gravity of this difficulty,
and even perhaps exaggerated it.   He could not see
without envy mixed with admiration the whole population
of Paris applauding Molière's comedies.   The intelligent
and direct contact of an entire people with the masterpieces of genius, while he felt it to be the true touch-
stone of the vitality of the latter, must, he declared, be
denied to a country like Italy, parcelled out into a number
of dialects.   He who was destined one day to unite all
the lofty minds of his country in a common sentiment of
admiration, did not then believe such unanimity possible,
or grieved that at any rate it could not be based upon
the comprehension of the public at large.   Fauriel
encouraged him with his authority, citing to him many
illustrious examples, even among Italian writers, and re-
minding him that all had more or less to struggle with
difficulties of the same kind."

These difficulties are further aggravated for the poet
by the severity of the code of the Italian Parnassus, where
the most severe restrictions on the use of language pre-
vail.   This limitation of the vocabulary must sometimes
induce considerable modification of poetical ideas, as
the deficiencies of a traveller's phrase-book sometimes
affects his choice of viands, and compel him in default
of a word for " roast-beef " to content himself with roast
mutton.   It may be suspected that in this sense there is
a good deal of poetical roast mutton in Italian literature.

But the limitation of the ideas treated in poetry renders
possible a corresponding limitation of language, while in
prose no such narrowing of the field is practicable.   Here
the literary banquet is of the most miscellaneous character,

calling into play all the resources of the *menu*, and re-
quiring the most homely comestibles to be duly named
and ticketed.

Now Manzoni's position on entering the field of letters
was this. He had no full command of any literary
language, writing Italian as one does a foreign tongue or
dead language, while the natural expression of his thoughts
was in Milanese dialect. So entirely was this the case,
that, having once published a prefatory treatise on the
drama in what passed as very fair French, he declares
that he found it far easier to write that language than
Italian. And in an appendix to his report on the Unity
of the Language he describes the difficulties attendant
on the composition of " I Promessi Sposi " as having
been such as " would move to pity," giving a vivid
picture of his blind groping in his memory and in books
for the Italian equivalents for phrases, which, presenting
themselves in dialect, or in Latin, or in a foreign language,
had to be " driven away like temptations."

The work written under these difficulties shows evident
traces of poverty of language, especially in its opening
chapters. The style, indeed, is always forcible from the
innate vigour of the ideas expressed; but they seem
rather to force the language to fit them than to be
naturally and easily clothed with it; and the effect produced is like that of one of Michael Angelo's great unfinished statues, in which the original energy of the
conception struggles through the rough-hewn block,
despite its want of finer shaping. Manzoni was himself
so keenly alive to this imperfection of his work that he
undertook a laborious course of study to enable him to
correct it. In this arduous task, which he called " giving
his rags a rinse in Arno," he sometimes spent, as he

tells us, days in search of a single word, gleaning chance phrases "from those who possessed them by right of birth." He was assisted by two Tuscan authors, Giambattista Niccolini and Gaëtano Cioni, and the identity of their corrections was an argument of the necessity for the changes proposed.

The result of these labours was the revised and Tuscanised edition of " I Promessi Sposi," published serially in 1840–42. The critics were by no means agreed at first as to what now seems the evident improvement, and even Giusti, the living vocabulary of racy Tuscan idiom, who boasted that he " wrote by ear," as untutored musicians sing and play, instead of ransacking dictionaries and going on reproducing " the ink of ink," was only converted to approval of the change in a scene described by Manzoni in a letter to Alfonso delle Valle di Casanuova :

"Giusti, in one of those familiar colloquies which are to me now at once a dear remembrance and a sad regret, said to me one day: 'What notion is this that has come into your head of making all these changes in your novel? For my part I liked it better as it was.' 'Giusti though you are,' thought I to myself, 'and on your own ground, you are out for once, and but let me only have you at my mercy, and I will make you sing another song.' So I said in reply : 'To explain the why and the wherefore of it all would tire out my lungs, to say nothing of your ears, but if your curiosity holds, I think that by a short experiment among us three (my son-in-law, Bista Giorgini, was present) we shall be able to come to an understanding. Let us take the two editions, open one at random, look out the corresponding place in the other; you two read some passages aloud, and where differences occur, judge for yourselves.' No sooner said than done. Giusti took up his *protégé*, and as he read, it was evident that he mouthed some phrases and expressions like a man trying a dish and finding a strange taste in it. Then, as he heard the variations read, the involuntary changes of his face plainly said, ' Ah, that is so,' and sometimes he would let fall under his breath a muttered ' That's right.' But lo and behold ! after a few sentences he stumbled upon one, long, involved, and intricate, ' Nexantem nodis, seque in sua membra plicantem,' like the serpent in Virgil's, as usual, magnificent simile ; and as he concluded it with evidently growing disgust, he burst out with, ' Oh, what a dreadful hodgepodge !' But, before the words were well out of his lips, he stopped awkward and mortified, I do not know whether for having given me too great a triumph or for some other cause ; but on hearing me burst out laughing, and on seeing on my face a look of great satisfaction, he rallied from his embarrassment and exclaimed, pointing his finger at me, 'See how pleased he is !' ' What ?' said I, ' do you think it nothing to have got you to contradict yourself so flagrantly !' The re-formed sentence was read, and it ran so smoothly, and extricated itself so completely from its involutions, that it restored us all three to our literary equilibrium."

It seems not unlikely that, in this want of a ready-made medium of expression, we have the clue to the otherwise unexplained mystery of Manzoni's cessation from literary labour when in the prime of life and vigour, as well as of the comparative sterility of Italian Romanticism subsequently, down even to the present day. The language is not yet nationalised ; seems, indeed, almost as far as ever from being so, and literary productiveness during the transition stage is not to be looked for.   " I Promessi Sposi " was written by a herculean effort, such as required, perhaps, the first vigour of the author's mind, and would scarcely be repeated after the initial impulse of his creative genius had spent itself.   It thus remains the unapproached masterpiece and monument of a whole epoch of letters.

Manzoni's difficulty in writing Italian extended even to the most ordinary correspondence, and is a sufficient explanation of the scantiness of his epistolary remains. Even in his old age the simplest letter was a matter of study, undergoing corrections innumerable, and only appearing in presentable shape when copied for the third time.   The letters thus produced are often models of simple expression, little suggestive of the pains bestowed on them.   One, addressed as a letter of introduction to Grossi, deserves to be quoted as an epigram :

'DEAR TOMMASO,—The bearer of this is one of the many who desire to make your acquaintance, and of the few who deserve it.

"ALESSANDRO MANZONI."

The comparison between Scott and Manzoni is the more inevitable, as the latter owned to having followed in the footsteps of his Scotch prototype.   "Then 'I Promessi Sposi' is my best work," said Scott on receiving this admission from its author, whom he once visited at his house in Milan.   The careers of the two great romance-writers offered, indeed, some parallels and many divergencies.   Both spoke as their vernacular a rude though forcible provincial idiom, yet attained such mastery over the literary languages of their respective countries as to produce in them works which are their chiefest glories. Both excelled alike in poetry and prose, yet attained their highest level in the latter. Both were keen students of history, and brought minute antiquarian research to furnish the raw material for their creative genius to work upon. But these traits of resemblance were balanced by greater dissimilarities. Alike in their keen sense of humour, in their sympathy with nature, in their wide comprehension of humanity, the two authors were diametrically opposite to each other in the attitude of mind accompanying these gifts. Both excel in their historical pictures of manners, but while the Scotchman creates a visionary past, disguised in the glow of his fervid imagination, the Italian calls it up stripped of its accessories, and unmasks its harsh and unlovely features. The one shows his actors in gala dress performing a stately pageant for the benefit of posterity, the other takes us behind the scenes of history, with its characters in everyday attire, and deprived of the glamour due to scenic illusion.

Both Scott and Manzoni were descended from a race of rude chieftains, lording it over a mountainous border country, but while the one idealised the feudal system in which his ancestors had borne sway, viewing it from its heroic side alone, the other, looking at it from beneath in its relation to the lower classes, stigmatised it as an instrument of social oppression. Both loved rural pursuits, and were accustomed from infancy to open-air life and picturesque scenery; but the childish eyes of the one were trained to the wild beauty of heath and glen, to the shifting skies of Scotland, with their fleeting mists and ragged glimpses of tearful blue, to brawling streams and grey silhouettes of hills undulating against the horizon;

the earliest vision of the other showed the ordered luxuri-
ance of the wide Lombard levels, the terraced flights of
vineyards sloping to the azure floor of Como, domed by
the steadfast serenity of Italian blue and fenced with
solemn snows by the silver battlements of Switzerland.
Thus, while Scott's landscape is shown in all the varying
moods of northern nature, Manzoni's is ever calm and
solemn, breathing the spirit of those broad skies and
level flakes of foliage which the Lombard and Venetian
masters love for their backgrounds.   Nor was the contrast
less between the private character and lives of the two
men, for, though both alike were lovable and genial,
while Scott carried into his affairs the prodigality of his
exuberant imagination, and died a victim to the pecuniary
embarrassments in which his splendid dreams ended,
Manzoni regulated his life with the strong common sense
of which he himself declared poetry to be but the supreme
exaltation.

EPILOGUE

THE intellectual prepotency of France among the Latin nations renders Italian literature little more than a branch of that of the neighbouring country. The thought and tendencies of Paris—and in this respect Paris is France—are everywhere predominant, and their influence can be traced through all the provinces of the world of letters. Of ability there is much, but of originality little, and of the individuality of character required to give a national stamp to works of genius, absolutely none. The novels are French novels in another language, the poems are variations on those of the French schools of *décadents*, *symbolistes*, *véristes*, or of some of the other subdivisions under which poetry may elect to classify itself.

Meanwhile the search for novelty extends even to the department of typography, and while rhyme is eschewed as out of date, while old metrical forms are revived or new ones invented, the very capitals heading the lines are superseded by the undistinguished uniformity of the commoners of the alphabet. The next reform will perhaps be to abandon the separateness of the lines in favour of continuous printing, leaving the *M. Jourdains* of criticism to discover whether they are reading verse or prose.

As in France, taste in subjects is often morbid, and the tone of thought pessimistic, a mood which in its ultimate results is destructive of all true art, as it obliterates chiaroscuro, and merges lights and shadows in a universal monotone without contrast or relief.   Thus the generation expectant of the Revolution was more fruitful of greatness than that which entered on its fruition, and the hopes of a second spring for Italian art as a consequence of political unification have been as yet belied.

The difficulty of language is yet unsolved, as the common speech of all classes is still the provincial dialect, and the sphere of literature remains apart from that of life.   Italy has not yet found her true identity in her newly consti-tuted organism, and speaks with an uncertain and hesi-tating voice.   It may be that she will not wake to her full utterance, will not gain free command of her new individuality until moral as well as political unity is attained by the close of the long struggle with the Papacy which divides her with a line of cleavage cutting more deeply to the roots of her being than the old frontiers of territorial demarcation.

The tendencies of her modern bards have been play-fully satirised by one of their number who has unhappily passed out of the ranks of living poets.   Felice Cavallotti, the brilliant leader of the Italian Republicans, orator, statesman, man of letters, tragically slain in a political duel outside the gates of Rome, was no lover of recent innovations, as the following *jeu d'esprit* on the tastes and tendencies of his contemporaries sufficiently shows.   It is headed " The Modern Elzevirs, by a Pensioner of the Muses," and was written in Milan *à propos* of the Feast of Santa Vittoria on December 23, 1877 :

> Santa Vittoria ! thou of toasts and speeches
>   And songs—to-day wilt have abundant store,
> While poets throng to enter glory's niches,
>   I leave them, pensioned off for evermore.

R

In casting me aside the count was reckoned
    At ten years' service—there or thereabout—
Now on the half-pay list, with pen infecund
    Afar from Pindus will my days run out.

Bards major, minor, minim, microscopic,
    I see go by, their several paths upon,
With thoughts and thoughtlets primed on every topic,
    While I stand melancholy looking on.

All ways from Tusculum by them are threaded,
    With trochees furnished for the coming years,
Metres with capitals no longer headed,
    And masterpieces masked as Elzevirs.

With shafts of scorn for pedants narrow-hearted,
    Skulls, misbirths, subjects for the surgeon's ward—
Worms to devour their lady-loves departed,
    And owls to strike the gruesome funeral chord.

With formulas for English misses hectic,
    Death-doomed by doctors—of consumption sick—
With Heine's woes and keen French dialectic,
    To the next world to send them double-quick.

Then to myself I say : " O latest fashion
    Of poesy—if this thy stock-in-trade,
Well have I done to leave the heights Parnassian,
    Blest be my pension and retirement's shade ! "

And thou, Vittoria, who in tones so various,
    Wilt hear thy name to-day the ear beguile,
Forgive my silence if no verse hilarious
    Of mine, salute thee in the modern style.

Reactionaries we, and bards pedantic,
    Whose homely thought in homespun garb appears,
Bare of exotic quips and graces antic,
    Of owls, and skulls, and worms, and Elzevirs.

Epilogue

Reactionaries we, and pedants loaded
  With metres out of date and out of time,
Who wear Parini's robe of cut exploded,
  And modes of Ugo's and Manzoni's prime.

But thou . . . Ideal of the ages olden,
  Until this tempest past and over be,
While yet the carnival of bards is holden,
  Come to my refuge and abide with me.

No time is this to trail our skirts obtruded
  In bygone fashion on the gazing town,
I know a haven placid and secluded,
  'Where we in peace can live the present down.

Fanned by the breezes from Verbano wafted,
  A cottage in a lonely vale doth hide,
There wine we'll quaff on the fair hillside grafted,
  And munch our chestnuts at our own fireside.

And thou wilt give the secret to my keeping,
  Which the blind Smyrniote immortal made,
And that which wrought the laurel wreath that, weeping,
  On Foscolo's dark bier our fathers laid.

Wilt show the veils wherewith Love zoned and cinctured
  The forms Praxiteles in dreams designed,
Rhymes that fair Galatea's soul so tinctured
  That she for a misshapen shepherd pined.

And as 'twixt sip and sip, with fingers plying
  The tongs, we stir to life the glowing brands,
Thou wilt impart the Exile's song undying
  That scourged the youth of the Italic lands.

To measure just wilt set the lines and strophes,
  And dictate rhymes that jeer and scoff shall curb,
Not cemeteries haunting, the sad trophies
  And urns of the departed to disturb.

Then, since some photographs I have secreted,
   Which once a vagrant stroller gave to me,
We, when our melodies we have completed,
   Art in its latest phases there will see.

Afar thus from the modern noise and riot,
   Antique Ideal, we two there alone
Will pass the hours in holy peace and quiet,
   Until this storm be past and over blown.

The day Cavallotti looked for has yet to dawn, and while the changed order has moved farther and farther away from the Old Ideal, the New Ideal still hides behind the horizon.

Printed by BALLANTYNE, HANSON & Co.
London & Edinburgh